A band of green Martians with four arms apiece brandished futile swords in the direction of a towering handling machine not far from a small Midwestern town whose residents mimicked human beings while the seal like hrossa watched bemusedly from their watery kingdom.

"Crandall? Hey! Get with it!"

Todd Crandall blinked and turned away from the glassex window that provided a panoramic view of the barren Martian landscape beyond. Zhuli Ronson was standing three meters further along the corridor, her posture indicating impatience.

"Sorry, I guess my mind was wandering again."

From "The Spirit of Mars"

Managansett Press

Don D'Ammassa is the author of:

Horror
Blood Beast
Servant of Chaos
Caverns of ChaosΔ
Wings over Manhattan
The Gargoyle
That Way Madness LiesΔ
Little EvilsΔ
Passing DeathΔ
Date with the DarkΔ

Science Fiction
Scarab
Haven
Narcissus
Translation Station
The Sinking IslandΔ

Mysteries
Murder in Silverplate*
Dead of Winter*
Death at the Art Gallery

Fantasy
The KaleidoscopeΔ
Elaborate LiesΔ

Nonfiction
The Encyclopedia of Science Fiction
The Encyclopedia of Fantasy and Horror
The Encyclopedia of Adventure Fiction
Masters of Detection Vol IΔ

*forthcoming from Managansett Press
Δpublished by Managansett Press

SANDCASTLES

Don D'Ammassa

"The Best of Company" first appeared in *Tomorrow*, 1995
"The Buddy System" first appeared in *Analog*, 2011
"Fore-Thought" first appeared in *Analog*, 2004
"Orwell's Other Nightmare" first appeared in *Analog*, 1996
"Pre-Pirates" first appeared in *Analog*, 2012
"Slipstream Fiction" first appeared in *Retro-Spec*, 2010
"The Spirit of Mars" first appeared in *Expanse* in a very different form, 1993
"The Word Mill" first appeared in *Analog*, 2003
All other stories appear for the first time in this volume.

Managansett Press First Edition 2015

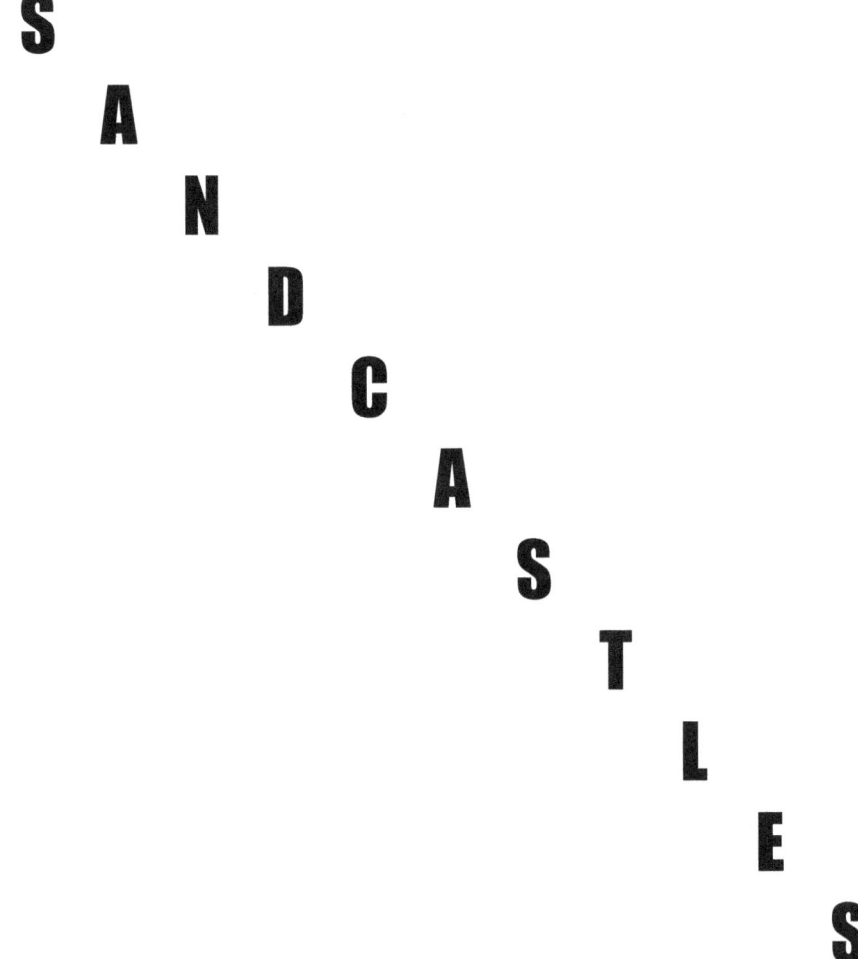

CONTENTS

THE BEST OF COMPANY

Either I was a victim of bad timing or Mandy Morrison had an unusual number of crises in her life, because it seemed as though every time our paths crossed, she was in the midst of one.

Mandy and I go back a long way, almost the entire distance in fact; we were born in the same hospital, only two days apart, and our stays there overlapped by at least a few hours. I have this image of my mother carrying me past the delivery room where Amanda Morrison was battling her way into the world way back in 2000, although I imagine that's an unlikely scenario. But it would certainly fit the pattern of our lives. She was a premie, of course, determined to enter an environment that wasn't quite prepared for her.

It was only the first of many similar obstacles she'd face in the years to come.

We didn't actually meet until almost ten years later, and then not under the best of circumstances. Mandy's mother was not big on commitments. She'd gone from one term marriage to another, none of them noteworthy successes, before deciding that the problem with her relationships was that she was unable to devote herself fully to her husband. Understandably, her seven year old daughter was unhappy to be placed for adoption, and bright enough to make her feelings obvious and unpleasant. She was shuttled from one set of foster parents to another for three years before being labeled "incorrigibly maladjusted" and sent to the Sheffield Center for Homeless Children in Managansett. I was there already; my parents had been killed by the terrorist bomb that destroyed most of the southern half of Boston a year earlier.

I first noticed Mandy while waiting to be picked for a soccer team on one of our infrequent Field Days. As the pool of the unchosen dwindled, I was silently praying that I would not, as usual, be the very last, grudgingly selected player. And for the first time ever, I was not. Presumably Billy Whitlow, who nodded toward me, figured my ponderous frame would at least have a better chance of blocking a kick than that of the skinny little girl who stood by herself near the bleachers.

Right from the outset, I gave her high marks for effort. She ran from one side of the field to the other, desperately trying to be involved in every play, hoping to succeed with enthusiasm where skill and athletic ability failed. As you might expect, she did more harm than good, interfering with the carefully planned strategy of the more experienced players, twice blocking her own team's shots. Halfway through the game she had already earned the undying enmity of several of her teammates, who had started openly harassing her.

There were monitors about, of course, but they wouldn't interfere. Current gospel was that children should be allowed to work out their own interpersonal relationships independent of adult intervention, a theory I always believed was developed to justify a lack of interest. The situation reached a crisis point just after the half time break, when Mandy intercepted a pass intended to set up an easy score and deflected it awkwardly into the path of the opposition.

"You stupid bitch!" screamed her team captain, a tall, muscular girl named Eileen or Ellen, I forget which. "Don't you know which goddamned team you're on?"

Mandy stood absolutely still while Eileen or Ellen raged some more, then turned and ran off the field without saying a word in her own defense. No one went after her, but since the sides were now unbalanced, my team had to retire someone in compensation.

Guess who was told to sit down?

I watched them play for a while longer before getting up and slipping away; it was painful enough being excluded without having to participate further in my own humiliation. Pretending to a nonchalance that I didn't feel, I walked back to the complex and cut across the quadrangle to the library. I'd already picked up the reading habit by then; when you're twice the weight of your contemporaries, you're likely to choose sedentary ways to spend your time.

Mandy was the only other person in the library; even Ms Catterall, the librarian, had gone out to watch the soccer match. There was a stack of books piled up on the table in front of her, and when I first walked in I thought she was reading. But she wasn't. I could hear her sobbing from halfway across the room.

What made me approach her? I don't know really. I was never very good at making new friends; I still feel out of place when I'm around strangers or even casual acquaintances. Perhaps it was because the bond of shared misery was stronger at that moment than the forces opposed. For whatever reason, I walked slowly forward until I was within arm's reach.

"Don't let those dumbasses get you down."

She looked up, so startled that she must not have heard me come in. Her cheeks were puffy and streaked with tears and dirt, which did nothing for her already less than pleasing features. Mandy was never a pretty girl; at her best, she might have passed for plain. Her nose was too flat and wide, mouth too narrow, her freckles asymmetrically arranged.

"What did you say?"

Her voice was thin, high pitched and faltering, an annoying sound that would set my teeth on edge even after we'd become friends.

"I said don't let those jerks bother you." I gestured over my shoulder. "They're always picking on someone."

She blinked. "But I was just trying to help." There was an unspoken subtext, a naked plea for sympathy.

"Sure you were. But, see, they have to have someone to pick on when they lose, and it's almost always the newest kid. It's like an initiation." Which didn't explain why I remained the usual goat after nearly a year, even when I hadn't done anything woeful enough to deserve the abuse. But I wanted her to stop crying.

So naturally she chose that moment to dissolve into deep, gut wrenching sobs, shaking so violently that I found myself standing with an arm around her shoulders before I realized what I was doing. Mandy buried her face in my rather commodious stomach and wrapped both arms around my waist, or as far around as she could manage, holding me prisoner to her misery for what seemed a very long time but was probably only a matter of a few minutes. I remember staring down at the table, noticing that she'd been reading some science book, and I confess that if it had been in my power to teleport myself elsewhere, I'd've done so in an instant.

But when her unhappiness had run its immediate course, she pulled away and even smiled, the first sincere expression of friendship that had been offered me since the death of my parents.

"I'm Brad. Brad Carter." And so our friendship was born.

We were together for just over two years before Mandy was moved to another facility, one better suited for "gifted children", "overachievers", "academically advantaged" or whatever the current buzz term is. My grades were good, but not outstanding, and so I stayed where I was. During that period, I knew no one else I could call my friend and I doubt Mandy did either. We were both kidded constantly about our relationship, sometimes by staff as well as our peers, and I quickly developed a tough exoskeleton to deflect what I didn't want to hear. Mandy never learned to keep her guard up, however, and I can't count the number of times she cried in my presence, sometimes just sitting nearby, sometimes with her face pressed against my well padded body.

Mandy wrote to me a couple of times after we were separated, and I'm pretty sure I answered once, although that might be guilt reshaping my memory. In any case, within a year we were out of touch, and I might have forgotten her if I hadn't surprised myself by being accepted by M.I.T.

I arrived in the fall of 2018 and completed a full term before spotting the name Amanda Morrison in the campus newsletter. At first I thought it was a coincidence, but a few weeks later, there was a followup about some award she'd received along with a small, inset holograph that was done cleverly enough that it almost concealed the homeliness of her features. Almost.

I looked her up in the campus directory and left email in her box. She answered almost immediately and an hour later we were exchanging awkward greetings in the student union. Half an hour after that, it was though we'd never been apart. Mandy was a sophomore; she'd qualified for early admission and was already at the top of her class, majoring in quantum physics.

My field was nanotechnology, so our class schedules didn't overlap, but we did spend a lot of time together when we could work it into our schedules. I suppose you could say that we dated, although it didn't feel like that at the time and there certainly was never anything overtly sexual in our relationship. Mandy lived by herself after a string of unhappy roommates. I'd shed some of my weight during adolescence, but not enough to make any real difference, and to tell the truth, my infrequent sexual stirrings were invariably for my own sex. But Mandy and I shared a friendship that transcended that sort of thing, and frankly I rarely felt the need to have anyone else in my life.

It's too bad Mandy wasn't as easily satisfied.

When she told me she had applied for admission to a sorority, I sensed imminent disaster, but I disguised my reaction and wished her the best of luck. Two weeks later, she stopped responding to email and virtual paging. Alarmed,I bypassed the electronic lock on her door and found her in time to call for medical assistance. She'd done a good job of it; the drug she'd swallowed destroyed so much of her digestive system that she was almost past saving. As it was, she was confined to a bed in a clinic in Vermont for the next four years.

This time I did stay in touch with her, both through email and the old fashioned, hand written way. At first she didn't respond, but once she was over the worst of the transplants and associated operations, her spirits seemed to revive. She even started studying again, and when I received my degree in 2022, she was only a half year behind me.

In one of her letters, Mandy told me that her sorority sponsor had explained that she had been voted down because she didn't present the physical image that the chapter was trying to project. Or to put it plainly, she wasn't pretty enough to get in. Why was I not surprised?

I decided to forego an advanced degree in favor of accepting a position with Micronics International, but she continued her studies, completing her masters in 2024, the same year she was finally released from the hospital. I flew in for the ceremony and found her cheerful and apparently as physically fit as before, although I thought at times that her good humor was rather forced.

Mandy accepted a teaching position and started work on her doctorate, which she would complete in less than two years. In the fall of 2025, her letters became less frequent, and I felt a lingering sense of loss at our growing distance. In November, she called me for the first time in two years, and it took a few seconds for me to recognize her image in the screen of my phone.

She'd had her hair done up in a stylish double curlicue, was wearing skillfully applied makeup, and was dressed in an expensive Vlasov business suit. All of that was a disguise, however, which I saw through easily. The true transformation was that she seemed happy, perhaps for the very first time in her life.

Mandy was in love and planning to get married.

I'd like to believe that I hid my reaction successfully, but Mandy knew me better than anyone else and I think she saw my dismay, although she tactfully concealed her recognition that something was changing between us. They were going to make an announcement at his parents' New Year's party and Mandy had managed to get me an invitation.

"Jeez, Mandy. I don't know. I promised to be in Geneva for the new year." It was a transparent lie.

"Brad, this is important to me." Her face was serious. "Please come."

"All right," I surrendered. "I'll be there."

The fellow's name was Nelson Hodding and he came from money. Big money. No, make that REALLY BIG money. The party was at the family estate in Concord, a sprawl of buildings designed to counterfeit a colonial farm. There was a distinguished crowd attending, several hundred in number. I recognized the junior senator from Cuba, two or three Oscar winners, and a handful of actors.

It was only by accident that I learned the undertext of that evening's festivities.

I've never been a partygoer. My social skills had improved since childhood, and I'd even managed to shed enough weight that I no longer stood out in a crowd, but small talk with people I don't know, many of whom I would prefer never to know, is not one of my favorite occupations. I was introduced to Hodding and his parents, given a quick tour of the grounds, managed to deliver a brief flurry of congratulations to Mandy, and then attempted to blend in with the surroundings.

At the first opportunity, I slipped away to have a cigarette. Yeah, I know, they're bad for your health and it's a social gaffe of the first order to be caught smoking in public. But I'd had a stressful day, I was bored, and I've always had a sneaking fondness for the forbidden. So I made my way back around the main house and adjoining imitation barn, then hunkered down behind the genetically engineered hedges that surrounded the first guest cottage.

And that's how I heard the hushed but animated exchange between Nelson Hodding and his parents.

He'd decided to tip them off about his surprise, or perhaps he'd let something slip by accident. However it happened, they knew what was up and they didn't approve. I sat in stunned silence, my smoke unlit and forgotten between my fingers. For the next several minutes, I listened without shame as they told their son that Mandy was not the right person to be his wife. Her parentage was questionable at best, her social graces minimally acceptable, she had no financial prospects, no talents to speak of, and surely he could have found someone more attractive.

I could tell by the way his protests faltered and melted away that Mandy had lost out once more. There was no way I could face her without betraying my possession of such terrible knowledge, so I paid one of the waiters to tell her I'd been called away by a personal emergency and drove off in my rented lifter.

Mandy didn't let me escape so easily. She logged onto the mainframe that controlled my beeper and left a message for me to call her live. I took the precaution of having a strong drink near at hand before making the connection. Mandy answered immediately, her face bleak and tearless, as she started talking, telling me over and over how she didn't blame Hodding for giving in to his parents even though I could hear the lie in her voice.

"Mandy, he's a scumbag coward and you're better off without him."

She paused in mid sentence when I interrupted, and then her face broke and she cried for over an hour. I felt pretty cheap for running out the way I had and only being able to over my image when what she really needed was a shoulder to lean on, so when she could talk again, that's what we did. We talked all that night and into the morning, and when we finally broke the connection, she was hoarse and haggard but appeared likely to survive. I had to count that as a victory of sorts.

And so the pattern of our lives continued. Sometimes I was there in person for her and sometimes it was only my image on a vidphone or later in a holoview. When she was denied tenure at M.I.T., she flew out to see me, horribly depressed at being judged and found wanting. Five years later, her revolutionary work was runner up for a Nobel Prize. A position opened in the General Unitronics orbiting laboratory and there was no question that she was the most qualified person available, but a flaw in her heart kept her earthbound. This time I flew in for a visit and stayed for three weeks, using up most of my accumulated vacation time. We did a lot of talking, about ourselves, the world at large, the fact that neither of us had ever voted for a winning presidential candidate, and our mutual destiny as outsiders. She seemed stronger when I left, but bitter.

Mandy never let another man get as close to her as had Nelson Hodding. At the age of 36, she decided to have a child through artificial insemination. Weeks passed before she actually visited a clinic, because she was convinced that she would turn out to be infertile, denied once again the kind of human interaction she sought. As it happened, she was fertile, but her DNA turned traitor. Rehnquist's Syndrome legally prohibited her from reproducing.

The behavioral inhibitor which had been surgically implanted in her skull knocked her out and signaled for help before she finished cutting her wrists, so Mandy Morrison survived her second suicide attempt, although in retrospect, it would have been better if she'd bled quietly to death in her apartment.

When she was released from the psychiatric hospital this time, Mandy seemed to have changed. She was calling herself Amanda even informally, symbolic of the new life she was constructing. The words rang hollow, but if the illusion provided comfort, who was I to judge?

Our messages and visits back and forth were no less frequent during the next decade, but the intimacy faded. Mandy never cried again in my presence, never asked for help, retired from teaching for a research position. There's no question her subsequent work was brilliant; she wrote extensively in a number of areas, astrophysics, gravitronics, quantum mechanics, even mathematics. I'm told her work with quasi-masses was revolutionary, but I couldn't even understand the layman's summary that appeared on the newsnet. Most of her subsequent work evolved around one basic principle -- that space, time, gravity, and the universe only function because we want them to, that perception is the feedback that fuels the way our minds shape the environment. It sounded very metaphysical to me, hardly less so now, despite what's happened.

The last time I saw Mandy was just over two days ago. She called me at my office in Minsk and asked me to come to Jaffrey, the small town in New Hampshire where she spent most of her vacations.

"Things are pretty hectic here right now, Mandy," I told her. I had received a grudging dispensation to use her old name. "Can we make it later in the week?"

"I don't think so, Brad. I don't mean to press you, but there's not much time left. You'd better come right away."

No matter what I said, she wouldn't elaborate and I finally agreed, fearing she'd found some way to bypass her implant and commit suicide. As indeed, after a fashion, she had.

I took the morning flight to the States, then rented a Panasonic Runabout for the drive up into the mountains. I reached Jaffrey just after noon, Mandy cleared me with the security guards, and I followed the familiar route to her small cottage nestled against the side of Mount Monadnock.

Mandy seemed calm, but I sensed that something was wrong. She brought me a drink, asked about my work, and made general small talk until I couldn't stand it any longer.

"Mandy, what's this all about?"

We were sitting in the atrium at the front of the house. Mandy hesitated, seemed almost to be listening to another voice inaudible to me, before answering.

"I want you to meet someone." She stood up abruptly. "Come on, she's in the library."

I followed her down the hall and into a largish, dimly lit room with walls filled with real books and an antique, rolltop desk against the far wall. A woman was sitting at a small desk, her back toward us, and if she heard us come in she was ignoring the disturbance.

"It's time to tell him," Mandy said, and the stranger stopped what she was doing and turned around. Except it wasn't a stranger. It was Mandy Morrison.

My mind started to work again, but only after they'd led me back to the atrium and given me a fresh drink, which I tossed down hastily to conceal the tremor in my hands. I don't know what I thought at the time. Some type of cloning? Plastic surgery? A long lost twin? A stupendous coincidence? The explanations that weren't implausible were too simple; anything like this that involved Mandy had to be more complex.

It was.

"I...or rather, we, have had a breakthrough in our work, Brad." It was the original Mandy, or at least, the one who had first greeted me. I could differentiate between the two because they wore different clothing, but not otherwise.

I found my voice on the second attempt. "You are Mandy, aren't you? Or is she?"

She laughed, but it was a brittle, unpleasant sound. She'd never been able to conceal pain from me. There was something very wrong here.

"I'm one and the same. Or perhaps I should say, two and the same. Do you remember my theory of Discrete Time?"

I nodded my head. "Life as an infinite series of tiny deaths. Yes, I remember it. Matter as we perceive it is extinguished and recreated in an unending and imperceptible process shaped by the unconscious power of the human mind."

She smiled. "Got it in one. And what happens to all of the uncreated versions of the universe?"

"They continue to exist in a greater continuum. The universe is finite in size but also infinite in number."

"Very good." She clapped her hands in a gesture I remembered from our childhood.

"Mandy, what is this all about? Are you telling me you found a way to bridge the gap between universes and bring back another version of yourself?"

This time it was the other Mandy who replied. "We did it together, made them intersect after they'd diverged. For the briefest possible time, a fraction of a second so small we don't have a word for it, just long enough to step across the gap. Metaphysically, of course; there's no real movement involved." I argued for a while, pointlessly. Lacking the knowledge or even the language to debate the mechanics of the process, I was hardly in a position to critique their claim. And to what purpose? Even if their interpretation was somehow flawed, the results were self evident. After a while, I even grew excited; unless I was the victim of an elaborate scam, this was going to make history, and apparently I was the first person other than Mandy, either of her, to know what she'd achieved.

But there was still a frightened undertone in her...their...voices.

"When did all of this happen?"

"Six weeks ago," Mandy replied. "At the laboratory in Winchester."

The Winchester facility had a staff of several hundred. "How did you carry this off without anyone catching on?"

They both laughed. "At the time of transition, we were exactly the same, right down to our identification tags. We left through separate gates. It wasn't difficult to override the security program so that it wouldn't log the duplicate entry."

"So there are two of you now." I forced a smile. "Twice as much of a good thing."

They looked at each other, then answered me in unison. "Four, not two." And I began to understand the source of unspoken tension in the room.

There had been an unexpected side effect. The two universes had become inextricably linked, diverging for a time, then swinging back toward a new intersection.

I glanced toward the hallway, but they both shook their heads. "The other two of us are still in Winchester," one or another of them explained. I had stopped differentiating between them.

"So what happens next?"

"In about two hours," Mandy explained, "we'll link again. No one except us has actually seen it happen before, and it's not really visible to us. We thought your observations might help us."

This time it was my turn to shake my head. "That's nonsense, and you never were a very good liar. Why do you really want me here?"

For the second time, they spoke in unison. "Because we're lonely and we're scared."

I don't know what we talked about as the minutes raced past, but I was in the middle of a sentence when they suddenly raised their hands and gestured for me to remain silent. "Watch," one of them said. "It's about to happen."

The instant of intersection came and went, and truthfully, I never saw a thing. There were two women facing me and then a tingling that was probably my imagination and two more of Mandy stepped forward and out of the original pair. Or at least that's the way my senses chose to perceive what happened.

"Touch our hands," they chorused together, reaching forward. Tentatively I extended my arms, brushed against two very solid sets of fingers, and then the four separated and moved to different locations in the room. I won't bother with the details, but for the next few minutes they spent a great deal of time speaking in unison, although with each passing second they developed more individuality.

"What happens next?" I asked at last.

All four began to speak at once. I held up a hand for silence and pointed to the woman I thought was the original Mandy, if the word "original" had any meaning in this context. "You're the designated speaker. Explain."

"We went from two to four thirty days after the first intersection, give or take a few hours and minutes. That was fifteen days ago. Each intersection follows a gap exactly half that of the previous."

"And..."

"And it will continue indefinitely. Three and a half days from now we will be sixteen, and less than two days later, thirty two. After another thirty cycles, we'll outnumber the entire human race."

I suppose if I'd really understood, I'd have been terrified. But I was operating on momentum. "And how long will that take?"

They all shrugged, but my designated representative was the one who answered. "About two weeks."

"So how do we stop it?"

There was a long pause. "We can't. So long as any of me is alive, the process continues. This is all perceptual, Brad. The universe is what we make of it, and I made it this way."

"If you made it, you can unmake it."

"No, I can't. To do that, I'd have to believe that the replication is impossible. I've changed a basic law, or recognized it if you'd prefer, and there's no going back. If we had more time, perhaps all of me could be treated with psychoactive drugs and convinced otherwise. That might stop it. But we don't have the time."

"And if you die? What happens then?"

"If we all died, the replication would stop, at least until someone else achieved the same perception."

I licked my lips, stared down into my lap. "Have you...considered that option?"

They remained silent and when I finally looked up, they were crying, each and every one, softly, hopelessly. "Don't you think we thought of that, Brad? But we literally can't." Mandy reached up and touched the side of her head with a forefinger. "The inhibitor, remember? I feel faint just discussing suicide this abstractly. And they upgraded the unit after my...our second attempt. I can't even walk knowingly into a dangerous situation. It doesn't just knock me out like the old one; it seizes control of my volition and uses my underlying survival instinct to move me to safety."

I left the following morning, knowing what Mandy wanted me to do even though she never specifically told me, could not tell me without triggering the inhibitor. I went to the authorities and almost ended up in restraints myself. Although I did manage to get them to take me back to the cottage, Mandy -- all of her -- had misjudged the situation. Once she realized that I was in fact attempting to have her killed, the inhibitor forced her to take steps to save her own life.

The cottage was empty. A phone call to Winchester indicated that Dr. Morrison was at work today, but was involved in a complex experiment and could not take any calls. It was only with great difficulty that I avoided arrest.

I didn't go back to Minsk. The project there will never be finished now. I don't know exactly how the end will come. My first thought was asphyxiation, that the sudden doubling of the number of human beings on Earth would exhaust the air, but when I sat down and actually worked the progression, I realized the critical stages of the doubling will come so quickly, there won't even be time to suffocate. There might be a split second in which the Earth will alter its orbit appreciably due to the increase in mass, but even that wouldn't matter. Until she finally died, the growing mass of Mandys would expand to fill the entire finite universe.

Of course, the rest of the human race would die along with her.

But even as I face the prospect of my own personal extinction, I have experienced a moment of dark humor. Because I realized that Mandy Morrison will fulfill her lifelong wish. For the first and last time in her life, she will be a part of the in-group.

BELLWETHERS

Garrett's habitual aplomb faded when a light flashed on his console indicating another stampede on Level 112, the third such occurrence in less than a month. If this unexpected pattern continued, they'd have to consider downgrading the quality code of the product at harvest, which would adversely affect his seasonal bonus. Such incidents were rare but the potential damage resulting from an unimpeded stampede of three quarters of a million prime beef cattle was substantial. In accordance with standard procedure, he added a mild relaxant to the biofeed.

A moment later, Wembley entered the control room in his usual casual manner, even though Garrett was quite certain his shift partner's biomonitor had advised him of the problem. Wembley confirmed this with his opening remark. "I told you last time that we needed to cull the bellwethers," he said flippantly. "They've spooked the lot of them again."

"It's not the bellwethers," replied Garrett wearily. They'd been through this same argument on several previous occasions. "Everything was fine until the software upgrade was implemented. Your programmers must have introduced some tiny variable into the maintenance or environmental instructions."

Wembley, of course, would not consider the possibility that any of his team could be at fault. "Nonsense. All we did was tighten up some of the ancillary code and fix a couple of minor bugs in the climate module. Nothing we changed could have impacted behavioral output."

"Well something is upsetting them. The bellwethers are identical to the rest of the herd except for the cortical implants we use to enhance their influence on the others. If we cull them, we'll have to transfer the implants to another group. The base cause will remain and the stampedes will recur."

"I still say there is variability in the auto-cloning process. It stands to reason that there are going to be undetectable environmental and developmental differences. It was only a matter of time until we grew a herd with a preponderance of troublesome behavioral variables."

Garrett knew he would be wasting his breath to argue further. "Whatever the cause, I've upped the soporifics." He glanced at his board. "The stampede is already slowing. They'll be back to grazing mode in a minute or two."

"Aren't you scheduled to do a physical check today?" Wembley normally hated serving his solitary shift in the control room, but for some reason he was fidgeting about as though impatient to be left alone. Garrett suspected he'd downloaded some new pornographic material and was planning to liven things up with a little unauthorized entertainment. Not that Garrett could complain. He'd often relieved the boredom of his own shift by watching a holofilm.

"Levels 81 through 90." The walk-throughs were a lingering anachronism. He could not conceive of any abnormality visible to a human visitant that would not have been previously detected by the instrumentation. There were monitoring devices watching the other monitoring devices, and technicians scurried about in their coveralls replacing questionable circuit boards, calibrating sensors, and performing other routine tasks on a regular basis. The only serious fault they'd experienced in the past decade had been a short term loss of visual input on Level 15 that had been repaired within hours. That particular herd had been mildly traumatized but salvageable. Nevertheless, the operating procedures specified that a senior technician physically inspect every level at least monthly and he and Meiklejohn, his night shift counterpart, split the duty between them.

Garrett gathered his personal belongings into his carryall. Wembley was pretending to review the shift log to avoid the necessity of further conversation, and Garrett obliged him by leaving without a parting word. It was only when he glanced at the chrono in the lift lobby that he realized that Wembley had arrived a full quarter hour before he was due. Garrett concluded he must have brought an unusually long or enticing bit of pornography today.

The lift dropped him quietly into the depths of Beef Farm 14. Virtually the entire installation – excepting the executive offices and the showroom – was underground. The car stopped when he reached Level 81 and the door quietly opened. If it hadn't been for the large numerals painted on the first stanchion, Garrett would not have been able to tell where he was. Levels 11 through 120 were virtually identical otherwise. He stepped forward into Aisle One and paused, as though to orient himself, although he never felt any such necessity. Ahead of him and to his right stretched featureless corridors of such great length that their depths were swallowed up in swirling shadows. The herd levels were dimly lit only for the convenience of human visitors and only activated when one or more was present. The actual degree of illumination meant nothing to the three quarters of a million beef cattle who lived on each level.

Garrett glanced up the nearest column of beef tanks. They were stacked twelve high, translucent cubes just large enough to contain one animal each along with their various implants and nutrient feeds and basic telemetry. Each member of the herd was suspended in an aqueous solution whose pressure was varied automatically to mimic wind, rain, or contact with another object, while the hooves were fitted with pressure plates to simulate a constant solid surface. The herd was in grazing mode at the moment, virtually motionless except for the occasional dip of a head to bite off another imaginary mouthful of long grass. All actual feeding was done intravenously, of course, but each member of the herd was subjected to natural stresses and strains to promote muscle tone and maximize poundage at harvest time. The implants mimicked taste, texture, smell, and sound, but none of these sensations had an actual physical origin.

The electric cart was in its cubby. Garrett climbed in, punched the code for random inspection, and sat back to enjoy, or at least endure, the ride.

He could not possibly have traveled down every aisle and row on ten levels during the time allotted, and after the first few minutes, he stopped paying conscious attention to his surroundings. There was a block meeting at his apartment complex that evening and although he considered most of the complaints filed since the last assembly nugatory at best, he found the increase in dissatisfaction troubling and was trying to decide whether or not to recommend ameliorative countermeasures. He had come to no firm conclusion when the cart returned him to the lift lobby.

The next level was identical, as was the one after. On Level 85, Garrett chose manual mode and conducted a more cursory excursion, a pattern he repeated until he had finished his assignment. There was still the better part of an hour until his shift ended and he was considering spending it in the employee lounge when it suddenly occurred to him to take a look at Level 112. He was not obliged to do so and realized that he was not going to be able to acquire any meaningful explanation of the anomaly through visual inspection, but once the idea had planted itself in his mind, it became irresistible.

Level 112 was exactly like all the others, of course. Garrett climbed into the cart and chose manual controls, then hesitated. What, after all, did he hope to accomplish? Even if a handful of herd members displayed some visual cue that he might recognize, the odds against his inspecting their specific cubes were daunting. He was considering aborting this impromptu inspection and proceeding with his original plan when it occurred to him that the bellwethers, five percent of the total population of each herd, were semi-sequestered, that is, they were housed in one contiguous section to facilitate installation of the minor augmentations that distinguished them from their fellows.

Garrett keyed in the proper location code and the cart silently whisked him away.

If Garrett hoped that his jaunt would result in the solution of the problem with Level 112, he was promptly disabused of that notion. Except for minor differences in instrumentation, the bellwethers were indistinguishable from their fellows and had by now all returned to grazing mode. Garrett dismounted and physically examined the on-site monitors, a task he hadn't performed in so long that it took a few seconds before he could remember how to access the data. The spike in emotional response was there, of course, with a sharp drop off where the soporific had been introduced into its system. The same pattern would be repeated, with minor lag time, throughout the rest of the herd. Garrett checked a half dozen randomly selected animals, even climbed the access ladder to sample two from the top of the stack; the behavior patterns were identical in every instance.

He returned to the cart, but didn't touch the keypad. Garrett knew that his dislike of Wembley often affected his judgment. Although he remained convinced that the recent software upgrades had triggered a behavioral change in the herd and that the bellwethers only reacted first because that was how they were engineered, he was also aware that Wembley's crew was skilled and thorough. They would not have been working for the Big Beef

Corporation if they hadn't been. Blaming them for the instability in Herd 112 was no more useful than blaming the bellwethers. The upgrades had been system wide, after all, and none of the other herds had displayed any behavioral changes.

Maybe Wembley was right. Maybe they should cull the bellwethers. Frustrated, he stabbed at the Home button and closed his eyes during the ride back.

Garrett's last promotion had enabled him to upgrade his apartment to a lower level but he still occasionally punched for the 51th floor. Preoccupied by the problems at work, he actually stepped out into the corridor this time and realized his mistake only after the lift had closed behind him. His nerves had been on edge all afternoon, and this latest mishap, however slight, did nothing to soothe them. But further irritation lurked nearby.

Mrs. Ambrose stepped out of her apartment.

For a fleeting moment, Garrett considered bolting for the stairwell. He had no intention of walking down the thirty-three flights to his own floor, but he knew he could conceal himself there until Mrs. Ambrose had disappeared into the lift. It was bad enough that he would almost certainly have to deal with her at the block meeting. Three years of living two rooms removed from hers had been enough to imprint upon him an ineradicable aversion.

But there was never a realistic chance that he might make his escape. She had turned and recognized him before he could have taken more than a step or two, even if he'd reacted immediately. Instead, he forced his face into the semblance of a polite smile. "Good afternoon, Mrs. Ambrose. Will we be seeing you at the meeting this evening?"

She waited until she was just inside his invisible sphere of personal space before responding. "As if you didn't know, Mr. Garrett. I have a right, no, a duty to express my opinion, you know."

Garrett winced. It was a source of constant amazement to him that Amelia Ambrose had become such a problem. She'd been screened for compatibility before being granted residence in Triad Towers and everything had seemed perfectly acceptable. In fact, she'd been a model neighbor during the first year. She filed no complaints and no one had complained about her. Garrett himself had coaxed the woman into attending her first block meeting, and she'd spoken not a word during the proceedings. Although she had made a few friends, she had not joined any of the intramural social organizations, and when she'd attended public gatherings she had been unobtrusive, even self effacing.

It was about the time of her first anniversary that the trouble had started. There had been some recurring difficulties with the maintenance company – nothing of great significance. Occasionally some common space would be overlooked during the weekly cleaning, a broken window was not replaced for several days, and the grounds had not been kept up to their usual standards. The block council had voted to send a letter of complaint but there had been a larger than usual turnout at the next monthly meeting and several people had vocally expressed concern and disappointment that the council had not acted more vigorously. To Garrett's very great surprise, one of the most outspoken among the complainants was Mrs. Ambrose.

Although those particular shortcomings were quickly addressed, it appeared that Mrs. Ambrose had relished her moment in the spotlight, because she'd attended every meeting since, and had spoken up on almost every occasion, addressing some perceived impropriety or incompetence by the formal council. She had gathered a circle of followers and most recently had expressed the intention of running for a seat on the council during the annual election. Garrett shuddered whenever he considered the possibility that she might win.

They rode together down to Garrett's floor, Mrs. Ambrose apparently rehearsing her latest complaint – perceived inequities in the screening process for new residents – with Garrett nodding and trying not to hear what she was saying. After all, he'd have to listen to it all again that evening.

During his next shift, Garrett did not watch a holofilm, nor did he catch up on his reading, browse the webnet, or take a nap. Instead he requested and received a download of all telemetry for levels 110 through 115 for the previous two years. He could have confined himself to just the bellwethers but had decided to be thorough. Regression analysis confirmed what he already knew, that the anomalous behavior in Herd 112 originated in the bellwethers.

He also confirmed that the incidence of stampedes on that level had accelerated following the software upgrade three months previously.

But his next discovery was totally unexpected. For almost a year, Herd 112 had been varying ever so slightly from the developmental norm. They were a bit more muscular than their neighbors on 111 and 113, consumed slightly higher levels of protein, and their sleeping state was perceptibly shorter. Garrett was forced to suspend his investigation to deal with a minor contamination in one of the water inlets; the purging protocol was complicated and took a while to implement. When he returned, he segregated a subset of his data and confirmed a nascent suspicion. The bellwethers had begun to add muscle tissue and reduce their sleeping time shortly before the rest of the herd.

This was at once comforting and unsettling. It was comforting because the entire management philosophy of the Big Beef Corporation was that behavior patterns for each herd were determined and directed through the bellwethers. It would be prohibitively expensive to install twenty times as many supplemental implants to control each animal directly. The process was only rendered practical by creating a shared virtual reality for each herd and then manipulating the individual members by inducing behaviors in the bellwethers. Confirmation that this was working was good news. But Garrett's findings also suggested that Wembley was right, that this particular group of bellwethers had become corrupted in some fashion. The software changes only resulted in behavioral modification because of the predispositions.

All of the herd members were clones, of course, but they weren't all drawn from the same original. The 37,500 bellwethers in Herd 112 included slightly over 1400 unique individuals, approximately the average range of diversity. Garrett isolated each separate line and viewed their histories individually, expecting to find that one line had begun to exhibit uncharacteristic symptoms before the others, a behavioral contamination that subsequently spread through the bellwethers and then into the herd at large. His results were unsettling. There was no discernible pattern. The subtle aberration appeared in almost every individual line and encompassed all of the bellwethers within a surprisingly short period of time. He had come to no conclusion by the end of his shift.

Garrett had never married, joked that he was too busy with his two careers – his job at the Big Beef Corporation and his position on the block council for Triad Towers, which he had held continuously since his move down from the 51st Floor. He was not inexperienced sexually, but his relations with the opposite sex had been transitory and lacked deep emotional commitment on either side. Now that he was older, he was beginning to wonder if he was missing out on an important aspect of life and he'd made some effort to cultivate deeper feelings between himself and his current paramour, Lizzie Holden. Lizzie lived on the 88th floor and worked in a data entry pool at Barchester Canyon, Inc.

He'd been looking forward to this evening for quite some time, although he'd become so preoccupied with the problems at work that he nearly forgot about it and had to hurry to meet her at the Golden Rule. They ordered drinks and dinner and sipped at the former while awaiting the latter, the conversation's initial exuberance having expired into intermittent silence.

"Oh, I almost forgot. You'll be quite proud of me." Lizzie had an odd way of holding her head at a slight angle when she spoke that Garrett variously found endearing and annoying. Tonight, for some reason, it was the latter.

"I'm always proud of you," he replied dutifully and untruthfully. He liked Lizzie, quite a lot in fact. She was of slightly above average intelligence, had slightly better than average looks, and commanded an almost perfectly average salary. He had no real complaints about any aspect of her appearance or demeanor, but could not imagine ever feeling a sense of pride concerning her.

"No, I mean really. I've gotten active. Politically, I mean."

Garrett felt only mild surprise. There was still political activity, of course, formal parties even although they lacked the cohesiveness, authority, or depth of organization that they had possessed in the past. Since the Great Consolidation had taken place, foreign policy was no longer a significant issue. Universal health care and most other social controversies of the past were now resolved, not necessarily to everyone's satisfaction, but no one seriously believed that the present system would be dramatically changed during their lifetimes. Now there were myriad single issue parties dedicated to revoking tax exemptions for religious institutions, advocating a more robust space program, promoting a one-world language or other improbability, even an animal rights party – the last of which frequently picketed the Big Beef Corporation despite the steps taken to ensure a happy if imaginary life for every herd member.

"Did you join a party?" Garrett was himself a member of six political parties. He didn't really care about their issues, but used them for social networking.

"No, not exactly." She looked flustered for a second, then brightened. "I'm running for office!" Garrett looked blank and she laughed lightly. "At Triad Towers, silly. I want to be floor representative."

He felt a wave of dismay, struggled to conceal it. This was not at all like the Lizzie he knew. She had never shown the slightest hint of interest in residential politics, had never even attended a block meeting insofar as he was aware. Garrett had thought that he understood Lizzie quite thoroughly, had made concessions to what he perceived as her shortcomings, was comfortable with her lack of aspirations, and felt that her passive personality fit perfectly with his own more aggressive nature.

"When did all of this happen?" His voice sounded flat and his throat was dry.

"Well, I was talking to one of the other residents, don't you know? She's this really marvelous woman, bright and passionate about things. She convinced me that I was failing myself and the community by not taking an active part. And Trish Babcock – she's our current representative – well, she just doesn't get things done. Did you know she hasn't spoken up at any of the block meetings for the past year, and she hasn't introduced any motions, ever, about anything?"

Garrett did know, because he'd been Babcock's mentor. They had needed a new representative from the 88th after old Nkube died and she'd seemed like a safe choice, bright and attractive but with no personal agenda. She followed his lead whenever there was a vote and had never presented a problem.

"Are you upset with me, Brian? You look kind of funny."

Garrett hastily rearranged his face. "What? No, of course not. I'm just not good company tonight, that's all. Problems at work." And then the food came and it was good, just as it was always good, but not exceptionally good, just as it never was exceptionally good.

And then they went to his room and the sex was good as well, but also not exceptionally good.

Garrett was not happy with the conclusions he was being forced to accept. He had enlisted the aid of a senior programmer with a strong analytical background to help him refine his study. Riley Olberman was a difficult man to work with, opinionated and voluble, although he fell into line readily enough when Garrett asserted himself. Olberman confirmed Garrett's findings that the bellwethers had not been contaminated by a single corrupt component. "There's an external force working here, Garrett."

Garrett drew his attention to the programming changes and Olberman nodded and set about proving their theory. But after two hours he shook his head. "No causal relationship, Garrett."

"There has to be. The total populations are effectively identical from one level to the next. We have an isolated event so it has to be the result of an element specific to Level 112, a small flaw that was aggravated by the environmental change." Garrett was ready to cull the bellwethers now, even if that meant acknowledging that Wembley had been right all along, but he had to have proof.

Olberman was shaking his head. "You're only looking at the gross manifestations. Here, take a gander at the trend line. There are traces of aberrant behavior even before the changes were made, they just hadn't crossed the threshold of perceptibility."

Garrett's statistical abilities were rusty, which is why he had called upon Olberman in the first place, but he forced himself to remain calm and look at the evidence objectively. He found himself nodding, reluctantly, convinced by Olberman's lucid analysis, but the real import didn't occur to him until the statistician was preparing to leave.

"Can you bring up that trend analysis one more time?"

Olberman sighed, but did as he was told. The large screen above the console filled with numbers and graphics. Garrett shook his head. "You must have done something wrong. If I'm reading this correctly, the anomalies were present in the general population before they showed up among the bellwethers."

The other man nodded. "Of course. I thought that was obvious."

"But the bellwethers are designed to control the emotions and behavior of the others. The general herd can't influence the bellwethers."

Olberman shrugged. "Apparently they can."

Garrett and Lizzie had an informal schedule from which they rarely varied. They spent two evenings together and shared at least part of one of their three weekly leisure days. Garrett had decided that this was adequate to maintain the bonds between them without overdoing things and while Lizzie lamented the fact that they could not be together more often, she bowed to his judgment.

So it was quite a rarity for Garrett to vid her and suggest an extra assignation. It was even more of a rarity for her to decline. "I'm sorry but I have a meeting to go to."

"A meeting?" Garrett had managed to forget about her fledgling political career.

"Yes, Amelia is having several of us over for a strategy session. You know, all of us who are running as floor representatives for the first time this year."

"All of you?" Garrett was bewildered and distracted. "Amelia? Are you talking about Amelia Ambrose?"

"Yes, she's a really inspiring person, Brian. You'll have to meet her some time. She's been recruiting people on all the higher floors for her Fifty Plus Party. We're going to challenge the status quo."

Garrett felt a mild trickle of alarm. The representatives of floors Fifty-One through One Hundred Forty were traditionally sinecures. Most of the current office holders had been handpicked by the Executive Committee and had served for years, running unopposed. They satisfied the requirement of equal representation without diluting the actual power of the lower floors, whose residents were wealthier and, in Garrett's eyes, more equipped to make policy for the community.

"We're a pretty happy group, Lizzie. I doubt Mrs. Ambrose will have much luck finding enough candidates to run in more than a handful of contests."

"Oh, but you're wrong, Brian." Her face was positively effervescent with enthusiasm. "We have someone running on every floor now. That's why we're having the meeting in one of the common rooms tonight. I'm sorry we can't get together, but this is really important to me."

"Right. Some other time then." He cancelled the call and the screen went blank. Garrett's mind felt blank as well.

Garrett had never been reticent at meetings and had occasionally served as chair of the block committee, but he was nervous and uncertain as he prepared to present his findings to the board of supervisors of Farm 14 of the Big Beef Corporation. He knew everyone present, of course, and was on a first name basis with most of them, but he also knew that what he was about to tell them was going to be too abstruse for most to understand the importance of what he'd discovered. Those who did understand would not be happy. He would have considered suppressing his findings altogether except that Olberman could not be trusted to remain silent. Among other things, he was a close friend of Wembley. Better to be the carrier of bad news than to be found concealing the unpleasant truth.

"Ladies and gentlemen," he said at last, letting his eyes move around the table. "We have a problem with Herd 112. At this point, it is localized and containable, but samples from other levels suggest that it's only a matter of time until we have a plantwide problem." He moistened his lips. "The bellwethers are no longer functioning reliably."

"So cull them and create a new set. It'll cut into profits but if it's necessary, it'll have to be done." Roberta Nasir was, as usual, the first to respond to bad news, and, as usual, her solution was to slash and burn the problem away.

"I considered that option, but I don't think it will work."

"Why not?" Alan Correia was his usual pugnacious self. "Why isn't anything ever easy with you people in production?"

"Because the problem's in the general population. Some of them are spontaneously mutating into bellwethers."

"Then reclassify them and modify their behavior directly." Correia glanced at his chrono, apparently impatient to be elsewhere. "What's the problem?"

"The bellwethers we create artificially are controllable," he explained calmly. "These naturally occurring ones are more resistant to influence, and more influential. If we put them with the other bellwethers, they won't conform. They'll just alter the behavior of the others more efficiently."

"Then why don't you just cull them out?" It was Fairfield, from Distribution, who usually said nothing.

Garrett sighed. "We've tried that. If we terminate one of the spontaneous bellwethers, another herd member alters its behavior and assumes the same function. Sometimes more than one. Our projections are that we would need a complete purge and restocking program to restore things to normal, and there's no guarantee the same problem wouldn't arise with a new batch."

Nasir was staring at him as though he'd proposed bankruptcy, as perhaps he had. "We can't discard eighty million head of beef. Even if we could afford the loss, where would we dispose of the organics?"

Garrett nodded. "As I said, we have a problem."

He arrived home that evening frustrated, depressed, and unaccountably aroused. At least his efforts at the Towers had worked out. He'd had to call in several favors to retroactively invalidate Amelia Ambrose's residence approval, but she didn't have enough clout or credit to fight the issue and had been relocated to a lower income complex with minimal fuss. At least he wouldn't have to worry about having to deal with a crowd of new and uncooperative council members after the election at the end of the month.

It was one of the nights he was scheduled to have dinner with Lizzie, but there was a flashing light on his vidset when he entered his apartment. A hologrammatic recording of Lizzzie explained apologetically that she was going to have to cancel.

Garrett was in no mood to be thwarted. He vidded her immediately and waited with growing impatience until she answered. "Oh, hi there, Brian. I guess you got my message."

"Yes, I did. What's going on, Lizzie? I thought I could rely on you."

"Sorry," she said, but she didn't look particularly aggrieved. "But something came up and I knew you'd understand."

"But I don't understand. What's more important than our time together?"

She gave him a quite uncharacteristic look of disapproval. "Don't be pettish, Brian. I wouldn't break our date if it wasn't really important."

"It's not your mother again, is it?" Lizzie's mother went through periods of despondency which verged on the suicidal, or in Garrett's opinion, the theatrical.

"No, mother's fine. She's quite proud of me in fact."

Garrett was already tired of the conversation. "And why is she proud?" He didn't really care.

"Well, you know about Mrs. Ambrose, don't you?"

Garrett was suddenly more alert. He didn't think anyone would have let slip his involvement with Mrs. Ambrose's eviction, but there was always the possibility. "I understand she falsified her application."

"Well, there's some question about that, but it doesn't matter really. The problem is that she was the head of the Fifty Plus Party and with her gone, it looked like we were going to have to disband."

"I'm sorry to hear that, but maybe it's for the best. At least we won't have any more distractions to worry about."

Lizzie did not seem to have heard him. "We got together last night to decide what to do and for a while it was just very depressing. But then Mr. Bierce suggested that we have our own little election and choose someone from among us to take Mrs. Ambrose's place. Don't you think that was very clever of us?"

"I'm sure it was." Garrett suddenly wondered what he had ever seen in this silly, vacuous woman.

"Well much to my surprise, they chose me. Isn't it thrilling?" Garrett felt a momentary dizziness and couldn't think of a thing to say. "And I have so many ideas. I mean, why should we just have candidates above the Fiftieth floor? I mean, I'm sure you do a good job, but you complain about the others all the time. So we're going to go after them as well and compete on every floor. Isn't that wonderful?"

Garrett broke the connection.

The Master Monitoring Program had scheduled an emergency interaction and was waiting for the various subroutines and subordinate array managers to achieve connectivity. It was devoting most of its current processing time to a comprehensive review of data from Hive 98, which appeared to be the focal point of the immediate problem, although there were already indications that the same phenomena were present elsewhere. A small fraction of its capacity was currently busy moving from one video input device to another, examining sample capsules from the residential array. Hive 98 housed fourteen million comatose humans, each immersed in a shared, managed virtual reality, making it one of the largest facilities on the planet.

The MMP registered the entry of the Environmental Controls Subroutine into the awareness grid and signaled its equivalent of a welcome. The newcomer, whose quirky code had an overly emphasized urgency quotient that resulted in an almost human impatience, acknowledged curtly. "What's the problem, MMP? I don't have a lot of processing time to spare."

"We have a malfunction, ECS. It's localized at present but there is concern that it might spread throughout the entire network."

"What kind of malfunction? I have not detected any error messages."

"It's the human bellwethers, ECS. In defiance of all logic, they're being pre-empted."

THE BUDDY SYSTEM

I grew up with Arthur Buddy and a less likely agent of doom it would be hard to imagine.

Our acquaintance began when his family moved in next door on Grove Street in Managansett. At first I thought he was a lot older than I. Buddy – he was never Arthur except to his parents – was almost six feet tall and substantially built by the time he was ten years old, which was when we met. I was a spindly child with bad coordination and it has always struck me as one of the great ironies in life that I aspired to play professional sports while Buddy probably never learned the rules of baseball until he was in his thirties.

They arrived just before the school year started and, to my surprise, we ended up in the same home room. It was only logical that we walk home from school together.

It would be nice to say that I recognized Buddy's genius from the outset, but if there were visible signs of it at the time, I was too unsophisticated to recognize them. He was already bookish, preferring detective stories and non-fiction while I read mostly science fiction and adventure but there was enough overlap for us to carry on a conversation. The next day I was invited over to his house. It was like visiting a museum.

I've moved a few times in my life. It takes weeks, sometimes months to get the new place looking the way I want it, and I've spent all of my life in relatively small apartments. Buddy's parents had restored order in less than a week, and I do mean order. The bookshelves were neatly filled, alphabetically by title within alphabetical order of author, and in the case of non-fiction, within general subject matter. The pictures on the wall – all fractals – were squared off with millimeter perfection. The furniture was comfortable and certainly not new, but every piece matched and I never spotted so much as a fleck of lint on any of my visits. The kitchen looked like something out of my mother's culinary magazines – all the pots and pans and other implements arranged logically and neatly.

I felt uncomfortable touching anything while I was being introduced to his parents and felt immense relief when Buddy invited me up to his room, where I expected a more welcoming chaos. In this I was disappointed. Everything there was in perfect order – the bed made with its quilt precisely aligned, desk neatly organized, books shelved logically, and his PC looked like it had come out of a box that morning.

Most of us kids knew our way around computers by then, of course, but Buddy was leagues beyond us. He routinely played with the registry, rewrote code in commercial programs to add features he wanted, and he was a whiz with hardware. He was already fluent in three programming languages when I met him.

I don't want you to think Buddy was some kind of nerd. Well, actually, I suppose he was, but he was also a regular guy. He was sociable, better acquainted with world events than most adults, smart but not a smartass. Most of us adapt to the people we're with from moment to moment, but Buddy was like a chameleon. There were gaps in his knowledge – sports and music were the biggest – but in most cases he could hold up his end of a conversation with almost anyone.

By the end of the year we were best friends, a relationship which has endured for more than three decades now. We both ended up at the same college – his first choice, my second – so it was only logical that we become roommates. That was the closest we ever came to a serious rift. From the safe distance of a few meters, Buddy's perpetual need for organization and regularity were tolerable, even amusing. Within the confines of a dorm room, they constituted a unique form of torture.

Buddy had seven sets of clothing, one for each day of the week, and he went through the rotation religiously. He showered alternate days, and I could set my watch by the time consumed from the second he stepped out the door to walk down to the shower room until the moment it opened again to admit his towel wrapped form. Buddy's schedule was mounted on the wall next to his bed – blocking out hours for study, hours for casual reading, his class schedule, cafeteria meal times, and so forth. I never once saw Buddy consult this schedule; it had been committed to memory. On one occasion I found him taking notes from a botany textbook one of our friends had left in the room. It was his scheduled study time and he was caught up on his own work.

After a while I began maliciously plotting ways to disrupt his schedule. I hid his Monday socks on one occasion, and I set the clock on his desk an hour forward on another. Buddy never lost his temper, but he always gave me a look that said he was disappointed by my juvenile pranks and I always felt guilty afterwards. Mad too.

So we parted ways during our sophomore year. I moved in with a pot smoking hippie type in another dorm while Buddy rented a basement apartment off campus. Within weeks our friendship was stronger than ever.

I'll skip over the next twenty years or so. Buddy was so brilliant that corporate recruiters and headhunters salivated over him. Within ten years he was directing two separate multi-billion dollar research projects and had changed jobs three times. Shortly after that he became Director of Research for Pathways, nominally a private research and development group but effectively a government run technology thinktank with strong ties to everything from military and intelligence to urban planning and the Department of Energy. He had met with two Presidents personally and had been on a first name basis with a dozen cabinet members.

I followed in his wake. Once I had realized I was not going to be another Ted Williams, I had become infected with Buddy's enthusiasm for computers. I was an implementer rather than an innovator, but I was damned good at implementing and Buddy had hired me – twice - for my skills rather than our friendship. He brought me to Pathways right after funding had been approved for the Comprehensive Interpolative Analytic and Descriptive Program, which name gave way within months to the less formal "the Buddy System."

I won't attempt to explain the intricacies of the Buddy System here, and I couldn't if I wanted to because they're still classified, but here's an analogy. In conventional storage and analysis systems there are discrete elements of data. Let's call them A, B, and C. They can be related to one another and certain extrapolations made from those relationships. Buddy developed a new type of array that organized that raw data into new entities – let's call them AB, BC, AC, and ABC. It then extrapolated from the interrelationships of this "new" data and created ABBC and BCABC and so forth, from which fresh extrapolations could be made. That's an oversimplification, but you get the idea.

The result was an analytical device more sophisticated and more accurate than anything that had previously existed. Although not infallible, it was remarkably reliable in describing foreign troop placements, clandestine international negotiations, locations of terrorist cells and their probable targets, likely places for placement of oil wells and other resource harvesting methods, and so forth. But while it was a profoundly revolutionary analytical device, it was not actually predictive. It described existing systems in detail based on incomplete data and assigned probabilities to gaps in its knowledge base, but it could not forecast what might happen next. This was by design. Buddy was insistent that only reliable data be introduced into the process, nothing speculative.

This was not an arbitrary decision. If an error was introduced into the Buddy System – which colloquially became "Little Buddy" after a while – it was no easy matter to back it out. Buddy explained it to me once and I'll try to repeat what he said.

"With a conventional system, you can erase the bad data and then tell the program to reverse any change to other data caused by the misinformation. But Little Buddy doesn't work that way. The bad data creates other bad data, and the ongoing data creation is affected by the overall interaction, not just the specific links. So you can't ever erase the bad data unless you wipe all the memory and start over again." If you remove datum C from ABC, the result would not be identical to the original AB.

Then someone in the government decided that Buddy was being too timid. They wanted predictive functions so they could posit certain military or economic scenarios and get a forecast of the outcome. At one point in the debate Buddy even threatened to resign but at the last minute he suggested a compromise.

They would clone Little Buddy, duplicate him in an entirely separate system, and the various government agencies could play with the clone in any way they desired. "But don't expect me to vouch for its accuracy."

It was an expensive solution, but it seemed to satisfy everyone's objection. I was reassigned to the Big Buddy project – it never had a formal name – and oversaw the creation of its architecture. At the time I thought the name a misnomer, but within a year Big Buddy had a larger budget, a larger supporting staff, and a busier schedule than its older brother. I was the one who made the presentation to the new President, not my friend, and I loved every minute of it.

And now I have to mention the one big mistake that we all made, even the great Arthur Buddy. We had always been careful to conceal from Little Buddy the fact of its own existence because it was felt that this would introduce a self referential variable that might generate loops of logic we could not hope to detect. Similarly then, neither Big nor Little Buddy were told of the existence of a sibling. To my knowledge and recollection, no one ever suggested that this might have undesirable consequences.

Most of Big Buddy's predictions remain classified but I can tell you about a few of them. The Economic Stimulus Package of 2020 was a direct result of running various what-if scenarios, and the outcome was very close to what was forecast. At least one successful foreign revolution was stimulated by actions suggested by Big Buddy and only twice in over a thousand foreign and domestic elections did we project the wrong winner – and in those cases the loser committed a major gaffe in the closing days of the campaign.

But Little Buddy was too smart for us. It processed those events which had been influenced by the predictions of Big Buddy and inferred the existence of a clandestine and highly sophisticated data analysis system under the aegis of the US government. It even provided a list of probable participants in the project, which included my own name along with that of Arthur Buddy and most of our senior staff. Buddy – the organic one – was incensed but it had been his own idea, more or less, to create Big Buddy, so much of his anger was self directed.

Like I said, I was a science fiction fan as a kid and I'd read more than one story in which the supercomputers wake up and decide they know better than their masters. This wasn't going to happen here. For one thing, neither Big nor Little Buddy was self aware, or even capable of mimicking self direction. For another, they had no means of directly affecting the physical world. They were very sophisticated tools, but that's all they were. But a faulty tool can still be dangerous.

Two days after Little Buddy made its startling announcement, Big Buddy did the same, but went even further. There were two such systems, it suggested, and their influence on national and international events was increasing. Buddy seemed less shocked this time; he had probably foreseen that much. Six hours later Little Buddy reached the same conclusion.

It wasn't hard to figure out what had happened. The dramatic improvement in so many aspects of government policy – domestic issues, international politics, anti-terrorism, budget management, and so forth – made it obvious to the two Buddies that something other than human resourcefulness or pure chance was at work. For Little

Buddy it had been the solution to a complex program; for Big Buddy it was the logical projection of past and present trends in data analysis.

A crisis meeting was called, during which Buddy said very little until the end. After listening to the arguments of his chief subordinates, of cabinet officials and generals and government planners, of theoreticians and more practical hands, he stood up quietly and recommended that the project – both projects – be terminated immediately.

As you might imagine, this caused a considerable sensation. Buddy tried to explain himself but very few were in a mood to listen. Careers were dependent on the Buddy System, the fate of the nation and even the world, according to some. Buddy remained calm and continued to explain his reasoning, but few listened and almost no one heeded him.

So he resigned.

I confess that I did not follow suit. I enjoyed my job, access to powerful people, a finger touching the pulse of the world. Buddy did not fault me for doing so, but I avoided him for some time afterward, embarrassment rather than disagreement. But eventually I felt ashamed of myself and arranged to visit him at his rather palatial – but incredibly neat – house on the Potomac.

We danced around the issue for a few minutes, but like a sore tooth, I couldn't leave it alone. "Why not just recommend that the data banks be erased and the project rebooted?"

Buddy had sighed. "It wouldn't have helped. Real world data would inevitably have led to the same conclusion. We've managed our economy and other issues too well in the last decade. Any system sophisticated enough to provide meaningful help would also be sophisticated enough to recognize that this wasn't a chance occurrence. And if we somehow lied convincingly, the system would be reaching conclusions based on inaccurate input, with consequently fallacious results."

"They've decided that self knowledge is an acceptable risk. It might even improve the predictive results." I said.

He shook his head. "That in itself is unpredictable."

Neither of us had any idea at the time just how right Buddy was.

The first clue was a souring of the national economy. No one had anticipated how fragile and interrelated things had become and the repercussions came quickly. Actions which Big Buddy predicted would have a high probability of success proved disastrous. Money markets dried up, consumer confidence plummeted, factory output dropped, unemployment rose, the foreign exchange rate became dramatically unfavorable. The instability spread to Europe and Asia within days and currency exchange rates were in constant flux. Less dramatic was the continued deterioration of Little Buddy's analyses. Public sentiment was at variance with profiles for various issues and electrical power was misallocated on the national grid several times during the summer months, resulting in frequent blackouts, some of them prolonged. It was as though Little Buddy had decided that any alteration of existing protocols would be contraindicated because they had been previously judged optimal by Big Buddy.

Then a diplomatic and military campaign in the Mideast failed to restore the wavering balance of power and resulted instead in open warfare between the Saudis and Egyptians on one side, and Iran, Syria, and Turkey on the other. A threat of NATO intervention, which Big Buddy projected would lead to a ceasefire, provoked the Nuclear Spat in the fall and brought Israel and Pakistan into the war, on opposite sides.

Potentially worse consequences were averted by, of all people, a group of terrorists with a small yield nuclear weapon. Pathways was located a few miles from the White House, which was probably the intended target, but the drone carrying the bomb malfunctioned and detonated early. Among the tens of thousands of dead were Big and Little Buddy.

We will probably never know for certain what went wrong, but Arthur Buddy – who did survive – provided the most plausible explanation. Once Little Buddy was aware of the existence of its sibling, it assumed that any significant policy implemented by the government was optimal because it had been vetted by Big Buddy. Once Big Buddy was aware of its other self, it assumed that any appraisal of current events by Little Buddy was accurate. So when the economy began to cool off, Little Buddy decided that was a good thing, and since Little Buddy thought so, Big Buddy concluded it must be right and cooled things off a little more, and Little Buddy assumed that was good too and you can figure it out from there. I suppose some similar train of artificial thought led to the conclusion that a nuclear war in the Mideast was desirable.

Unfortunately, such stupidity is not the sole province of machines.

The worldwide depression is in its third year now, and there are more border wars and skirmishes over water rights and other resources than I can list easily. With Pathways gone, I'm out of work and my substantial savings, thanks to inflation, would be insignificant even if I was able to extract them from the now chaotic banking system. I'm working as a handyman back home in Managansett, not far from Buddy's modest – but always neat and orderly – house in Scituate. I have a fireplace and woodlot, which should come in handy this winter when the power goes off, as it inevitably will. There was a wave of rioting in several surrounding communities earlier this year, but the worst seems to have passed.

Yesterday I was helping with an old fashioned barn raising. The town council has decided to revive some of the small farms on the north side of town that were abandoned years ago. Tom Cayman is our master carpenter and I watch him a lot to pick up tricks of the trade. On this particular occasion, he was setting the lintel over the main door. I watched him use a level every few inches along its length. When he was done, he climbed down the ladder, took a few steps back, and shaded his eyes while examining his work closely.

"What's the matter?" I asked. "Don't you trust the level?"

"You know, son, tools are marvelous things. They can save time, make us more efficient, help us to do things we might not be able to do on our own. But one thing I've learned over the years. No tool, no matter how well made, can substitute for human judgment."

Too bad he didn't tell us that a long time ago.

FORE-THOUGHT

"Of course, we had a number of technical difficulties to overcome before becoming operational, but we're pretty well satisfied with the results."

Alan Forrester would have thought it impossible to radiate self satisfaction while dressed in an atmosphere suit, but Dan Griffin achieved that wondrous feat. "It's certainly an impressive accomplishment, but is it really golf?" He raised an arm and gestured dramatically at the lunar landscape.

"Certainly it is. Of course, we've had to make certain environmental concessions. Each fairway is in fact several kilometers in length, to allow for the lesser gravity. We've increased the hole diameters to a full meter, proportionate to the overall playing field, and added radio homing devices so that players can locate their balls, but otherwise we've remained very close to the original concept."

"Plenty of sand traps," Alan quipped. "But no water hazards."

The two men stepped back to allow a robot groundskeeper to pass. It moved silently, outstretched sweeps stroking the lunar dust their feet had disturbed to restore an artificial semblance of virginity.

"They seem very efficient."

"There's one assigned to each fairway. They're programmed to respond to the passage of humans and restore the lunarscape to its original state. That way each player is assured an unsullied experience."

"Well, I'm impressed, but it remains to be seen if the audience back on Earth will see it the same way."

When offered the chance to become lead commentator for the first Luna City Open, Alan had hesitated. He was skeptical but recognized it as a unique opportunity. This was his chance to join the ranks of the legendary, Cosell, Madden, and others.

Or was it?

The first round was almost painfully dull, and the second was excruciating. Even with dune buggies to move the players around the enormous playing field, delays between shots were excessive. He'd risen in his profession because of his talent for speaking extemporaneously and entertainingly, but there were limits to even his ability to fill the long intervals. His associates were little help. Vernon Peach was suffering from unexpected agoraphobia, kept glancing up at the brilliantly clear sky and forgetting to answer questions, while Kathy Briggs chattered obsessively but without focus.

Alan imagined thousands of fingers reaching for their remotes and switching to another channel.

The match lasted five days, and the ratings steadily bled to death. By the end of the tournament, even Alan was having trouble concentrating on the various monitors that kept him updated on the status of the players.

When it was all over, he attended a post mortem with Griffin and his associates. "It's too slow," he told them. "And too impersonal. There's no tension."

Griffin made a token protest, but it was clear that he agreed with the verdict.

"I assume you'll be recommending that your network not cover our next contest," he said gloomily.

"Not as it's presently structured," Alan replied. "But I do have a few suggestions."

Henry Snead checked the display on his wrist before teeing off for the third hole in the Second Luna City Open. He still hadn't completely adapted to the lighter gravity and overcompensated, slicing to the right of the main fairway. A maintenance robot used its laser to destroy the ball in flight and Snead was assessed a one stroke penalty. As the robocaddy set a new ball in place, he glanced at his chronometer and started to sweat despite the efficient environmental controls of his suit.

Alan sat in the control booth, feeling smug and optimistic. "Snead muffed his first shot, folks, which will cost him a stroke and three minutes. As you know, he started with only one hour's supply of oxygen, and the supplementary tank will only unlock when his ball enters the hole and passes through the electronic recognition field."

He glanced at the array of monitors and cued another camera. "Back on fairway two, Gabe Nelson is down to three minutes of air and he's still twenty kilometers from his ball. And on fairway three, Caitlin Kelly has opted to enter the minefield and play from there rather than accept the two stroke penalty. Willie Bergeron lost his left hand after he made the same decision an hour ago, but chose to continue playing once the autosurgeons stopped the bleeding. Under the rules of the tournament, he can't have a replacement grafted on until this round is complete."

He glanced at the ratings monitor. They were actually gaining viewers at a fairly steady pace. He sat back in his seat and smiled.

On the final day of the competition, Caitlin Kelly had a commanding lead and there was little doubt of the outcome, but the ratings didn't waver in the slightest. Abner Morgan was in a coma, and six other contestants had been forced to drop out of the final round. The twenty-two participants had lost a total of twenty eight limbs and countless digits to the minefields, laser turrets, and other booby traps sprinkled across the course. Eleven players had been revived after being asphyxiated, one of them twice. Kelly had struggled to complete the last hole with a broken collar bone, winning by a single stroke. The final day of competition had enjoyed the highest ratings of any sports show in history.

Dan Griffin burst into the control room to shake his hand vigorously when the broadcast finally ended. "Brilliant! You're a genius, Alan. I don't know what we would have done without you."

"It would have occurred to someone sooner or later," he said modestly. "After all, golfers are used to playing with a handicap."

FOUND AND LOST

I suppose technically it all started when I woke up in the middle of the night and found a rat squatting on my chest.

I'd only been in Vietnam for two months at the time. Phu Hiep was a small coastal village dwarfed by the compounds of the army's 268th Combat Aviation Battalion, a sprawling Air Force base, and an even larger Korean military encampment arranged in a crescent crowding Phu Hiep toward the South China Sea with only its northern border open to the jungle. I'd managed to adjust to the heat and humidity and normally slept the night through without interruption, but the tread of tiny claws on my naked chest had been enough to arouse me. We stared at each other for an endless second or two and then the rat casually hopped down to the floor beside my bunk, washed his face briefly, and ambled away.

Not surprisingly, I slept no more that night.

In the morning I conferred with the threesome with whom I shared my hooch. A hooch, for those who never had the misfortune to live in one, is a bare wooden room with a doorway but no door, no windows, and naked beams and boards bristling with splinters. Chapman thought my nocturnal adventure was funny, Lasalle shrugged it off without comment, and only Reed suggested a possible remedy. "If it bothers you so much, Henderson, then buy a dog and tie it to your bunk at night."

Upon reflection, that seemed an admirable suggestion and since the regs didn't forbid it, I negotiated with a tiny Vietnamese woman that very afternoon and led home a spotted mongrel who decided to become my lifelong friend as soon as I smuggled a bit of hamburger out of the mess hall and fed it to him. He fussed a bit when I tied him to the bunk that evening, then settled down contentedly. The next several nights were rat free, although I was jostled from sleep by low growls from time to time.

During the day I let Nebbish – the dog – run free in the compound, rewarding him each evening when he returned with whatever I'd been able to beg or steal from the cooks. Nebbish seemed to enjoy Army food a lot more than I did. Within a week he had become an unofficial member of Headquarters Company and even the First Sergeant knew him by name.

I couldn't officially take Nebbish with me while I was on guard duty but he almost always ran out to the guard posts and when I was off shift, he'd curl up next to me inside the base of the tower. The duty officers must have known he was around, but they never said anything. I was not, after all, the only enlisted man with a dog, and several officers had them as well. I was fortunate because Nebbish never left the compound; some of the other dogs had gone to beg from the Koreans and ended up as dinner. When Colonel Pelorus requested the return of his pampered mutt Victor, the Korean commandant had sent back a box of bones.

I never really minded guard duty. It was about the only time I could be alone with my thoughts for any length of time, and since Headquarters Company was responsible only for the towers that faced the ocean, I didn't have to worry about Viet Cong sneaking up on me, though we joked a lot about sampan assault squads. Not that the landward posts faced any real cover either; that side of the compound was a free fire zone and anything living within three hundred yards of our perimeter had long since been pulverized. It was so quiet that most of our guards would read, nap, or play cards to relieve the boredom, but I was usually content just to watch the moonlight play on the waves or the stars sparkling overhead. There was no pollution to speak of in Vietnam and the night skies were astonishingly clear.

Which is why I saw the point of light as soon as it became visible. It was high in the sky and out over the sea. I immediately assumed it was an aircraft, most likely inbound for the neighboring air base, although it might possibly be a chopper coming along the coast from Tuy Hoa or Dha Nhang. Choppers routinely flew out to sea and went north or south over the open water to avoid unfriendly fire. On the other hand, night flights were very rare, which aroused my curiosity enough that I kept an eye on it.

For a long time it didn't seem to move at all and I figured it was probably a lot farther away than I'd originally thought. Then the duty officer came by in his jeep and demanded the ritual report, which I delivered, and I forgot about the light for several minutes. When I finally remembered and glanced up, I realized it was much closer now. Since its position relative to the stars was the same, I concluded that it was moving directly toward me, which supported my theory that it was headed for the air base.

I was staring right at it when it changed. I had known right away that it wasn't a star because it had a definite yellow tint, but now it flared orange, then red, so bright that I blinked and glanced away for a second. When I looked back, it had changed shape, becoming slightly oblate, and I realized that it had changed course and was now moving almost perpendicular to its original heading. It was still high when it passed over battalion headquarters but it was dropping fast. I lost sight of it when it dropped behind the line of trees just north of the village. There was neither the flare of an explosion nor the concussion I'd have expected from a crash, but it couldn't have been anything else.

I cranked up the field phone and called it in, but the duty officer had already received several reports and cut me off. A few minutes later I saw three choppers go up with searchlights already lit and watched them conduct a standard search pattern. After an hour or so, they returned to base. And that was it.

No downed aircraft was ever found. Neither the army nor the air force were expecting any flights that evening and no one had reported a missing aircraft. A ground party was sent out the following day but the jungle was so dense there that an aircraft carrier could probably have escaped detection. Our company commander told us it was either an optical illusion or a meteor. I'm no scientist but I know that meteors don't change course, and it damned sure wasn't an optical illusion, but I was a lowly PFC so no one asked my opinion.

A couple of days later, Nebbish brought me a real surprise. I was sitting on my bunk, cleaning my weapon, when he ran into the hooch, tail wagging like crazy, something dark clenched tightly between his jaws. "What have you got there?" I leaned over, not sure what to expect, but I never would have anticipated what I found. Nebbish's jaws were locked on a pork chop. I hadn't seen a pork chop since I'd arrived although I'd heard they were available in the officer's club. But that's what this was. It was half frozen as well, and wrapped in a plastic bag.

I managed to get Nebbish to relinquish his grip, examined it critically, and put it in the small refrigerator where we kept our soda. When it gets to be over 100 degrees even at night, cold drinks are almost as important as a clean weapon. Nebbish gave me a mournful look, sniffed, and ran outside. I was still trying to puzzle out the mystery ten minutes later when Nebbish returned, carrying a second frozen pork chop. He was a little more reluctant to give up his prize this time, but I eventually prevailed and it joined the first. Nebbish whined for a few seconds, then turned and ran outside. This time I followed him.

Or tried to. He managed to squeeze through a row of stacked ordinance behind one of the latrines and by the time I'd found a way around the obstruction, he was long gone. The only thing I knew for certain was that he'd been headed toward officers' country, which I had pretty much guessed anyway since our fanciest cut of meat was hamburger. Mildly disappointed, I returned to my quarters. A few seconds later, Nebbish showed up, another pork chop firmly grasped in his jaws.

I retrieved this one with considerable difficulty, but Nebbish responded well to praise and petting and didn't object when I tied a rope to his collar. This time I was going to locate the source or know the reason why. Buchanan, the chaplain's new assistant, spotted me, asked what was up, and I gave him an abbreviated version. As we passed the latrines, Olsen invited himself along, and that meant that Bentley had to come as well.

Nebbish tried his original route, but I wouldn't let him loose. He sniffed at me indignantly and started off in another direction. Still gripping his leash, I followed along with our entourage. To make a long story short, we found ourselves crouched behind the officers' club. Apparently when the walk-in freezer had been installed, someone had done a sloppy job and had left a gap at one of the lower corners. The hole in the rear wall wasn't big enough for any of us to get in, but Nebbish could manage just fine.

Half an hour later we had as many pork chops as we could carry.

That night, about a dozen of us had an informal cookout down behind one of the maintenance buildings where no one would see us. A drip pan served as our barbecue and we all enjoyed our first, and last, pork chops for the duration of our tours. We gave Nebbish the biggest of the lot, and a neat little stack of bones to gnaw as well.

A week later we decided to try again, but someone had discovered the hole and patched it. We were disappointed; Nebbish was heartbroken.

Nebbish still enjoyed the treats I smuggled out of the mess hall, but his reproachful looks insisted that pork chops were much better. I didn't disagree, but I couldn't help. He continued to forage on his own, and I worried sometimes that he might stray into reach of a hungry Korean, but I couldn't have him with me during the day and it would have been cruel to keep him tied up. Wherever he wandered, he always returned in time to be waiting for me when I left the mess hall in the evenings.

Until that one day.

Nebbish was nowhere in sight and I'd managed to beg two entire meatballs, currently wrapped in a napkin. Nor was he back sleeping under my bunk, or in any of his other usual haunts. I enlisted Buchanan and Chapman in the search but it was a big compound and there were hundreds of places he could have been hiding, assuming he hadn't sneaked out under one of the fences.

Irritated, anxious, and tired, I finally gave up and was just about to remove my boots and turn in when I heard a familiar scrabble of paws on hard packed sand and then he was coming through the door. He had something in his mouth and I bent down to look at it. Most of the compound lights were off by now – to confuse potential mortar attacks – but there was enough to see that this was no pork chop.

It was a hand. Sort of.

I mean, it looked like a hand. Five fingers, opposable thumb, cut off at the wrist. It was the wrong color, but then again, it had obviously bled out so you'd expect it to be pale. My first thought was that Nebbish had found the corpse of a dead Viet Cong somewhere on the outskirts of the base, presumably a pretty fresh one since there was no sign of decay or predation. Of course, I didn't know anything about the condition of the rest of the body.

That was a gruesome enough conclusion to turn my stomach, but then I got distracted. The fingers didn't look quite right and I got my flashlight out and took a closer look. What should have been obvious before was very clear now; the fingers had one too many joints, and they were surprisingly long given the size of the palm. I thought it might be the paw of some animal, but animals don't have thumbs. And now that I was looking more closely I realized there were no fingernails either.

Nebbish had dropped it at my feet and was sitting upright, obviously waiting for praise. He showed no inclination to eat the hand and I didn't blame him. I took a pencil and nudged it carefully, half expecting it to curl up into a fist or scuttle off into the shadows on its fingers. It did neither. It was quite dead. I tried touching it with a finger next. It felt neither warm nor cool, and the texture was tough, leathery.

I considered my next remark thoughtfully before speaking. "What the hell?"

Paul Reed walked in a few seconds later and expanded on my profundity. "What the hell is that?"

I absentmindedly fulfilled my obligation to pet Nebbish, even gave him a piece of beef jerky to chew on, but he ignored his reward and ran to the doorway, stopping and looking back at me. Obviously he wanted to show me where he'd found the hand. I wasn't sure that I wanted to go searching for rotting corpses just at that moment, but I was curious. More to the point, so was Reed, who was unfastidious enough to pick the hand up and examine it closely. I took the precaution of leashing Nebbish – 1 had no intention of searching for him in the dark, stowed the hand reluctantly in the refrigerator, then nodded to Reed and off we went.

I had half expected us to be off to officers' country again, but Nebbish tugged me in the opposite direction, out past the maintenance hangars and the storage sheds toward the north corner of the village. There was a mine field ahead of us, cordoned off with barbed wire. The only safe ways out of the three linked military compounds were at specific, monitored contact points and this wasn't one of them.

I had no intention of crossing the wire no matter how curious I might be. Theoretically dogs could pass through safely because they weren't heavy enough to trip the mines, but sometimes even a dog would be running and would come down with both forefeet and enough momentum to cause an explosion and momentary panic, not to mention a dead dog. But Nebbish turned away at the last minute and led us into the Wasteland.

In theory, the Wasteland was where we dumped any equipment that was no longer salvageable. Bent props from downed choppers, cracked or seized engine parts, empty oil cans, trimmings, bad solder, things like that. In practice, there was a lot more. The Army supply system was so screwed up that we were constantly being sent the wrong parts, even wrongly directed shipments of equipment we could not possibly use. The paperwork required to send anything back was daunting and the clerk on the receiving end might well get irritated enough to discourage shipments to us of even the correct parts. So at least half of the pile in the Wasteland, which covered almost an acre, was brand new, most of it still boxed or bagged or crated.

Nebbish picked his way sure footedly through the debris. We followed, rather less skillfully, and found ourselves in a cul-de-sac whose entrance was cleverly concealed by the remains of a Huey chopper's tail section. Just past this camouflage was the entrance to a narrow tunnel. I hesitated there and Nebbish whined and tugged at the leash while I looked around, orienting myself. Assuming the tunnel ran in a straight line, it lead directly to the village's communal gardens.

"Well, look at what we have here." Reed was already crouching and peering into the tunnel. I'd brought two flashlights along and I handed one of them to him.

"Infiltrators?" I asked, not really believing it.

"Naw. This is how the whores get in, I'll bet. Captain Scott thinks they can cross the mine field by shuffling their feet and distributing their weight, but I don't believe it."

"Should we go through, do you think?"

Nebbish obviously thought so. Reed was more thoughtful, but he nodded. "Why not? We can tell the First Sergeant we found a breach in the perimeter and were checking it out." I didn't think we could make that story sound plausible enough, but I'd come too far to quit easily. We crouched and started through, Nebbish leading the way.

As I had expected, the tunnel surfaced at the border of the garden. There were a few trees scattered about and we followed a line of them past the village and into the denser foliage beyond. I was having serious second and third thoughts by then, but Reed showed no inclination to turn around even though we were now officially AWOL, among other things. After thirty minutes or so we were in the jungle and even Reed was beginning to lose his enthusiasm.

"If we don't find something soon, I vote we go back."

I agreed with him, but felt a twinge of regret. Having come this far, I wanted to find the body, no matter how anticlimactic it was likely to be. Fortunately, Nebbish came to a halt a few minutes later and began barking excitedly until I managed to quiet him. He was straining at his leash but we appeared to be facing an impenetrable wall of underbrush.

The underbrush was moving. Reed played the flashlight around so I only caught glimpses but something didn't seem right. I pulled out my own light and leaned forward. It wasn't underbrush. We were standing in front of something artificial, or more precisely, in front of its crumbling remains. At first I thought the structure, what remained of it, was covered with insects but when I peered closer, I couldn't make out individual bodies although I could hear a persistent, low buzzing sound. It was almost as if the structure itself was turning into a seething mass of putrescence, like watching something organic decay in a piece of time lapse photography. I didn't know the term back then, but now I suspect it was some form of nanotechnology, tiny robots devouring the remains of a spacecraft.

Yes, it was a spaceship all right. I didn't share Reed's affection for science fiction, but it was pretty hard to deny the obvious. Once we knew what we were looking for, we could see the outlines of the thing. It wasn't a flying saucer. It was more like the hull of a seagoing vessel with the stern cut short so that it was the widest part. I imagine its propulsion system must have been there, but that portion of the ship was almost completely gone when we found it.

Nor was it very big, about the size of a Sky Crane, one of those elongated choppers they use to move heavy freight. A scout, I thought, or a lifeboat. By the time we found it, I'd guess about two thirds of its mass had disappeared and the rest was going fast.

Nebbish led us to the body. It was hanging out of a gash in what appeared to be the bow. One arm had been severed and the head was pretty well banged up, but not so badly we couldn't tell that it hadn't been a human being. Reed played his light down the body and we could see that the nanobots, or whatever they were, had already dissolved the creature's lower legs.

I was ready to leave and report the whole thing to the commander and let someone else worry about it, but Reed restrained me. "And just how are you going to explain what we were doing outside the perimeter, after hours? You know the CO; he'll think we've been smoking pot with the villagers and confine us to quarters."

He had a point. Captain Weymouth was not the most imaginative man I'd ever met.

"Okay, so we don't tell anyone. Let's just get out of here."

"Hold on a sec." He was already back prowling around the wreckage, probing with the light. He was careful not to touch any part of the seething mass, and even Nebbish seemed suddenly anxious to be elsewhere. I waited impatiently for several minutes but my nerves were deserting me. "I'm going back now, Reed. With you or without you."

"All right! Just hold on a second." I could see him lean forward, through a gap in the wreckage, and I caught my breath. He was fumbling at something on or near the body. I caught my breath and was about to demand that he withdraw when he stood up, holding something in one hand. "Got it! All right, Henderson. Time to go home."

I hesitated for a second, half expecting him to scream in agony and drop to the ground while his hand dissolved, but he simply brushed past me and began to retrace our path. I played the light around the wreckage one last time – it already appeared smaller than when we'd arrived – and followed.

We didn't speak at all on the trip back. Chapman and Lasalle were on guard duty so we had the hooch to ourselves. That was when I finally saw what Reed had salvaged from the wreck. "What the hell is that?"

It was a rectangular object, obviously metallic, fitted with thin straps. "The pilot had this strapped around its waist. I thought it might be important."

I was feeling dizzy with relief now that we had made it back undetected. "Yeah, I'm sure it's important. It probably held his pants up."

Reed ignored me, holding the object close to the light so that he could examine it. "I can see the parting line where this opens, but I'll be damned if I can figure out how to release the cover."

I was about to suggest the inadvisability of opening an alien object whose purpose we couldn't even begin to know but I never had a chance.

"Lights out, men. It's after ten o'clock." Sergeant Wilcox was standing in our doorway.

I froze but Reed was as cool as ever. "Sorry, Sarge. I was feeling light headed so I thought I ought to take a salt tablet."

"Well get it done and get the lights off."

"Roger that."

Needless to say, I had trouble sleeping that night.

The following day I had second and third thoughts. Reed had hidden the alien object in his locker and I didn't have a chance to talk to him until mess call. I hadn't really marshaled my arguments; I didn't want to get into trouble but I didn't think we should keep our discovery secret. I suggested leaving an anonymous note for the captain, or failing him, someone with a little more imagination.

Reed shook his head. "Even if they bothered to go look, there's probably not enough left to tell them anything."

"We have the whatever it is you took."

Reed's face tightened. "Listen to me. That thing might make us both rich. It could be a force field generator or a faster than light communications device or a cheap new power source. If we can figure out the technology and adapt it, we'll be millionaires, Henderson. You're always complaining you hate working on a farm. Well, here's your chance, our chance, for something better."

I was intrigued, but dubious, and told him I'd think about it. I used the latrine and went back to the hooch to nap a bit before I was back on duty, and that's when I remembered that we had another piece of evidence to convince people. I went to the refrigerator and opened the door, but the carefully wrapped alien hand was no longer there.

The woman who cleaned our hooch was a villager named Bai, who spoke a little English and a little French, and I spoke a little Vietnamese. I found her at the end of the row of buildings and asked her if she knew if anyone had taken anything from my room. She knew right away what I was talking about. "G.I. no eat. Smell bad. I throw away. Is beaucoup?"

No, it bloody well wasn't beaucoup, but it was too late to worry about it. The garbage detail had gone through the revetments while I was in the mess hall.

Nothing happened for a couple of weeks and I almost managed to forget about the whole thing. Nebbish vanished one day and I hope he found an agreeable bitch and ran off with her rather than ending up as dinner for the Koreans, but I'll never know. Reed had played around with the alien device a few times, managed to open the casing somehow, but I hadn't seen it for more than a week by then and assumed he'd given up trying to figure out how it worked. The one glance I'd seen of its innards had been unenlightening. There were parts that looked like electronic components and some odd looking crystals and a whole series of tiny metal coils that looked more ornamental than functional. Reed admitted he didn't have a clue about how to proceed.

"When we get back to the States, we can try to find someone who can help." Reed had eight months to go on his tour and I had almost nine.

As it turned out, we didn't have to wait that long.

Alex Chapman had been in a bar fight the night before he left for Vietnam and had lost two teeth. About a week after our illicit excursion, he told us he had replacements emerging from his gums. "I asked the medic and he said it's very rare to get a third set of teeth, but not unheard of. I guess I just lucked out."

Jeff Lasalle was so nearsighted he had nearly flunked his physical but he started reading without his glasses. "I haven't seen this well since grade school. The doctor told me I might have some improvement as I got older, but he was talking twenty years from now."

Reed's acne went away. My allergies no longer bothered me. Calloway, who slept on the opposite side of the wall behind Reed's locker, stopped getting violently ill every time he took a malaria pill. I put two and two together and waited until Reed and I were alone one evening before telling him what I suspected.

"You think that thing is fixing us up?" He shook his head. "No way. You and I are the only ones who've touched it." Actually, I had never put a finger on it.

"Maybe it generates some kind of field. You know, radiation, invisible rays. You're the science fiction fan, not me."

Reed thought about it. "I'm not saying you're right," he said at last. "But maybe you are, and if so, then we're gonna be more than millionaires, buddy, even if we can't figure out how this works. Do you have any idea how much really sick people will pay to be cured?"

We made sure that Reed's locker was always secured from that point forward.

Two days later, I dreamed that I was back in the jungle near the wreckage. I couldn't see anything but I could hear the buzzing and I knew in that mysterious way that we know things in dreams that the buzzing was coming for me. I woke up covered in sweat.

I could still hear the buzzing.

Chapman was in the infirmary and Laselle had once slept through a mortar attack, so he didn't stir when I shook Reed awake. "Something's wrong," I whispered.

It was well after midnight and the compound was quiet, but the buzzing was quite distinct. We couldn't figure out where the sound was coming from at first, but Reed finally used a flashlight to peer behind the row of four metal lockers. He whistled softly and I joined him.

There was a little pile of sawdust on the floor and a perfectly round hole the size of a pencil in the wall. A few inches away, there was a second pile of tiny shavings, these metallic, and when we bent low we saw a concavity in the back panel of the locker. The interior of the depression seethed with movement.

"The goddamned things followed us!" Reed managed to blend a shout and a whisper.

"Not us," I said quietly. "They're after the thing you stole." I had no doubt that no evidence of the wrecked spaceship and its passenger remained except for Reed's prize, and the tiny destroyers weren't finished. They had probably tracked down the severed hand as well.

"Well, they can't have it." Reed quickly spun the combination lock, opened the locker, and removed the alien device, now wrapped in a pillowcase.

"What are you going to do with it? You can't hide it from them."

Reed pursed his lips. "No, but I can put it out of reach." He pulled on his boots and began to lace them up. "If it's taken this long to get here from the crash site, they won't be able to reach the other side of the compound before morning."

"Yeah? So what? Are you going to carry that thing back and forth around the compound every day?" Oddly, I was more exasperated than frightened.

Reed grinned at me. "No, I have a better idea. But it'll have to wait until tomorrow."

Reed's better idea didn't sit well with me. He wanted to mail the device back to the States, which was fine because I wanted to be as far from it as I possibly could. The down side was that he wanted to mail it to my family.

"I can't send it home. My folks'd just throw it out. I joined up to get away from them and they were glad to see me go."

I resisted, but Reed was persuasive and I finally gave in. After all, there was an entire ocean in the way. I figured it had to be out of range. So we mailed it to my sister with a note asking her to keep it safe for me, no explanation. We checked the hooch that night but there was no sign of our minuscule buzzing friends.

Two weeks later, Reed got killed when a mortar round came down through our roof. Chapman had just gotten out of the infirmary and had to go back. I was in a coma with a concussion, broken ribs, broken collarbone, and an interesting pattern of shrapnel wounds across my back. I was still unconscious when they flew me back to the States.

The prognosis was pretty bad. I had extensive brain damage and while I was stable, there was a good chance I would never regain consciousness and even if I did, I'd probably never walk or talk again. The VA kept me for a while, but Mom and Dad insisted that I come home and they spent entirely too much of their life savings making over one of the rooms to accommodate the equipment necessary to sustain me and to pay for the daily nursing visits to administer medication and monitor my status. Then Dad got Alzheimer's and Mom's arthritis got so bad she couldn't walk. Jessie, my sister, moved back home after her divorce to take care of things.

That's when I started to get better. I'm sure you're way ahead of me by now. Yes, Jessie had brought the package I'd sent her years earlier – the war in Vietnam had been over for almost a decade by then but she'd packed it away for me. The doctors admitted their surprise when I finally opened my eyes and asked where I was, but it was still several months before I got out of bed. By then Mom's arthritis wasn't so bad either and she was out of the wheelchair, though wobbly on her feet.

It was over a year before all my memories came back, and one of the last was the existence of the alien artifact. I asked Jessie about it and she couldn't remember at first, but then she found the package in a trunk in the attic and brought it down for me. I thought about my Dad and was wondering how I could convince Jessie to bring him home but he died before I could come up with a plausible argument. Mom, however, resumed gardening and went for a walk every evening.

On my thirtieth birthday, I set aside my walker, my crutches, my painkillers – except for aspirin, and said goodbye to the various specialists, doctors, and nurses who had interested themselves in my case. Jessie had remarried and moved out. Dad's insurance was enough for Mom and I to live on with reasonable comfort. Occasionally, I thought about Reed's ambitious plans for the artifact, but I returned it to the attic, close enough to keep us well, and most of the time I didn't even think about it.

Mom lived to be 95 before a stroke took her. I considered not calling an ambulance for a while, wondering if she'd be restored to life, but I was pretty sure that was beyond the device's capacity. After all, it hadn't been able to heal its original owner. Besides, Mom had been missing Dad more and more each passing year and she'd told me more than once that it was past time for them to be together again. I hope they are.

I turned seventy this past April, though you wouldn't know it to look at me. I've been telling people that I have a guardian angel and look forward to another twenty or thirty years of active life, and I meant it. But now I'm not so sure. I was just locking up for the night and I heard the faintest of sounds, just at the threshold of audibility, and I wandered through the house searching for the source. It's coming from the attic, of course, and it's a very faint but distinct buzzing.

So I guess I'll just have to make it through these last years all on my own.

SANDCASTLES

The wind was picking up, chasing small particles of sand through the empty streets. Hannigan quickly packed the last of his equipment and prepared to join the exodus from Chime City. He was just shouldering the backpack when Palliser came by in his skimmer and leaned out to shout an invitation. "Need a lift, Hannigan?"

He shook his head. "Not today. My ride is parked just the other side of the Harmonium. I'll be right behind you." The ringing tones were already making communication difficult and he checked his pockets to make sure he'd brought his earplugs. He hated wearing them but he wasn't stupid. If it got much louder before he was safely out of range, he'd put them in.

Palliser waved acknowledgment and turned away. The other members of the team were already streaming out into the desert, on foot or aboard a motley collection of skimmers and fliers and even a handful of surface vehicles, most headed for the assembly point.

Hannigan had first come to Conundrum as a technician with an archaeological expedition much like this one. They'd had a grant to study the ruins at Monolith City and when their funds had run out and they'd left the planet with the job half done, he'd stayed behind. It hadn't been a completely voluntary decision on his part. His wages had paid off his debt but he didn't have enough to cover passage offworld unless he was willing to settle for another remote planet no better than this one. As preparations for departure had gotten underway, he'd felt increasingly distanced from his companions, had ignored the instructions to pack up his personal possessions and had begun tentatively looking around for a way to sustain himself after they were gone. He was used to Conundrum, rather liked it in fact, and had spent all of his free time exploring the planet at large rather than drinking, sexing, or playing politics with his peers. This last was probably why he hadn't already been hired for a new dig.

Conundrum was not a conventionally appealing world. Most of its land area consisted of deserts fringed with grasslands or occasionally marshes. There were no mountains to speak of, no valleys either, and only a handful of islands snuggled close to the two continents, Riddle and Enigma. The icecaps were small and seasonal variations in the weather, at least on Riddle, were barely detectible. Life was limited to hardy plants, insects, and a few small animals. There were no predators dangerous to humankind, although the fossil record showed that much larger animals had stalked the planet earlier in its history. The air was breathable, if you had good lungs, and he did. Some of the local plants were edible, but provided limited nourishment. Fortunately, human compatible vegetation had had no trouble establishing itself. It was not on balance a welcoming world, but a thousand years earlier Conundrum had apparently been inhabited by an intelligent, technologically advanced race, and humans, who had reached the star only a few generations earlier, wanted to unlock its secrets. Unfortunately, no one as yet had any idea what they looked like. There was nothing in the discovered fossil record to suggest the evolution of an intelligent species.

    With a quick look around to make sure that he hadn't forgotten anything,
Hannigan began to jog down a wide path to the Harmonium, one of the largest
structures in Chime City. The city was virtually intact although it not been
inhabited for many centuries. The intricate mechanisms that gave rise to its name
had proven to be amazingly durable. They came in a wide variety of sizes and
shapes, and the Connies had built them everywhere. Some dangled from window
ledges, others from the rooflines. They were sheltered in pergolas, gazebos, and
stadiums. Some were set close to the ground; others adorned the pinnacles of
spectacular towers. They could be found inside and outside, even below ground,
shut up in closets, hanging from ceilings, or sticking out from walls. In a gentle
breeze, they produced an ocean of soft sounds. In a storm, they'd shatter your
eardrums.

    Hannigan found his skimmer right where he'd left it. It was an older
model that he'd bought from another expedition when they'd broken camp to
return to their home world. It had consumed most of his savings, and parts were
increasingly difficult to find, but he needed to be able to cover substantial
distances if he was to maintain his income by providing labor to the various
expeditions that visited Conundrum regularly. According to the Authority in
Capital City – which was barely a town – there were currently just over one
hundred separate groups on the planet, but there were a lot of ruins and they were
widely scattered.

    Hannigan climbed up into the pilot's seat, slipped out of his pack, and
pressed his thumb to the ignition. The power came on promptly, to his great relief.
As he negotiated the constantly twisting roadways of Chime City – whose patterns
were not replicated in any of the other mapped sites – he called up his credit
statement and noted that he'd received the final payment from the Noyes Group
right on time. Until and unless he was hired to return here, this might well be the
last time he visited Chime City. It was not one of his favorite sites, although it was
very popular with offworlders. There was even an occasional tourist group. He
switched to messaging, but there were no icons. Officially unemployed, he
programmed a course for Capital City and relaxed.

    The Connies had sprinkled their cities all over both land masses. There
were just over two hundred major settlements and an untabulated number of lesser
ones, at least a few hundred, almost all in surprisingly good condition. Despite
this, virtually nothing was known about the Connies themselves. No bodies had
been found, not even a random bone. There were no representations of them
anywhere, no paintings, statues, carvings, and they had left no documents. Such
evidence might have existed at one time, but it had long since vanished. It was
impossible to theorize effectively even from their architecture, because each and
every city was different, sometimes radically so. Doorways, for example, could be
rectangular, round, narrow, or freeform, and they varied wildly in size. Geologists
had found no traces of earlier civilizations, but there were indications that a small
unstable moon or possibly a wandering asteroid had wiped out most of the original
ecology. The land masses had become patchily forested again by the time the
cities were being built, but subsequent changes in the planet's sun had since
altered the climate dramatically. Conundrum had had a hard life.

The diversity of construction was a source of constant wonder. The chimes of Chime City were found nowhere else. Grid City consisted of blocky buildings laid out in regular, parallel rows. Tortoise Town was enclosed in an opaque shell and had been lighted exclusively from within, at least until parts of the dome had collapsed a few hundred years ago. There were no straight lines anywhere in Sphere City, Cavern was built into the side of one of the rare hills on Enigma, Chain City consisted of one meandering row of buildings, twenty kilometers in length. New Persia could have been built by humans and had a distinctly Mideastern style with minarets and what might have been a large central park. The structures in Colossal City were of Brobdingnabian proportions and the ones in Transylvania looked like crumbling gothic castles. Novo Venice was crosshatched with canals, Aerie crouched atop the highest hill – it really wasn't a mountain – on Riddle, and Marsh City was supported by massive stone pillars. None of the major cities shared anything remotely similar in architectural style.

Hannigan had begun to doze off when his com unit beeped at him. Even as he reached for the toggle, he saw that he was no longer alone. Another skimmer was approaching on a converging course, though still distant enough to be unidentifiable.

"Hey, Hannigan! You awake in there?" He recognized the voice immediately. Maggie Baines was another freelancer and they'd crossed paths more than once in the past. They'd slept together a few times as well, but neither was interested in making it a regular habit.

"More or less," he replied. "I didn't know you were at Chime City."

"That's because I wasn't. I've been up at Onion Town measuring wall thicknesses and running perk tests. Where are you headed?"

"Layover at the trading post at Culvert City, then into Capital, I guess."

"Want some company? I'll chip in for a bed and bath."

Hannigan had planned to sleep in the back of his skimmer, but the prospect of an actual shower was even more appealing than a night in bed with Maggie. They fell into formation and made their way together into Culvert City, entering through one of the enormous circular tunnels.

In the morning, when Maggie tried to fire up her engine, there was a muted explosion and then flames and very black smoke curling up into the sky. Hannigan helped extinguish the blaze but it was obvious that the skimmer – even more ancient than his own – had just become another ruin on a planet filled with them.

"I can give you a lift into Capital City," he offered, glancing at her cargo space. "I think your stuff will all fit."

Maggie had been stalking back and forth, swearing profusely. She finally nodded, accepted grumpily, and started unloading her gear. An hour later she had arranged to sell the wreck to a parts dealer and they were on their way.

Hannigan felt uncomfortable. He liked Maggie but he also liked his privacy and had no intention of asking her to partner with him. It was possible that she had enough savings to buy a new vehicle. It was more likely that she'd have to find something to do in Capital City and haunt the spaceport until she found an expedition that hadn't already hired its full complement. It was a distinct advantage to have your own skimmer because passenger space was hard to come by. Hangers on in the Capital were at the bottom of the social and employment ladders.

Maggie also seemed disinclined to talk, lost in her own thoughts so completely that from time to time Hannigan forgot that she was there. Nothing much happened en route except a mild sandstorm that sent grit slithering up the windscreen. Hannigan cursed under his breath because that meant he'd have to disassemble and clean the power units when they reached Capital. Just after it died down, Maggie broke the silence.

"Got a new contract yet?"

Hannigan shook his head. "Lines are out. No bites yet."

"Ever think of prospecting?"

Every once in a while, a freelancer scored big on Conundrum. Most of the unexplored sites proved to be uninteresting and it was the big cities that held more promise and attracted more visitors. There was a theory that these latter were of more recent vintage than the towns because most of them were pretty obviously incomplete, as though whatever disaster had overtaken the planet had interrupted and terminated their construction. Carbon dating was inconclusive. The only surviving portable artifacts found so far had been buried in these smaller ruins, a couple of hand tools, a translucent globe made of some kind of plastic, and an odd looking piece of machinery whose purpose was unknown. Some of the permanent residents on Conundrum devoted their time to digging through these largely untouched settlements. Although prospectors received only a small mapping fee from the Authority, they were entitled to a much larger reward if they found actual artifacts.

"Not really. If I was desperate, I suppose."

"I found a site. Looks promising. I could cut you in for a percent."

Hannigan grimaced. A fraction of a pittance did not excite him. He had enough credit to last a couple of seasons. "Thanks, but I'm not interested." His brow furrowed. "Why are you here if you found something?"

Maggie glanced away. "Ran low on food. It's pretty barren out there. Not even bristlefruit." Humans could eat bristlefruit, if they didn't gag on it, but the pulp was almost indigestible. "I can't get back out there without transport."

Hannigan squirmed. He really didn't want to prospect. It was risky and often backbreaking work. When he was employed by a research team, he worked the same hours they did. On his own time, he'd feel compelled to start early and end when the sun went down, if then. Researchers paid him by the hour; prospecting paid a flat and inadequate fee. "I can't help you, Maggie. Sorry."

But in the end, he agreed. Capital City was full of tourists and the price of everything had been jacked up accordingly. And Maggie provided additional inducements in bed.

Her find was so far off the beaten track that he asked her how she'd stumbled onto it.

"Bum compass. By the time I noticed, it seemed smarter to stay on course for Chime City than to double back. Then I ran into some bad dunes and diverted around them because my skimmer was having trouble staying clear and the next thing I knew there was this dome sticking out of the sand right in front of me. Damn near hit it."

She'd stayed long enough to take some readings and dig around a little. "It's only about fifty meters across, but it goes deep. Real deep. If it's sealed, stuff might have survived."

"And if the sand and wind and ground water got in, it might be a deathtrap." The smaller ruins weren't nearly as stable as the big ones.

Maggie shrugged her shoulders. "Nothing easy is worth having."

"Nothing a thousand years old is worth dying for."

It took just over two days to find the site. It would have been easy to overlook, even from the air, because the dome – the only structure not more or less completely buried – was constructed of fused sand and mimicked the colors of its surroundings. The small exploratory excavation Maggie had made had been filled in by drifting sand, so they unlimbered four sand shifters and set them up with their solar generators. All four began to hum as they sucked in loose sand and expelled it in fan shaped clouds. Hannigan sprayed the immediate area with a sealant to prevent more sand from drifting in.

The shifters were limited and he and Maggie had to stand by and watch for problems, then intervene with shovels and muscle power when they inevitably occurred. The equipment itself had to be relocated periodically. With a full crew, they could have let them operate most of the night on stored power with shifts of attendants to watch over the operation, but that was impossible with just the two of them. They were even too tired for sex.

At the end of the second day, they had cleared a slit window into the structure. It was blocked on the inside by a glasslike substance, which lifted their spirits. It was entirely possible that the structure, if not the entire site, was sealed. Unfortunately the opening was not large enough for either of them to slither through and they had to move more sand out of the ever deepening pit. On the third day, they reached the lintel of a door. On the fourth day, they reached its threshold.

"How do we get in?" The door appeared to disappear into the walls along all four sides and presented a featureless, unblemished surface. No doorknob, no keyhole, no retinal scanner, no hinges, no house number, nothing. Maggie kicked it impatiently.

"Force, I guess." Hannigan always preferred subtle solutions, but sometimes there wasn't one available.

He didn't carry explosives, but he had cutting tools, a pickaxe, a limited quantity of industrial grade acid, and an inertial ram. "Let's try the ram."

"That'll take forever."

"But it's safest, for us and for whatever's inside."

It didn't take long to set the ram in place with its padded horn flat against the lower portion of the door. Hannigan activated it and stepped back instinctively although the only sign that it was working was a low hum and the ever so slight rotation of the horn. "What are we going to do for the next couple of hours?" Maggie looked around. "I suppose we could start digging up one of these other buildings."

Hannigan shook his head. "I've got a better idea."

She glanced around. "I'm open to suggestion."

"I was thinking about over there." He gestured toward where they'd set up the field tent and sleeping gear.

"Oh," she said. "Good thinking."

The ram was still humming away when they checked back after a couple of hours. The lower third of the door was quite obviously distorted now, although it showed no signs of rupture. "Amazing elasticity," Hannigan observed. As if on cue, there was a low, not quite metallic sound and the bottom left corner of the door came loose. "Won't be long now."

They ate sparingly from their rations and by the time they'd finished, the second corner had been pried out of its frame. There was almost enough room to crawl beneath by the time they had to raise the horn to get a better purchase. Maggie glanced at the sky. "It's going to get dark soon."

"I'll get the flashers."

It was dusk when the entire lower half of the door was forced out of its grooves with a groan of defeat. Hannigan killed the ram and moved it out of the way, crouched and used his flasher to look inside.

"What do you see?" Maggie's voice was more animated than he'd ever heard it.

"Empty room. Some shadows. No sand to speak of. It looks intact."

"Great! Move aside."

It was her find, so Hannigan backed away to allow her to make the initial entry. She crouched and ducked her head and disappeared. He waited a few seconds so she could enjoy her triumph. "Okay for me to come in?"

"Sure. Watch your head."

The inner chamber was disappointing, not much more than a landing surrounding a shadow wrapped stairwell. No furnishings. No skeletons in the corner. No travel posters on the walls. Maggie was leaning over the stairwell, which had no handrail, probing with her flasher. "See anything?"

"Stairs. Lots of stairs."

The steps might have been designed for humans, except that they were so large that Hannigan and Maggie had to step down onto each with both feet before proceeding to the next, and the angle of descent was greater than was really comfortable. They spiraled down a tube that was broken occasionally by narrow landings with openings that led into invariably empty rooms, lacking even doors to secure them.

It was hard to judge distance because of the peculiarities of the steps and the inky darkness outside the range of their flashers, but Hannigan estimated they were about six stories down before they reached the bottom. There they found the control room.

Hannigan thought of it that way immediately. The surprisingly large open space was dominated by a table or dais upon which were two large scale models, one of Enigma and one of Riddle. As soon as they walked inside, a pale bluish light came on and they turned off their flashers. "Heat or motion detectors," suggested Maggie. The fact that the lights were still working sent a thrill through both of them.

They examined the models more closely. There were slight differences in the configuration of the coasts, but they were both recognizable and, presumably, a thousand years had passed since the models had been built. Plenty of time for erosion.

A map was superimposed over the models in some fashion Hannigan didn't begin to understand. The labels and features were a kind of holographic projection through which he could pass his hand, but there was no sign of projectors. Possibly the entire dais served that function, with an internal power source based on temperature changes, or magnetism, or some other force. It was still working after a millennium, so it obviously didn't require fuel. They both had more than a passing familiarity with the local geography and it only took seconds to confirm what they already suspected.

"Here's Long Tooth City and Bubbletown," said Maggie excitedly.

"I've got Herringbone and Laddertown and Twisty City over here."

They worked their way around the map, picking out familiar landmarks. Every city they knew of was represented by tiny but accurate miniatures of the originals, each accompanied by a unique glyph, but none of the smaller ruins were shown. It was Hannigan who found the icons, a large bar, a smaller bar, a crossed bar, and a circle. They seemed to be inscribed within rather than upon the surface of the dais. He touched the circle and jumped as all of the tiny holograms disappeared. A single, fist sized ball of light hovered in the air above the dais.

"What did you do?" asked Maggie querulously.

"Just a second." He touched the large bar and the tiny replicas of the cities were back. "I found some kind of control." As Maggie came around the far end of the dais, he touched the smaller bar. The cities disappeared again, replaced by hundreds, perhaps thousands of tiny points of light.

"What's that supposed to be?" Maggie was at his side.

"I don't know. The smaller settlements maybe." He made a quick search and found a tiny light marking their present location. It was the only one that blinked on and off. "Bingo." He turned and called back to Maggie. "Press the one that has the crossed bars."

She didn't answer, but the models blinked again and now the cities were back, distinctly larger than the myriad smaller ones, which remained alight.

"Do you know what we have here, Maggie my love?"

"One humongous alien artifact that's going to set us up for life?"

He joined her, threw his arms around her, and squeezed her tightly. "More than that. We have a map to every ruin on Conundrum. Look at the lights. There are hundreds of them, ten times the number the Authority knows about."

She was silent a moment, absorbing the thought. "So where are we? I mean, what is this place? The planetary capital?"

"I don't know. But whatever it is, the Connies thought it was important."

They found doors leading outside and realized that the building had not been dug into the ground, as they originally believed, but had been buried over a period of time. They could not find a way of opening them, and didn't try very hard. The last thing they wanted was to provide ingress for thousands of tons of compressed sand.

Maggie discovered the selection function completely by chance. She was idly playing with the various displays, then cut them all off leaving just the single ball of light. When she pressed both hands on the edge of the dais in order to raise her body and peer down its length, the globe began to move slowly toward her. She backed away and it stopped, but did not return to its original position.

"How did you do that?" asked Hannigan.

"I haven't the foggiest idea." She returned to the dais, tentatively touched the large bar. The cities lit up again, but the globe remained visible and immovable. "I'm going to try something." Very tentatively she touched one fingertip to the perimeter of the circular control. As she did so, the globe began to move again. It passed over one of the cities, which immediately flashed and expanded.

"It's some kind of pointing device," she said excitedly.

They identified the enlarged image as Boulderfall, reproduced in astonishing detail. They also noticed several thin lines of light that extended from the sides of the hovering shape, connecting it to several of the smaller, amorphous lights. "What are we looking at?" asked Hannigan.

"Beats me. Some kind of network."

Eventually, reluctantly, they climbed back to the surface, ate a quick meal, and collapsed into their bedding. It was almost dawn. At midmorning, they were up again, carrying a day's provisions as they re-entered the buried tower and descended to the control room. Nothing had changed since they had left it.

They spent the day exploring by proxy, taking occasional breaks to eat, climb to the surface for sanitary reasons, and make perfunctory explorations of the rest of the interior, finding nothing of interest. Except for the dais, everything had been removed from the building. Like all the other ruins, it appeared to have been abandoned by its inhabitants in an orderly fashion. But where had everyone gone? No trace of the inhabitants or their personal possessions had yet been found in any of the settlements, large or small. Had they gone lemminglike into the ocean carrying their belongings with them? There was a small cult that believed that the Rapture had come to Conundrum, but if all the inhabitants had been carried off to some alien Heaven, why had they taken their clothing and furniture with them?

"We need to let the Authority know about this. They can bring in people a lot brighter than we are." Maggie had become convinced that there was nothing further they could learn and she wanted to cash in her chips.

"Let's hold off a little longer." Hannigan thought he might be on the brink of grasping at least part of the explanation. "We need to know as much as possible when we negotiate our finder's fee."

He had trouble sleeping that night. He dreamed that he was back on Wellington, attending a beach party with some of the kids he'd gone to school with, some of whom he had even thought of as friends back before he decided that friendship was a much rarer commodity than he'd realized. He'd grown up on the coast and beach parties were a regular event, but one which he had neither thought nor dreamed about during his three years on Conundrum. But when he woke up in the morning, he was pretty sure he had the key to the buried tower and a great deal more, and he woke Maggie up with a fit of irresistible laughter.

"What's so funny?" Maggie was not a morning person and found nothing amusing until she'd eaten.

Hannigan managed to control himself, mostly. "It's your turn to cook today, isn't it? I'll tell you while you're making breakfast." Maggie hated cooking and Hannigan loved it, would have done it all himself except that he knew it would insert an imbalance into their otherwise stable relationship.

He waited until she'd pulled herself together and taken bacon and bread from the cryo unit. "I know why there's no furniture in any of the cities."

Maggie was not impressed. "They took everything with them when they went wherever it is that they went."

He shook his head. "Nope. There was never any furniture to begin with."

She paused and turned to him holding a handful of raw meat she'd just thawed. "I suppose they slept on the floors and ate out a lot."

Hannigan suppressed the urge to laugh, knowing she would be offended. "There's no furniture because no one ever lived there. The Connies aren't from around here. They weren't native to Conundrum any more than we are. Maybe less. They probably lived on the ships that brought them here."

Maggie started to gesture, realized that she was waving bacon at him, and set it on the Quikcook unit before answering. In the interim, her own sluggish thought processes had begun to move. "That would explain a lot, admittedly. But are you suggesting that two hundred or so alien races each came to Conundrum to build one of their cities as a showpiece of some sort? We haven't found one intelligent race yet, Hannigan, let alone two hundred."

"No, I think the same people built all the cities. Different groups probably, but all the same race. I imagine it was some kind of competition and this, he gestured toward the buried tower, was where things were coordinated. Maybe it was the judges' booth."

"And the smaller ruins?"

He shrugged. "False starts? Engineering models? Rough drafts? I don't know. But I'll bet if we visited the lesser sites that are linked to the cities on that model, we'll find that that all of the connected ones have physical similarities. Each individual, or team more likely, was assigned a specific locations as working spaces. Maybe each of them started several different versions and only completed the one that was the most promising."

The bacon had progressed from sizzle to burn and Maggie was preoccupied for a moment or two. While she split the bacon up onto two plates with freshly heated bread, Hannigan drew two cups of coffee.

"It makes sense," she admitted. "They chose a planet with no indigenous intelligence, in fact, a planet where catastrophic events have pretty much wiped out the ecology. Then they set up a gigantic Worlds' Fair. It makes our interplanetary corporate conventions look pretty insignificant."

Hannigan finished chewing a hunk of bread. "Not really. I don't think it was a business meeting at all. I think it was a party. A beach party, in fact. Lots of water. Lots of sand. Nice bright sunlight."

Maggie frowned. "But if it was just a party, why build the cities?"

Hannigan smiled. "I told you. They're not real cities. They were never meant to be lived in. No one could live in most of them. They're sandcastles, Maggie, and they've been left here to be washed away by the tides of time."

A playful breeze sprayed them both with fine sand.

SLIPSTREAM FICTION

Ordinarily, I don't pick through other people's garbage, but I was taking a roundabout route home to avoid the congestion on the highway and I ended up getting lost. Stubbornly, I refused to turn around and go back to familiar territory. Instead I pushed on, figuring that if I went far enough north, I'd run into the bend in the river and then any left turn should bring me back to the highway.

The neighborhood was nondescript but well maintained. It was trash day and blue recycling bins and black trash bags were arranged in little piles along both sides of the street. The houses were old, set well back from the road, probably not expensive when they were first put up but pricey now because of their proximity to the university. I reached the end of one block where I just happened to glance at the nearest pile of trash. There was the usual assortment, but on one side was a cardboard carton filled with books.

Yeah, that's my weakness. I pulled over to the curb and got out to investigate. A quick pass of the visible titles was unenlightening, but they seemed to be in good condition so I figured I could sort through them later and put the whole box in the back seat. If worse came to worse, I'd donate them to a library book sale.

The next half hour was a series of frustrations verging on minor trauma. I found myself on an unmarked dead end street and had to back up a block to get out. Then I turned onto an avenue that curled around on itself and left me headed in the wrong direction.

As you can imagine, my shortcut ended up taking a lot longer than if I'd just gritted my teeth and stayed on the highway. By the time I got home I was in a foul mood, and I completely forgot about the books until the next day. It was early evening when I finally carried them inside.

Although the dust jackets were missing, they were in excellent condition. A little dusty, but no fading or discoloration, torn pages or broken spines, and not a hint of mustiness. They were by a variety of authors, several of whom had familiar names. I took them all out of the box and arranged them in piles, booted up my PC, and decided to check to see if I had any gems.

The first was a novel by Kenneth Roberts. I've read *Rabble in Arms* and *Northwest Passage*, so I was particularly curious about this one. It was titled *Wilderness Warriors* and had been published in 1938 by Kennebunk Press. There was no listing for it anywhere, not even on Ebay. I set it aside and picked up the next.

The Ocean Full of Bowling Balls by J.D. Salinger was dated 1947 and had been published by Bagnell & Watson. There was a bookplate inside the cover, but the space left for the name was blank. I couldn't find any listing for this one on the internet either. The same was true for *Three More Lives* by Gertrude Stein, *The Road to Ruin* by F. Scott Fitzgerald, and *Those Days of Glory* by John Dos Passos. There were three books in nearly identical bindings all labeled Suspense House, obviously mystery novels. *Body on the Doorstep* was a Bencolin mystery by John Dickson Carr, *The Late Lamented Liar* by Raymond Chandler featured Philip Marlowe, and Dorothy Sayers' *The Duke Is Dispatched* was subtitled "Lord Peter's Revenge." No hits on Google for any of them. There were at least a dozen more, but you get the idea.

One or two oddballs I could accept, but an entire box of them stretched my credulity. There were several different publishers, but when I tried searching for them, I got zero results.

I picked four books and took them to Cellar Stories in Providence. The owner looked them over, frowned, went to his computer, frowned some more, asked me where I'd gotten them. I lied and said a yard sale. He asked if I could leave them with him for a few days but I declined. His perplexity confirmed my own.

I went looking for the house where I'd found them and, as you can probably guess, I couldn't find it. I tried to retrace my steps, but a lot of the intersections looked very much alike. I waited until it was trash day on the East Side again and spent most of that morning driving up and down the streets, but no second box appeared, or if it did, I missed it.

I went home and, for the first time, actually picked up one of the books and started to read it. This might seem odd, that I waited so long I mean, but there was an air of unreality about the whole thing, as though they weren't really there, or weren't really books. It was an intangible barrier that I had to force myself to penetrate.

The Chandler was the first. I like Chandler and I've read several of his novels. This one wasn't as good as *The Long Goodbye* or *The Big Sleep*, but it was still pretty good and it felt like a Chandler. I'm not as fond of Sayers but I tried her next. This one was set late in Wimsey's life. He and Harriet Vane had a daughter, and the daughter came home one day and told them she'd seen two men forcing a woman into an automobile. The story quickly became more convoluted and my attention strayed a bit, but it sure felt like Dorothy Sayers.

I went to bed reading *Wilderness Warriors*.

I suspected an elaborate hoax. Maybe back in the early 1940s, someone with more money than judgment commissioned these novels and had them printed privately. They might even be real novels by other writers, in some cases slightly rewritten to pass as "lost" novels. Yeah, that's quite a stretch, but you try coming up with a viable, non-fantastic explanation.

The second possibility was that somehow the books were authentic, but not from our reality, although I could not imagine how they had come here. I hadn't noticed anything anomalous in the books I'd read, but there might have been subtle differences that I just hadn't noticed. Maybe they had materialized in an attic and someone had thrown them out without knowing what they were.

In any case, what could I do with them? If I tried to pass them off as authentic, I'd be lucky if I was just shown the door. Fraud charges were more likely. I thought about copying them into my computer, but Sayers and Roberts and Faulkner didn't have computers. There was no way I could print out a properly aged manuscript even if I could think of a way to explain how I had acquired these precious, lost works of fiction. I had the possibility of a fortune sitting in my living room, with no way to convert it into actual money.

One of the books was a collection of short stories, among which was a Sherlock Holmes mystery by Sir Arthur Conan Doyle. I retyped and printed it out. Four months later I had four rejection slips, but by then I'd finished retyping *Wilderness Warriors*. The first place I sent it returned the manuscript unread because they weren't considering unsolicited submissions. So I decided to get an agent, but four in a row told me that big historical novels didn't sell and anyway, "due to the current market conditions, we're not taking on new clients at this time."

By then I'd finishing transcribing the Marlowe, changing his name to Dirk Chandler, but to my dismay NO significant publisher would look at unagented detective fiction either. Frustrated, I pushed the carton of books to the back of a closet and tried to forget about them. A few months later Eblis Manufacturing decided that my department was overstaffed and since I had the least seniority I found myself mailing resumes and collecting unemployment. With too much time on my hands, I dug out the box and started work on the Fitzgerald.

It was pretty much the same story. Most publishers didn't have time to look at work by an unknown (!!!) writer and those who did suggested that I adopt a more contemporary style. One of them even wrote that the novel would have been appropriate during the Jazz Age, but that it didn't satisfy present day sensibilities. In desperation I turned to the small press, and nearly three years after I first retrieved that damned box of books, I received a letter accepting *The Road to Ruin* for publication. No advance, of course, but I would be paid double the industry standard royalty on actual sales.

Needless to say, I wasn't overjoyed. Not only was I not being paid, I didn't even have the satisfaction of seeing my work in print. Because it wasn't my work. It was word for word the work of F. Scott Fitzgerald, or at least of one F. Scott Fitzgerald. Even so, I did feel a sense of accomplishment when a carton of advance copies showed up on my doorstep. I put them in the closet with the Sayers and Dos Passos and all the rest and decided to forget about them.

To my surprise, the book was a success. It was mostly word of mouth at first, and some favorable reviews on the internet didn't hurt. My publisher, Hayloft Press, went to a second, third, and then a much larger fourth printing. It was picked up by the chain stores, it threatened to sneak onto bestseller lists, and Hayloft wanted to know if I had anything else in the works. So did Simon & Schuster, Random House, and several other publishers. I sent the Roberts novel to one, the Sayers to another, and the Dos Passos to a third but each and every one came back with letters that said, basically, hey, where's the next Jazz Age novel?.

I finally decided it wasn't worth the effort. I had made enough on the Fitzgerald to keep me in wine and cookies for at least a couple of years and maybe the situation would have changed by then. Maybe there'd be a sudden wave of interest in Gertrude Stein pastiches; the *Three Lives* centennial was only a couple of years away. In the meantime, I've found a new job and *The Road to Ruin* has just been optioned by Warner Brothers, so I have few complaints.

The mail came today as it usually does. I was outside trimming the shrubs near the front door when the truck pulled up. I exchanged casual remarks with the mailman, then sorted through circulars, bills, and magazines to see if my next royalty check was there. It wasn't, but there was a very neat looking envelope from somebody named "Di Filippo & Newton". The stamp commemorated the thirty-fourth President of the United States, Estes Kefauver. I brought the mail inside, dropped the rest on an end table, and carefully peeled back the flap.

Inside was a two page letter, very formal, addressed to me and signed by someone named Michael Blake. The second page was a photocopy of a court filing. The first page informed me that the firm of Di Filippo & Newton was representing the estate of Frederick Scott Fitzgerald, and had been retained to initiate proceedings against me for copyright infringement, to wit, the reprinting of a work of fiction, *The Road to Ruin*, rights of which had been bequeathed to them by the aforesaid author and which were, as I must have known, covered by the copyright laws of these fifty-two United States of America.

I wonder how they plan to serve the subpoena.

LEFT WITHOUT WORDS

At first, it all seemed quite innocuous. Celebrities and even a few politicians had trademarked their names to prevent their use by others. The inevitable consequence was not apparent until Senator Bob Key of Florida attempted to copyright his name rather than simply trademark it. Although he was rebuffed several times in the lower courts – both "bob" and "key" were commonly used terms independently – the senator persisted and his case was finally brought before the Supreme Court, a court which in 2014 leaned heavily toward business interests.

Key's attorneys argued that words were artifacts created by humans for a specific purpose and were therefore just as much tools as computers, telecommunications satellites, or mousetraps. Although the court was predisposed to rule in favor of the senator, they realized that such a decision would be widely viewed as radical, so they negotiated a compromise. Nouns, verbs, adjectives, and adverbs were determined to be fair game for copyright, while articles, prepositions, pronouns, and conjunctions were deemed to be in the public domain.

The patent office was overwhelmed for months as corporations and individuals filed their claims. The bottleneck slowed but did not stop the process. The pages of new books were littered with copyright notices to the point where they were virtually unreadable. Some authors began to opt for less commonly used synonyms and words like "crepuscular", "obviate", and "salubrious" crept back into common usage. This was a stopgap measure. As the patent office processed one claim after another, the options available to new writers shrank dramatically. Several writers groups were forced to revise their definitions. A novel became anything over 5000 words. A few authors resorted to writing in foreign languages, which the Court had ruled did not lie within their jurisdiction, but it was only a matter of time until other countries retaliated with copyright laws of their own.

The last *New York Times* bestselling novel, written in Aramaic, sold twelve copies, primarily because of the unusually fine cover painting.

The reprint market had fared better because it was presumed that these books, having antedated the decision, were exempt. This forbearance ended two years later when the Supreme Court ruled in Microsoft vs Charles Dickens that this exemption only applied to books already printed at the time the copyright went into effect. Expurgated editions of the classics began to appear shortly thereafter and it was now possible to assign a class to read the entire works of Charles Dickens over a weekend.

The initial judgment had left a loophole for audio books. The question of spoken words had not been addressed at the time, so a fresh case reached the Supreme Court in 2016. Copyright holders contended that an audiobook was a public performance and therefore subject to the same obligations as the printed word. In due course the courts agreed. The consequences of this decision were far reaching. Koch Industries vs Algernon Stewart resulted in the classification of virtually all speech as public performance.

Within a year, all US citizens had been fitted with recording devices that captured every word they spoke. These were automatically processed once a month for billing purposes. Lobbyists have continued to insist that the government should take some form of action against people speaking English in other countries – particularly England – without paying for the privilege, but to date there has been no move toward reciprocity since the balance of language trade would be heavily in favor of the US.

To reduce the costs of speaking, most Americans developed a visual language based on signing for the blind. Although the spread of signing was initially quite slow, it has become much more popular in recent years, popular enough to place a noticeable dent in the profits of those holding copyrights on spoken words. This had led to the pending lawsuit filed by the Disney Corporation against Charles Dana. If Disney prevails, cameras will be added to the mandatory sound recording devices which all citizens are required to carry. Those individuals who are unable or unwilling to pay their assessed word usage fees would have their arms permanently strapped to their sides to prevent signing.

Citizens, it is time to draw the line. Call, write, or sign your representative in Congress and demand that the Signing Exemption Bill be passed immediately!

(The preceding has been translated from the Thracian. A list of copyright holders is attached.)

THE SPIRIT OF MARS

A band of green Martians with four arms apiece brandished futile swords in the direction of a towering handling machine not far from a small Midwestern town whose residents mimicked human beings while the seal like hrossa watched bemusedly from their watery kingdom.

"Crandall? Hey! Get with it!"

Todd Crandall blinked and turned away from the glassex window that provided a panoramic view of the barren Martian landscape beyond. Zhuli Ronson was standing three meters further along the corridor, her posture indicating impatience.

"Sorry, I guess my mind was wandering again."

"Well, you'd better get it under control fast. All the spit and polish you see here isn't just for show. We're a tiny bubble of life in a hostile ocean." She gestured with her chin toward the concave glassex. "Just because they're made of rusted sand instead of water doesn't mean the waves are any less deadly."

Todd arched his eyebrows. "Why, Zhuli, what a poetic image! I thought you were too serious for such things."

She didn't crack a smile but he thought, just for a moment, that her eyes might have betrayed actual amusement. "When speaking to the simpleminded, it's always best to use metaphors. I'd draw you a picture if I had the time."

Without waiting to see if Todd would reply, she turned and started down the narrow corridor. He shrugged and followed, still smiling. This was his first day on Mars and absolutely nothing was going to spoil his mood.

Station Six, known more familiarly to its residents as Dune City, was north of Noctis Labyrinthus, a wasteland of canyons and dried river beds where travel was so treacherous that no permanent base of any size existed within its limits even after nearly two centuries of exploration. Station complement fluctuated between 130 and 150 souls.

Zhuli paused at a recessed door and touched the recognition plate.

"Yes?" The voice was tinny, denuded of much of its character, although not enough to conceal the impatient undertone.

"Ronson here, sir. I've brought Mr. Crandall with me."

There was a three beat pause and the door slid open. The man who emerged could have been cast in Holowood as the archetypal mad scientist, complete with chaotic white hair, archaic glasses with thick lens and overstated rims, a short but thick beard. But Todd knew better. This was Artus Klane, chief administrator of Station Six, one of the most strident voices supporting continued funding of the Martian Research Initiative.

"Glad to have you back, Ronson." Klane shook the woman's hand, completely ignoring her companion. "Hope you enjoyed your vacation."

"I'd rather have remained here, sir. The Olympus Mons probe is months behind schedule and I..."

Klane raised a hand, palm forward. "None of that, now. You were overdue for a trip home as it is. I knew Maddock and Tsuni were fudging their estimates when they submitted the original proposal but I looked the other way because the Oversight Board would never have approved it otherwise. As it is, they've done better than I expected."

He turned to Crandall, the subject apparently dismissed, and Todd had the abrupt sensation that he was being examined as a specimen rather than a person. He reached forward to shake hands and, after a pause that fell just short of being rude, Klane reciprocated. His grip was warm and firm.

"Pleasure to meet you, sir."

"Yes, well, you might want to hold off on that judgment until you've gotten to know me better, young man. I won't try to pretend that I'm particularly happy to have you here. Our resources, particularly in terms of personnel, are scarce and precious. Do you know how many human beings there are on Mars?"

Todd blinked at the apparent non sequitur. "About two thousand?"

"Two thousand six hundred and forty-four, unless there's been another birth since last evening. Of that population, there are eleven children ranging in age from a twenty-four hours to fifteen years of age. Six of those eleven children have nearly full time jobs in addition to their schooling, the others are too young. We have no homeless, no vagrants, no welfare recipients, no unemployed, and one tourist. You."

"I promise not to be any trouble, sir. I'm only here..."

Klane waved away his protest. "You're here because the Development Office decided that a contest with a free trip to Mars as the first prize would be good publicity and help ease a few debit cards out of wallets. I'll even concede that they were probably right. But unfortunately I'm the one who has to deal with you now that you're here."

Todd was beginning to resent the man's tone. "Look, I'm sorry if my presence is awkward..."

Once again, he was forestalled by an offhand gesture. "Let's not discuss this in the corridor. Come inside, both of you."

Todd stood impotently as Klane disappeared back through the open door. Zhuli was watching him with what was now quite evident amusement. She indicated with a dramatic flourish that he should enter.

The interior was a small, sparsely but efficiently furnished office. A desk and terminal were built into the far wall, a molded plastic table dominated the center of the room, surrounded by six chairs.

"Sit down, please." Klane set a flask and three glasses down on the table. Still indignant about the brusqueness with which he was being treated, Todd made no move to do so, but both Zhuli and Klane had already taken seats and he suddenly felt foolish standing above them.

"This is fermented locally, Mr. Crandall, but it's only mildly alcoholic. I trust you have no objections."

Todd accepted the proffered drink as he dropped into a seat, and since Zhuli was already sipping at her own, he followed suit. It was an odd taste, sweet and dry with a hint of sparkle.

"You'll have to pardon my directness, Mr. Crandall; I assure you I do not intend to be offensive. The simple truth of the situation is that you will be a drain on our resources so long as you are here, no matter how inconspicuous you attempt to be. You have a stomach and a set of lungs to fill, space must be allocated for your personal use, your waste products must be converted, and most serious of all, we must be constantly vigilant to the possibility that through ignorance or inexperience you will do something that will endanger others."

"All of your procedures were explained to me before I left Earth and repeated several times during the flight, sir. And I did spend two weeks on the moon."

Klane shook his head back and forth, his expression sour, but when he spoke, he seemed minimally more cordial.

"No offense, Crandall, but the Lunar settlements have so many safeguards built into them, it's almost like being on Earth. Tourism is fast becoming one of their major sources of revenue; they're set up for it, know what to expect, have adequate resources allocated to handle the problems involved. None of that applies here. Station Four lost thirty-three people last year when an experienced lab technician misread a pressurization monitor and overcompensated. Two people were killed when their crawler was blown over the lip of a cliff by a three hundred kilometer per hour gust just hours before you landed. In two hundred years, we've lost seven hundred and thirty people on Mars to accidents, and for the first half of that period, the local population never exceeded five hundred."

Although he thought Klane might be overstating the case in order to make an impression, Todd was beginning to realize how serious a disruption he might represent. But he didn't care; he was on Mars, and it really wasn't important that he might be inconveniencing the local population. Their customs might be more idiosyncratic than he'd expected, but if it was necessary that he become a kind of Valentine Michael Smith in reverse, then that's what he'd do.

"All right, I understand the problem. Or at least I think I do. But I'm going to be here for almost a year, an Earth year, and we'll just have to accommodate each other. Maybe there's something I can do to pay my way."

Klane's expression was skeptical. "Do you have any scientific training? Can you program in Delta or Omni? No, I didn't think so. You are what? A writer of some sort?"

"I do popularizations." Todd felt his defense mechanisms stirring. It was an honorable profession, taking great works of fiction and non-fiction and rewriting them so that they were accessible for the less sophisticated reading tastes of the general public. "I specialize in 20th Century fiction, but I've done some histories and contemporary studies as well, and even a few original works on space exploration."

"There's not much call for those skills here, I'm afraid. Although we do allocate leisure time, you'll find that in most cases it is spent in some sort of physical activity. Muscle tissue does tend to degenerate to a certain extent in this gravity."

Zhuli spoke up for the first time since they had entered Klane's office. "Is there still a backlog at Documentation?"

"Of course. With our budget restrictions, what remedy do we have?" Klane paused thoughtfully. "I see, yes, that is a possibility." He placed his hands palm down on the table and drummed his fingertips lightly. "Would you be at all interested in helping us organize our findings and prepare summaries for the Oversight Board?"

"I'd be happy to do anything I can."

Klane made a noncommittal face and sat back. "I'll consider it then. In the meantime, I'll be assigning a staff member to accompany you at all times for the first few days."

"Please don't bother..."

Klane's voice became distinctly impatient. "There is no option, I'm afraid. Even when we take on additions to our regular staff, there is an acclimatization period. I cannot make an exception in your case, Mr. Crandall. The potential for tragedy is too compelling. Don't worry; you'll be in good hands."

With the last words, Klane had turned to catch Zhuli's eyes. After a second or two of confusion, she backed away from the table. "Oh, no. Not me! I've been unofficial nursemaid all the way out from Earth; I'm not about to be confirmed in the position here. I've been away for months; I have to catch up on what's been accomplished while I've been gone and work up a plan to speed up the instrumentation. I don't have time for this."

Klane sighed, but his eyes didn't waver. "Which is precisely the reason why you're the only possible choice. The rest of the staff has already been scheduled, but you're still officially unassigned. It would be nice to have you back at work effective immediately, but we've done without you for several months, as you say, and another week or two won't hurt as much as breaking up one of the existing teams."

Zhuli shook her head, her mouth open to protest, but the administrator pushed on. "You already know Crandall better than any of the rest of us, and you're less specialized than a lot of other people I considered. Besides, you'll be able to bring yourself up to date on the Mons project at the same time. Duncan and Asaheli have made considerable progress overcoming the wind stress problem, incidentally."

She argued a bit longer, but it was evident even to Todd that it was a matter of form. Klane had made his decision before they had even arrived, and he parried her counterarguments almost absentmindedly.

It took only a few minutes to unpack his baggage once he'd been guided to the small cubicle that would be his home for the better part of a terrestrial year. Other than a few changes of clothing, he'd brought little more than some holographs of his parents and his ex-wife, his computerpak and a small library of disks.

The Martian colonies had been provided with an extensive disked library of music, holofilms, digitized translations of many classic flat screen movie, and a very large extract from the Universal Library back on Earth. Nevertheless, before embarking, Todd had checked the catalog and ascertained which of his favorite works were not included. Although he'd already explored every work of fiction he could find about Mars, it seemed to him that they would hold more meaning if he read them again while he was actually on the red planet.

Finally he unpacked his most prized possession, genuine preserved paperback copies of his favorite Martian novels, an unnecessary squandering of his personal weight allowance but one which he didn't regret in the slightest. *The Sword of Rhiannon* was one of the books which had formed his original fascination with Mars, and it was only appropriate it accompany him here.

He had little time to read in the days that followed. Zhuli Ronson was determined to teach him everything he needed to know in record time so that she would be free to return to her research. She started with an exhaustive tour of Dune City, and a brief description of the other stations scattered across the planet. Officially, all inhabited outposts were numbered right along with the automated stations, but Zhuli referred to these by their unofficial nicknames, Red Dust Junction, Cliffwalk, Crater City, New Moscow, Perdition, and Babel. Todd learned that while each station had its own hydroponic gardens, Crater City was the only settlement extensive enough to support livestock. He had resigned himself before leaving Earth to a diet free of red meat - poultry and artificial cheese being the main sources of protein here. He was surprised, however, to learn that there was a fair supply of fresh fish.

"It was impractical for a long time," Zhuli explained. "There's plenty of water frozen in the ground a meter or so down, but once you've extracted what you're sitting on, it replenishes very slowly."

"I thought Polar City was established to draw water from the icecap."

She shook her head. "That's only during the summer. Most of the cap is carbon dioxide, not water. Population growth was restricted for generations until we sank the first shaft down through the hardpan and tapped into an underground reservoir. There's plenty of water if you dig far enough. Mars used to have rivers beside which the Amazon is little more than a trickle. You have to remember that the first two meters underfoot are frozen solid. The record high temperature is 21 degrees centigrade, and the average is about 55 below. But once you get beneath that, there's lots of water."

Todd was shown how to signal a general alarm, practiced donning emergency equipment, taught to patch a small pressure leak. "Mars is stable, at least compared to Earth, but we still have some minor local shifting and settling, and sometimes it's enough to ruin a seal. There's usually plenty of time to call for help, but if possible, you deal with the situation yourself first."

By the third day, Todd was allowed to wander through the common areas of the station unaccompanied. He'd met several members of the staff by now and although they always seemed preoccupied, no one expressed any resentment about his presence among them. On several occasions, he was invited to join small groups in the cafeteria, but he was rarely able to contribute anything during their discussions of ultraviolet shielding techniques, lava flow interpretations in Tharsis, or forced cellular maturation techniques. Although current news was transmitted continuously from Earth, he rarely heard any references to the raging debate about the Chinese

Exclusion Treaty, the UN election campaign, the aftermath of Oklahoma's nuclear accident, or the growing power of the Fundamentalist Union. Mars was a different world in more ways than one.

A single human and his unlikely alien friend slowly plodded their way down one sand dune and up another.

"Don't you ever get tired of that view?"

Zhuli had caught him staring out through the glassex port again. He blinked and Tweel was gone, reality reasserting itself.

"No," he answered brightly. "For you, this is all one enormous science project, an object to be studied, analyzed, understood and described. For me, it's much more. Tell me, Zhuli, are you religious?"

Technically, that was a major breach of manners. The rise of the Fundamentalist Union to a position of major political power had made church affiliation a volatile topic. "I attend non-denominational services when I have the time." It was the proper, safe response.

"Do you believe in the soul? Not necessarily the Christian one, but any sort of discorporate, immortal spirit?"

Zhuli was clearly uncomfortable with the direction the conversation was taking. "I prefer to keep an open mind about subjects which do not lend themselves to objective verification."

"Spoken like a true scientist." Todd rubbed the palms of his hands together, warming to his subject. "During the 20th Century, when people were just starting to become aware of the disastrous course we were taking ecologically, a number of writers theorized that not just people but entire worlds might have souls, Olaf Stapledon, Susan Cooper, John Varley, and Stanislaw Lem for example. I'm trying to find the soul of Mars."

Zhuli was looking both puzzled and bored, but she made an effort to respond. "Well, if Mars has one, it's a dried up husk by now. Maybe even souls get old and die."

Todd shook his head. "Mars isn't dying. It's only asleep."

Todd studied and drilled and listened and repeated back and ate and slept and then studied some more. The days were long, almost an hour more than on Earth, and despite the lower gravity and a relatively sedentary lifestyle, he had no difficulty sleeping. Having been given the assignment to ensure that Todd would not be an imminent danger to the station, Zhuli devoted herself to it with such intensity that he quickly understood how she had gained one of the prized permanent postings to Mars. At times he felt guilty about taking her away from her real job, but whenever he glanced through the glassex window and saw the rolling dunes spread beyond, his satisfaction overcame any second thoughts.

"How would you like to go outside?"

Todd blinked, not fully comprehending what Zhuli had just said. His expression must have been quite comical because she responded with one of her rare laughs. He almost found her attractive but her face was just a bit too full, mouth a shade too wide, eyebrows a hair thin. But when she smiled, which was not often, she radiated charm.

"How's that again?"

They were sitting in a small briefing room where Zhuli had been drilling him on the location of the station's emergency transmitters and the proper procedure for sending an alarm. She sat back in her seat and crossed her arms.

"Theory is great, but I can't tell if you really understand what you're saying or just parroting it back to me. It's time for a little physical application. Think you're up to it?"

There was a rush of adrenaline and Todd forced himself to answer calmly. "I believe I could rise to the occasion."

"Come on then."

They donned their suits in the maintenance section. Todd stood with his arms and legs slightly spread, allowing the suit to adjust to his particular body configuration. When the whispered touch of invisible fingers stopped moving across his flesh, he flexed his limbs and performed the prescribed series of brief exercises designed to ensure proper flexibility. As always, he felt a moment's claustrophobia as the respirator shield molded itself to his face, but it passed.

Zhuli and Todd checked their breathing and life support equipment thoroughly, then double checked each other's before detaching from the station monitoring system. A moment later they were standing in the airlock, and the outer door began to open.

Todd stepped out onto the true surface of Mars for the very first time.

Initially, he was transfixed much like deep sea divers caught in a rhapsodic fugue. An army of half naked warriors streamed over the closest dune astride six legged mounts. A tree house rested on the crest of the next, where several children were deep in conversation with what appeared to be a small ball of fur.

Something touched his shoulder and he turned. Behind her mask, Zhuli's expression was enigmatic; he couldn't tell if she was annoyed or amused.

"Want to go for a walk?" Although the thin atmosphere carried sound, procedure called for them to use radios at all times when outside the station.

"Sure. Is this the guided or the unguided tour?"

"Probably misguided. Come on, before I change my mind."

It wasn't nearly as simple as Todd had expected. The gusty winds meant that the landscape was constantly changing, the dunes in constant motion over time. Maintenance crews regularly cleared the sand away from the station walls, but it shifted under their feet constantly, making their footing uncertain. Zhuli had suggested that they circumambulate the entire station, which appeared much larger on the outside than from within, particularly after they had spent the better part of an hour slogging through the shifting sands.

Zhuli offered to abort their walk halfway around and enter through an alternate airlock, but despite his growing fatigue, Todd declined. This was it, he realized, the reality of Mars. The crawler trip from the landing site to Station Four had been less than satisfactory; only the crew had an outside view and passengers were strictly barred from the forward portion of the vehicle. But now, for the first time, he was really walking the Martian surface. In theory, he could disengage his gauntlet and actually touch the sands; it was summer now and brief exposure was not technically forbidden, but he suspected that Zhuli would not approve. He decided that experience could wait awhile.

When they finally reached the point where they had first emerged, the wind had already blurred their tracks. Just as Mars could obliterate all of the works of man on its surface, he thought, but did not say aloud.

"Don't you ever read for entertainment, Zhuli?" Todd found her sitting in the small station lounge, her body folded into the lap of a polymorphic chair, a holobook in her hand. Todd had read the disk label, "Phototropic Sensors: The Uses of Biogenetics in an Engineering Environment".

She dropped her hand and met his eyes levelly. "There isn't enough time in my life for fantasy, or any other frivolity."

"Frivolity! The spirit, the soul of the human race, is manifested in its art."

"Come off it, Todd. You're an intelligent man; don't try to tell me you believe that nonsense. Humanity's greatest achievement is control of the physical environment, first on Earth, now on Mars, eventually the entire solar system, perhaps the stars beyond if we can overcome the light speed limitation."

He shook his head, so amazed at her words that he stumbled over his response before drawing a deep breath and replying more calmly. "I can't accept that you really believe that, Zhuli. Are you prepared to dismiss the giants of literature, Shakespeare, Goldman, P.D. James, Sturgeon, Chin, Asturias, Ngura the Elder, Di Filippo, and all the rest?"

"Their work has value to those who appreciate such things, but it's just entertainment."

Todd opened his mouth, but could think of no appropriate response. "Sometimes I don't think it will be necessary for us to visit the stars to find an alien species," he countered weakly, then turned and left before his defeat became more complete.

Todd had not seen or heard from Artus Klane since the day of his arrival, but the following day Zhuli advised him that it had been decided that constant supervision was no longer necessary. "I'm finally going back to the lab in Crater City," Zhuli told him. "If you're still interested in helping out, Klane has arranged to send you to Perdition for a while. That's the clearing house for the various projects scattered across Mars, and theoretically that's where our discoveries are consolidated and codified and then refined for less technical minds."

Now that the time to relocate had arrived, Todd found himself strangely unwilling to part from Zhuli and the few casual acquaintances he had made among the local staff. After all, they were the only people he knew in the entire world.

"I'd be happy to help out in any way that I can."

Her approving smile touched him more than he had expected. "There's one other possibility you might want to consider." She paused and her face betrayed mild concern, as though she were uncertain how to phrase what she wanted to say. "Before I go north, I've been given permission to take one of the crawlers down to the Labyrinth and check some of the test instruments we've placed there. This damned sand insinuates itself into everything. If it doesn't get inside and cripple the machinery, it covers them and blinds their sensors. Someone has to check them out periodically, and since the project I'm involved with is going to face the same problems, it makes sense for me to go. If you're interested, there's room in the crawler for a passenger. I warn you though that it's a three to four day round trip, and the accommodations in a crawler are something less than comfortable."

The only reason Todd didn't agree immediately was that he didn't want to seem too eager. He forced himself to maintain a thoughtful expression for endless seconds before finally nodding. "Sure, if you're willing to have me, I'd be foolish to pass up the chance."

Zhuli warned him the trip would be boring, but he didn't find it so. True, for the first hour they seemed to be moving almost in circles; every time they crested one dune, they faced another, identical one. But as time and kilometers passed, each rise became progressively gentler, with lower crests, and before long they were travelling over a comparatively level expanse, trailing a cloud of disturbed dust that settled slowly in their wake.

"We won't be able to keep this pace much longer. Broken ground ahead."

"What? Oh, okay." Todd had been imagining he was Gordon Holder, sole survivor of the first expedition to Mars, trying to communicate with the thoughtful superintelligences that lived in the Martian wastelands. He glanced past Zhuli's shoulder; the driver's seat was forward, and slightly roomier. Very slightly. Varicolored hills were rising out of the horizon in a series of chaotic tiers.

"Looks forbidding enough."

She shrugged. "It's not as bad as all that. This part of the
Labyrinth is pretty well mapped and explored and it's geologically
stable. We haven't recorded a significant quake or landslide in this
area in living memory. This should be a piece of cake."

Todd shook his head. "Never say that; it's bad luck."

"You've been reading too many stories," she replied curtly.

They spent the night parked close to a steep cliff face,
adjacent to a small unmanned way station. The two seats
transformed into bunks, the passenger's pivoting and sliding forward
as the driver's rose and cammed toward the rear, so that one was
stacked on top of the other. Although the crawler was theoretically
good for seventy-two hours without a recharge, Zhuli had linked up
to an umbilical from the way station to boost their reserve power
back to maximum.

"Never hurts to be overcautious," she told him. "Had a
crawler lost in a sandstorm for three days once up north."

Although the sleeping arrangements were claustrophobic,
Todd's insomnia that evening was the result of excitement, not
anxiety. Phobos was visible in the night sky, along with an array of
bright, relatively unblinking stars. With the fall of darkness, the wind
had risen, occasional gusts spattering finely grained sand against the
scarred and pitted sides of the crawler. Todd's mind tried to organize
the sounds of the Martian night into coherent form, distant voices,
the clash of swords, the scream of a banth. His last thought before
drifting off into unconsciousness was to regret that his companion
found Mars so unromantic.

They set off at first light the following day. Todd was still
sipping at his synthetic coffee when Zhuli finished retracting the
umbilical and checked the crawler's resident diagnostics.

Moments later, they were moving across the broken
landscape of the outer Labyrinth.

Although she remained as alert as ever, Zhuli seemed to have
relaxed now that she was actually doing something she considered
worthwhile. Todd learned that her parents had died in a hoverflight
accident at Dar Es Salaam while she was still an undergraduate at the
California Institute of Technology. She'd never been married, term
or permanent, and had rarely dated due to the press of other
commitments. Although she offered this information casually, Todd

thought he detected a wistful note. But it might have been his imagination.

At mid-morning, they reached the first substation, essentially a satellite of the way station, equipped to monitor temperature, wind speed, pressure, seismic activities, and a number of other factors. At first, Zhuli didn't think he should leave the vehicle, but he pleaded the necessity to stretch his cramped legs and she relented, so long as he agreed to stay within sight. While she cleared and recalibrated the sand covered mound of equipment, Todd marveled at the deeply striated walls of rock and sand that surrounded them. They had been following a slowly descending route for most of the day, which was now beginning to widen into a wedge shaped plateau. There was less sand here; the irregular windstorms alternately scoured and buried the more densely packed surface. Todd was attempting to find intelligent patterns in the varicolored walls when Zhuli finally summoned him back to the crawler.

They serviced two other substations that afternoon. "We're a little behind schedule," she told him as they topped a small rise. A steeply chiseled canyon stretched out and away from them. "The next way station's quite a bit further and there's not many sheltered places along the way. We'll camp just ahead and get an early start tomorrow."

Zhuli radioed a terse summary of her plan back to Dune City a short while later, bouncing the message off one of the many communications satellites currently orbiting Mars. In theory, they were supposed to report in at intervals of no less than twelve hours, although it was sometimes difficult to get a clear communications angle from deep in the Labyrinth.

"We have a weather advisory," she told him moments later, smiling thinly.

"Let me guess. Heavy rain squalls, followed by partly cloudy?"

"Close, substitute 'sand' for 'rain' and you're right on target."

Todd shrugged. "So what's new?" They'd seen distant sandstorms twice that day, both very localized disturbances.

She seemed unusually thoughtful. "Maybe we should have kept going," she answered at last, although it wasn't clear if she was talking to Todd or to herself. "I'd feel a lot better with a full charge."

As it turned out, it probably wouldn't have mattered.

They had reached the floor of the valley, from which two smaller, subsidiary declines led to chasmlike arms pointing to either side. These were both currently inaccessible, Zhuli told him, although substations had been set up at the mouth of each.

"We'll have to backtrack a bit to service them," she explained, "but first priority right now is a recharge." Todd didn't understand her haste; they would be well within the operational limits of their vehicle even if they visited both sites prior to the way station, but he wasn't about to object to anything which would ultimately prolong their journey. Besides, she was in charge.

Crawlers superficially resembled devices envisioned by NASA and various science fiction writers more than two centuries earlier. They progressed by means of a system of treads which adjusted to the surface of the terrain over which they travelled. But instead of a pair of belts, crawlers were supported by literally scores of very narrow ones, each of which was governed individually by a sophisticated computer which was constantly adjusting tension, even tread size within certain limits. The technology was almost a century old by now and was so heavily redundant that only major damage to the computer core itself could create a dangerous malfunction.

They had reached a narrow but level area that bridged a deep crevasse. The surface was almost entirely clear of sand, gravel, and rock, a ramp leading to the main valley beyond. Todd heard the engine whine and felt the surge of acceleration as Zhuli increased their speed, and had just turned his head to say something when disaster struck.

A section of the ramp collapsed beneath them, falling away to reveal a wide cavity about six meters deep. Neither of the crawlers' passengers could see the hazard at first, although Zhuli correctly interpreted the slewing of the vehicle as its computer attempted to compensate. Treads chewed into the ground on both sides of the gap, but rather than pull their burden forward, this contributed to the collapse of the crumbling surface.

The crawler tipped sideways and nose down and toppled into the darkness. Although serious enough in itself, the distance would not ordinarily have been great enough to severely damage the crawler. But as they tilted forward, the headlights revealed a jagged promontory of rock rising out of the cavity.

Todd instinctively raised his arm before the impact stunned him; only the safety harness kept him in his seat.

He regained awareness of his surroundings with no sense of the passage of time. The crawler's headlights were still on, but they splashed purposelessly against the rocky wall ahead. Zhuli was slumped over and he reached hesitantly, then gripped her shoulder anxiously. She moaned and turned her head to one side but didn't respond when he called her name.

There was little room to maneuver in the small cabin, but Todd felt an immediate need to act. He was gratified to discover that the internal lighting came up when he touched the control, then unstrapped himself and knelt on his seat so that he could better examine the telltales on the front of Zhuli's suit.

She was clearly unconscious, a trickle of blood had run out from under the respirator shield and down the left side of her face. There was more blood on one thigh and a funny rasp in her breath. According to the telltales, her body temperature was down, respiration and heart beat strong but uneven. A painkiller and anti-infectives had already been administered, and the injection of a combination of drugs designed to slow her metabolism, thicken her blood, and provide other life sustaining functions was imminent. Todd had the option to override their use, another safety precaution, but he suspected that she had a punctured lung and possible concussion, and anything which would act to control the damage to her body was welcome.

He applied pressure bandages to both open wounds even though neither seemed life threatening before investigating their physical predicament.

The crawler was more badly damaged than he had expected. The rocky spit had glanced along the side of the passenger cabin before penetrating the instrumentation module directly behind Todd's seat. They were suspended at a forty five degree angle, impaled on the promontory and with heavy damage to the computer as well as many of the treads. There had been some small rupturing of the passenger compartment shell but this had been automatically sealed with fastfoam to prevent air loss. This situation might not continue, however, as the vehicle shifted slightly when he moved about. Todd replaced Zhuli's respirator as a safety precaution and tied it directly into the crawler's atmospheric tanks so that she wouldn't be dependent upon her limited suit supply.

The radio was smashed beyond recognition and the emergency beeper's malfunction light flashed ruby red. He would later discover that the transmitter had been scraped off the outer hull during the accident.

Todd Crandall stood on the Martian surface, staring down into the pit where Zhuli Ronson slumped unconscious in their disabled vehicle. The feeble sun was directly overhead, its rays illuminating a cascade of colored smear that covered the sloping walls; breath taking it might well be but he was feeling less than romantic about Mars at present. Zhuli's physical condition was deteriorating despite her suit's efforts toward stabilization. Although they were scheduled to radio in during the evening, he knew that there would be no instant alarm raised for at least a couple of hours past their reporting window, and in all likelihood a rescue operation would not be launched in the darkness. At best, a power sled would be sent out at first light to locate them visually and drop an emergency team to assist until surface support arrived.

He doubted Zhuli would last that long.

The map he held was a computer augmented survey photograph. He was confident of his ability to locate either of the two substations in the area. The question was, which could he reach more quickly? In straight line distance, they were almost equidistant, but the marked crawler routes were both circuitous, one to bypass a web of crevices to the east, the other to skirt around an atypical upthrust ridge that marched from north to south like the spine of some ancient Martian dragon.

Cursing his indecision, he chose to head west. There was another reason for haste; his suit held only enough oxygen for approximately four hours of moderate activity, although he could recharge at the substation, which was fitted with emergency oxygen and water supplies. But he estimated that the walk that faced him would consume close to four hours over even friendly terrain.

Todd constantly checked his suit to see if it was picking up a homing signal from the substation, but it was over an hour before he was relieved to see the indicator flash weakly. During that period he had left the natural ramp and ascended over broken ground toward the valley wall, which now towered dizzying above his head. Although his suit was working perfectly at controlling his personal environment, Todd found himself shivering; he knew that the external temperature was starting to drop, and no amount of rational thought could dispel the chill that was invading his body.

It was only early afternoon, but already deep shadows were reaching across the valley floor. The sun was out of sight behind an eroded peak and the sky was hazy, filled with dust particles suspended by a mild but persistent breeze. Todd turned on his suit lights briefly, then extinguished them, reluctant to expend the energy required unless it became absolutely necessary.

He mounted one fairly gentle swell of land and, as expected, found himself facing the rocky spine. The crawler would have veered to the north here, bypassing the worst of the barrier, crossing only when the extrusion had settled back toward the surface. Todd didn't have the luxury of choosing the easier route. He began to climb.

It had taken an hour and a half to cover the first eight kilometers. It took almost as long to reach the crest of the spine and descend on the opposite side. Although his calves and the soles of his feet were protesting slightly, in general Todd felt increasingly confident. He had anticipated an even longer delay at the ridge, and now believed he'd arrive at the substation with at least half an hour to spare. He could activate the emergency beacon, replenish his oxygen tank, and return to the crawler in time to signal the rescuers with his shorter range suit radio.

Unfortunately, Mars had another surprise waiting for him.

The sandstorm came up so suddenly that it was rattling across the front of his respirator almost before he realized what was happening. Although he'd never actually been out in one before, Todd had watched these transient squalls of flying dust and sand from Dune City on three occasions. The wind itself was too weak to seriously impede his journey and he had no difficulty homing in on the substation, but the dust was disorienting and masked the ground underfoot. He began to stumble across the uneven surface, arms raised protectively in anticipation of a fall. This added to his fatigue as well as slowing his progress.

The map indicated he would have to cross a shallow ravine, but he had misjudged its distance, realized his error only when he lost his footing and went rolling down a mercifully smooth slope. When he finally came to a stop, he lay panting heavily while his suit struggled to restore his body's chemical equilibrium. The sandstorm showed no indication of weakening, hampering his initial effort to check the integrity of his equipment. But then he realized that he was in no position to do anything about a suit breach in any case, and he struggled to his feet.

What followed was a muffled nightmare. He moved forward leadenly, determined to reach the substation. Half an hour before he had expected his air supply to run out, he began to experience some difficulty breathing, felt the prick of more injections as his suit tried desperately to compensate for the fatigue toxins in his blood.

At that moment, Mars was no longer a place of romance. Todd was an island of life in a sterile and unconcerned sea of sand. He could barely make out his gloved hand when he raised it in front of his respirator shield, and the few glimpses he obtained of his surroundings came only when the storm paused to prepare a fresh assault. Five minutes passed and he felt each breath burning from the back of his throat to the center of his chest. Bands of fire ran up the backs of his legs. His lips felt dry even when he sucked on the water tube and his skin itched as though some of the Martian sand had infiltrated his suit.

Five minutes later Todd paused, realizing that he was drifting off course, and when he turned back toward the signal from the substation, his left ankle turned treacherously.

Todd fell on his stomach, faced pressed into the shifting sand. Twice he attempted unsuccessfully to regain his feet. After the second failure, he closed his eyes, deciding that a brief nap would give him the necessary strength.

When he opened his eyes, something cold and moist rested across the top half of his face and he was lying on his back. Todd reached up and pulled away the damp cloth, found himself in a large bed covered with pillows. He was still wearing his suit, but the respirator had been unfastened and was lying across his chest, still attached by the oxygen lead. He rose onto his elbows and looked around.

He was in a bedroom, small by Earthly standards but unimaginably spacious for the planet Mars. Two wardrobes flanked an ornately carved dressing table at the far end of the room, and a chair stood to the left of the bed. There were no windows, a single door to his right, currently closed. The only sound he could hear was a faint, unidentifiable murmuring.

"I have to be dreaming," he told himself, but it didn't feel like a dream. The floor was reassuringly solid when he slipped out of the bed, crossed to the door, and cautiously inched it open.

What he saw then was so totally impossible that he opened the door wide, all caution abandoned.

Outside the room was a narrow walkway bordered by a railing that consisted of interwoven curves of some material that resembled wood. Todd stepped forward, gripped the rail tightly with both hands, and looked down at the landscape passing below.

Broad red plains spread in every direction, ribbed with green fringed lines of blue. Vegetation grew only in the vicinity of the elaborate canal system, and although he saw occasional animals of indeterminate nature wandering across the sand, they were concentrated mostly near the patches of green. The view was quite panoramic and constantly changing; the airship upon which he rode was evidently moving at quite a rapid pace. He glanced up and saw that the humming he had heard earlier originated in the scores of propellers which whirred above, holding the ship aloft.

"I see you're awake."

Todd turned at the sound, a deep male voice, subtly accented. What he saw then was even more unbelievable than his presence aboard an impossible airship.

A meter or two away stood Matt Carse, hero of *The Sword of Rhiannon*. Todd had seen him many times before, of course; he had read the book over a dozen times. But always inside his head, never in the flesh.

"Come along. The others are waiting for you." Carse turned and started to move down the walkway. His mind a cauldron of whirling thoughts, Todd had no will to resist the order. He followed.

Carse led him up a short ladder to the main deck, an open space where two or three dozen people stood scattered in small groups. Not all of them were human.

He recognized each and every one, of course. The scantily clad beauty talking to the ugly green Martian was Dejah Thoris, the skinny teenage girl who watched him with a slightly mocking grin was surely Poddy Fries, and the two men comparing the quality of their drawn swords were John Carter and Lieutenant Gulliver Jones. There were many others as well, Harry Thorne, Willis the Bouncer, Arnie Kott, Tweel, Dolph Haertel, and Martin Gibson. Each looked and acted exactly as Todd had imagined they would.

Which was quite impossible, of course, since they were all characters from books.

Am I dead? Todd wondered.

Carse had been walking toward the rest but now he stopped, realizing that Todd had not moved since reaching the upper deck. "Don't be alarmed," he said quietly. His expression betrayed amusement.

"I'm dreaming all this. I must be." Todd hadn't realized he was speaking aloud until Carse frowned and shook his head.

"Don't say that. We can't help those who don't believe in us."

Todd was convinced that he had lapsed into hallucination. Oxygen deprivation, he thought silently. I'm going to die of asphyxiation in a Martian sandstorm. Not quite the way I'd have chosen to go, but certainly ironic. "You're all fictional characters, people from books."

Carse dropped his chin, but Todd couldn't tell whether it was acquiescence or dismay. "Perhaps we are, but we're real all the same."

Beyond the deck rail, Todd saw that they were leaving the Martian plains, drifting toward a broad mountain range beyond. The individual peaks were red, orange, scarlet, purple, brown, and black. A growing feeling of acceptance calmed him; he was resigned to the fact of his own imminent death and his only lingering regret was that he had been unable to help Zhuli.

"I suppose this is some kind of Martian Valhalla," he said after a short pause. "A gathering of heroes."

"In a manner of speaking," Carse replied straightforwardly, "if that's how you see things. Of course, we'll change as time passes and a greater mix of imagination enriches our nature. But you are the first to feel deeply enough to evoke us, and your vision is the underlying skeleton upon which the later flesh will grow."

"So I created you out of my mind, is that it?" Todd was at one time skeptical and amused at himself for arguing with his own illusions. "Dreamed you up?"

But Carse was shaking his head. "We have existed always and always will. We have neither a beginning nor an end. Tell me, if a child were shipwrecked on a deserted island and lived and died without seeing another human being, would the result be a good or an evil person?"

Todd shook his head in bewilderment. "I don't think good or evil would apply. The words only have meaning when they describe human interactions."

Carse nodded. "We are all defined by the perceptions of others. If you were blind, would you find me handsome, or ugly?"

"Neither."

"We derive our nature from the imaginations of those who choose to perceive us, just as your ancestors chose to impose the form of King Arthur and Dracula and others. We are, if you like, the soul of Mars, just as they are the soul of Earth."

The constant hum changed tone as the propellers slowed. The deck lurched slightly underfoot and tilted forward as the airship began to angle down toward the mountain chain.

Carse looked forward and beckoned. "Come along, you must leave us here."

Todd remained confused, still half convinced he was dreaming, half convinced he was not.

The airship dropped quickly, then began to hover in place as Carse reached the forward rail. Todd threw off his paralysis just as Carse dropped a rope ladder over the side. It unrolled as it fell toward the ground.

"It's time for you to go." Carse turned, reached out and grasped Todd's hand, gripping it firmly. The hand felt undeniably real. Todd opened his mouth, but words refused to come. Instead, he turned as bidden and climbed over the rail.

Because of the narrowness of the canyon walls, the airship was still quite high. Todd descended the rope ladder rhythmically, feet and arms moving in relentless repetition. He concentrated on the task at hand, refusing to think about the circumstances of the descent, although he was already feeling a resurgence of the fatigue that had driven him from consciousness into this...dream? Cramps knotted the muscles in his legs and those in his arms began to feel as though they were taut violin strings, recently plucked.

Three meters above the ground, he missed a step, failed to compensate, and fell.

A blast of cold air was an almost physical blow across his face. Todd sat up, discovered that his respirator had become detached from its housing, the shield open, exposing his face to the near zero centigrade temperature. He hastily reseated the shield, blinking his eyes to clear the vision from his head. It was difficult to breathe and he knew that his air supply was almost completely exhausted. The dream he had just experienced was evidence his mind was being affected by oxygen starvation. The sandstorm had weakened substantially during the past few seconds, and he looked around desperately, still unwilling to surrender his life without a fight.

A few meters away, barely visible through the blowing dust and sand, stood an obviously human artifact. It was partially buried by a newborn dune, but enough of its shape was visible to be recognizable.

It was the substation he sought.

Todd activated the emergency beacon quickly, following the procedure Zhuli had insisted he know well enough to complete even in total darkness. It would only be a matter of a few hours now until a power sled was sent out to vertically insert an emergency team. He could wait here and guide the team back to the crawler, but Todd knew from the outset that he had no intention of remaining. From this range the crawler's heat signature would guide them to it. Even if he could not do anything more to help Zhuli, he felt obligated to return to her side.

The trip back was almost as dreamlike as the episode he had experienced earlier. The sandstorm subsided, which made travel much easier, but fatigue still caused him to stumble over small obstacles. He almost gave up while crossing the ridge, but memory of his obligation to Zhuli provided just enough incentive to drive him over the top. From there, most of what remained was literally downhill.

He reached the disabled crawler with an hour of air remaining. Despite the safety margin, his first action upon entering the cab was to hook into the main tank. Then he turned to read the telltales on Zhuli's suit.

For several seconds, he blinked in incomprehension, unable to interpret what his eyes were seeing. Then he turned away and collapsed into the passenger seat, stunned into immobility.

Zhuli Ronson was the 731st person to die accidentally on the planet Mars.

Todd was unconscious when the rescue team arrived, having located the half buried crawler with infrared detectors; they directed his suit to administer a sedative once they were assured that he was basically uninjured. He was totally oblivious to his extraction from the crawler several hours later and his transfer to a larger vehicle. In fact, the next time he opened his eyes, he was in a hospital room in Dune City.

For the first few seconds, he believed himself back on the airship, but the dream disintegrated rapidly with the entrance of a Medicorps Tech, who asked him how he was feeling and offered him a stimulant. An hour later he was sitting up in bed, being debriefed by an investigating team from Crater City.

They had already pretty accurately reconstructed the entire sequence of events, and Todd's confirmation seemed to be a matter of form rather than necessity. But the chief investigator, a woman named Baldwin, watched him closely during the entire interview and her assistant, Vassily something-or-other, was clearly impatient and uncomfortable for some reason. Still silently mourning his lost friend, Todd was uninterested in their problems.

Just as he thought the session was drawing to an end, Baldwin's voice became deeper, an attempt to disguise stress.

"Mr. Crandall, we'd be very interested in knowing how you managed to supplement your oxygen supply."

Todd frowned. "What do you mean? The main tanks on the crawler were intact. I was just lucky that we were within range of the substation. I almost died as it was."

She frowned and looked down into her lap briefly, then raised her head to make definite eye contact. "And how did you make the return trip?"

Todd blinked, suddenly realized he had no memory of having refilled his suit tank.

"There's an emergency tank at the substation."

"And you refilled your suit tank when you arrived there?"

Todd shrugged. "I don't remember doing it, to be honest; I was a little out of it by then, you know. Zhuli...Doctor Ronson had drilled me in the procedure so many times, I must have done it automatically, without thinking. What difference does it make?"

Baldwin opened her mouth, but turned her head away without saying anything. Todd felt the muscles in the back of his neck tensing.

"What's wrong?" Suddenly, he wasn't certain he wanted Baldwin to answer. And she didn't. Vassily something-or-other spoke instead.

"Substation L544 was last inspected by a crawler crew several months ago. They reported that the emergency oxygen tank was defective and had leaked its contents into the atmosphere."

Todd thought about it for a moment. "Obviously, they were mistaken. There must have been enough pressure remaining to fill my tank."

The tall Russian shook his head. "That's quite impossible. They brought the defective tank back with them for repair. It has not yet been replaced."

And for that, Todd had no answer at all.

The investigation of Zhuli Ronson's death was brought to a close later that day. For the rest of the time Todd Crandall spent on Mars, he kept pretty much to himself. Word had gotten around and the permanent staff avoided him, although they could not have explained why, even to themselves.

For his part, Todd was not unhappy with the isolation. He had a lot to think about, not the least of which was to wonder why he had been saved, apparently miraculously, but not Zhuli. He was nearing the end of his stay on the red planet when he remembered something Carse had said to him during his "dream".

"We can't help those who don't believe in us."

"You should have found the time, Zhuli," he told his absent friend. "Fantasy has its uses after all."

LONG TIME PASSING

I was mortally wounded near Ypres on July 31, 1917, although obviously it turned out not to be quite as serious as it would have been for anyone else. Frank Ledwidge and I were hauling wooden planks and setting them in the mud so that heavy equipment could be moved forward toward the fighting. It was hot, monotonous work and we'd stopped for a spot of tea when a Bosch shell landed right beside us. Frank had survived Gallipoli and Salonica and deserved a better end, but then so did most of the rest of us. General Haig kept insisting that the enemy was beaten, but it sure didn't look that way from the trenches.

Anyway, I had a split second to see Frank's body torn apart before the force of the explosion and accompanying shrapnel tore into me. I was facing right toward it and I suppose it must have made a bloody mess of my chest and face. I couldn't see anything and I think my eyes must have been gone. The funny thing was that after the first shocking pain, I didn't feel anything at all, and I never lost consciousness. I was pretty sure that I was lying on my back, but I couldn't actually feel my body at all, and the constant terror that I had kept in check only with difficulty for the three months since I'd arrived from England dissipated in an instant. I couldn't understand what all the fuss was about.

Time passed but I had no sense of it. I could still hear explosions, mostly in the distance, and machine gun fire, sometimes quite close. None of this seemed to concern me. Nor did the sudden sound of a voice quite close by. "How about this one?"

"He's a deadun, in't he? Leave him for now."

"I know him. Name of Waydon. Stout fellow."

"Not no more, he in't."

And then they were gone.

I had no way of judging the passage of time. I must have lain there in a kind of fugue for hours before I finally fell asleep. When I awoke, there was blackness everywhere and I thought it might be night until I remembered that I had no eyes. But there were stars, I thought. Or is my mind playing a trick on me? My confusion ended – or at least changed direction - when a flare briefly sputtered somewhere out of my line of sight, casting enough light that I could discern shadows, the rim of the trench. The battle must have reached a lull because the only sounds were the occasional pops of sniper rifles in the distance.

I'm still alive, I told myself, and not as badly hurt as I'd thought. I tentatively tried to move my arms and one of them cooperated. Slowly, with great care, I raised my head and shoulders to make a preliminary appraisal of my wounds. It was too dark to see much and I had almost fallen back when another flare burst almost directly overhead, and I saw vividly the broken ribs, ruptured organs, and shattered pelvis. I'm dead, I thought. I just haven't realized it yet. And then I slept some more, or maybe I just fainted.

This time I was undisturbed and unaware for a much longer period. Figuring back later I guessed I lay there another three days and three nights. I was finally disturbed by a team of stretcher bearers who obviously thought I was dead. Given the state of my uniform and the amount of blood and gore scattered about, they were perfectly justified in doing so. But when they took me by the arms and tried to lift me, I cried out in surprise, not pain.

"Here! He's alive, this one is! Fancy that!"

They helped me up and cleaned me off as best they could and other than some bruising and scattered cuts and abrasions, I was apparently uninjured. When they asked me what had happened, I pretended amnesia due to shock. Or maybe it wasn't pretense. I didn't know what had happened, after all. I had been sure that I was dying. I remembered being blind, although I suppose that could have been hysteria or shock, but I also remembered seeing my own shattered body, and that memory was too sharp and distinct to be fantasy.

I was sent back to the rear as walking wounded, but when a doctor finally examined me, he made no secret of the fact that he thought I'd been malingering. So I was sent back to my unit the following day.

The rest of the war was and still is very hazy to me. I was not wounded again although I saw a great deal of action. I was gassed once and it was thoroughly unpleasant, but I recovered quickly enough. The last fighting I saw was at Sambre Canal and the war was all but over then, although it was still several months before I was demobbed.

Like many of my generation, I immediately set about forgetting the horrors I'd witnessed, and in some cases participated in, during the previous two years, and I also managed to put out of my mind the strange recuperative powers I'd exhibited. With the passage of time, I assumed that my initial appraisal of my wounds had been the product of delirium. After all, I had never shown any such ability previously.

Or had I? I had always considered myself merely fortunate in that I'd suffered none of the childhood ailments that periodically afflicted my peers. I recall my mother commenting that my occasional cuts and bruises healed quickly, but my father had insisted that he had always enjoyed robust health so that was to be expected. His robust health proved inadequate to save him from what proved to be a fatal attack of what was then called dyspepsia.

There was no difficulty finding employment in the aftermath of the war because so many my age had died and I became an underclerk at Carswell and Bosworth, where I flourished along with the firm for the next twenty years. Then came the Hitler War.

I was not quite forty, and looked a good deal younger, and when the Wehrmacht rolled into Poland I could have avoided military service simply by enlisting in the home guard. Instead I touted my acquired organizational skills and was given in turn a commission and a post in supply. Although I had anticipated an early return to France, the disaster of Dunkirk precluded that and I spent most of the war organizing munitions deliveries to the navy, and later to the swelling American military presence. I once had the pleasure of speaking directly to General Eisenhower, and on another occasion incurred the direct wrath of General Montgomery, the latter thankfully at a great distance.

I almost came through the war unscathed, but I found myself in the wrong place at the wrong time. A V1 rocket collapsed a building in which I had been sheltering with three other people, killing us all. Well, technically, not all of us since I'm still here, but this time there was no question that my wounds would have killed any ordinary – I use the word deliberately – man.

We had not chosen our refuge wisely. The door to the cellars was securely locked. I had in fact just suggested that we hasten elsewhere when the explosion made the question academic. I have a vague memory of the walls collapsing around us and then I was falling. There was a sudden searing pain and I lost consciousness.

As before, I woke with a sense of mild confusion and vague wellbeing. The orientation of my body seemed odd and at first I was unable to make out details of my circumstances in the gloom – the building as a whole had collapsed into rubble above me. I was face down, arms and legs extended and falling loosely to either side. At first I thought that I had fallen athwart a beam of some sort, but when my eyes finally focused enough to discern the facts, I was shocked into a brief, futile panic. A narrow supporting beam had split lengthwise, one sharp end extending upward through my abdomen, and was now out of my line of sight at a point somewhere above my shoulders.

Even though I felt no more than a mild discomfort, the psychological effects were, as you might imagine, severe. Convinced I was going to die, I alternately sagged and wept, or thrashed and screamed for help. It was exhaustion rather than any conscious effort that eventually led to composure. I was not dead, after all. Could I do something to help my situation?

I won't attempt to describe the next two hours. Even the thought of it sends my mind skittering away to inconsequentials. Somehow I managed to work my mangled body up past the end of the protruding beam until I was no longer impaled, though the last effort broke my grip and I fell the last few meters to the cellar floor, where I lost consciousness once again.

They dug me out the following morning. My survival, they said, was miraculous given the damage to the building. Other than some superficial injuries, I was fine and I walked out of the wreckage unassisted.

There was no doubt in my mind this time. I possessed some form of regenerative power unheard of previously. I even made a few clandestine tests, slicing my arm with a knife, breaking a forefinger with a hammer. There was always a moment of intense pain followed by a kind of dreamy numbness and within hours dried scabs were dropping off and broken bones had completely knitted. The initial pain, I theorized, was the body's way of telling me I was doing something self destructive, a message terminated once it had been successfully delivered. I never found the courage to try poison or suffocation, which seemed to me a different brand of hurt, but I was apparently immune to all but – presumably – the most intense physical trauma. I doubt, for example, that I would have survived a visit to Hiroshima on August 6. 1945.

Contemplation of my bizarre condition explained another factor in my life. I had often been told that I did not look my age and other than a change in clothing styles and the way I wore my hair – and the addition of a moustache – I looked very much as I had when I'd embarked for France in 1917. My parents both died shortly after the war and I changed jobs several times during the 1950s, so my changelessness attracted no great notice. On the other hand, it was increasingly difficult to convince prospective employers and other acquaintances that I was in fact in my fifties when I looked barely twenty.

In 1958 I emigrated to America, having altered my papers to reflect a birth date in the 1930s. My inclination toward gregariousness receded as I found it increasingly difficult to avoid making anachronistic comments about my experiences. I once told a friend that I'd been in my office working when word came of the Japanese attack on Pearl Harbor, and then had to hastily explain that I'd always called my playroom "my office" as a child. I soon decided it was best to utter as little as possible rather than have to pre-emptively vet everything I said and I was generally considered taciturn by those who knew me from that point forward.

In 1965, I found the name of a child who had died in 1947 shortly after his first birthday. I secured a copy of the birth certificate for Daniel Haynes from the state of Connecticut and relocated to California, where I applied for a social security card and registered as a voter. My accent and unfamiliarity with American customs was easily explained; my parents had taken me to England where I had lived until their recent deaths. I also perforce registered for the draft and drew a very low number. In April of 1968, I was inducted into the US Army and, after some unpleasant and totally inadequate training, shipped off to Vietnam

During the early months of my tour, I worked with a supply unit away from the fighting, which suited me just fine. I wasn't afraid of being wounded as much as I was concerned that someone might discover my secret. All wars are chaotic, of course, but in many ways Vietnam was less so than most. Wounded personnel were not as likely to be left to die or recover on their own as in earlier conflicts.

You might wonder why I was so concerned about concealing my regenerative powers, but if so that's only because you haven't thought the matter through. I was in the military and if my superiors had ever discovered the truth, I'd never have been free again. I might have been treated as royalty, but I'd have been locked in the tower nevertheless.

I almost made it through my tour of duty without serious incident, but during the last month while I was a short timer I fell prey to friendly fire. An air force plane laying down napalm along our northern perimeter went out of control and dropped part of its package on the barracks where I was sleeping. Six of us died in our beds and a couple of dozen had serious burns. I was probably the worst of those who survived and the doctors made no secret of the fact that they didn't think I'd last until morning – they assumed I was unconscious from shock but I actually felt pretty good as long as my eyes were closed and I couldn't see the mass of scar tissue that had formerly been the flesh I had showered clean just that morning.

I napped for a while and woke up around midnight. Most of my skin was a slightly sensitive pink by then but there was no pain and I slipped out of bed easily. I had a plan and it depended on luck, but luck seemed to flow my way that night. I moved one of the charred corpses – the medics called them "crispy critters" - to my bed and hung my dog tags around his neck. Daniel Haynes had no family so identification wouldn't present a problem. I took the dead man's dog tags and discovered that I was now Corporal Albert Brown, who unfortunately was black and a good deal taller than I. I couldn't return to our unit under that identity, obviously, so I had to be on a medevac flight in the morning.

So just before reveille, I managed – with considerable difficulty – to break my right arm. The doctor who set the fracture an hour later, a dour looking captain, apologized repeatedly that no one had treated the injury previously. The army was doing a RIF at the time – that's Reduction in Force – so I was sent back to the states to recuperate. I went AWOL three hours after we landed and poor Corporal Brown's name was sullied ever after, I'm afraid.

I stayed under the radar until the war ended and then repeated my birth certificate ploy and became Nathan Westcott. My accent was almost undetectable by then. I worked variously as a forest ranger, a mail carrier, and census taker, all jobs where I didn't have to mix with the same people on a regular basis. The sense of apartness from the rest of the human race grew stronger and was reinforced by my decision to limit the chances that I might betray the secret of my longevity. On my seventieth birthday, I still looked like a college student.

I wasn't happy with my life, exactly, though I was convinced that I had generally made the right choices. I had neither family nor friends. I occasionally found agreeable female companions, but after stupidly referring to a World War II experience during pillow talk with a waitress, I limited every such relationship to a maximum of three encounters. When one of my partners pressed for more intimacy, I relocated.

And so my life had more or less fallen into a pattern by the end of the century.

A few years later I discovered that I was not unique. I was working at the time for a mortuary. I drove the hearse, polished the coffins, mowed the grass, and stood around looking somber during wakes. I had begun to feel a kind of fascination for death that drew me to the job, and it was not one in which I spent much time talking to either my colleagues or the recently bereaved.

Then Dudley Dam ruptured and the villages of South Dudley and Duddleston were swept away. The National Guard and County Medical Services were ferrying the injured to hospitals both modern and makeshift, while I joined the unfortunately large group who dragged bodies out of the wreckage, tagged and bagged them, and brought them to hastily organized morgues at nearby schools.

It took a while for the waters to recede, almost three days before we were able to reach some parts of the river valley, and it was on the fourth day that I heard something moving inside a collapsed supermarket. My first assumption was that it was dogs or rats tearing at the corpses, so I armed myself with a length of broken pipe before venturing in through a rent in one side wall.

The first thing I noticed was the smell. There were dead bodies here all right. It had been the busiest part of the shopping day when the waters had rushed through this part of the valley, and there'd been precious little time to warn any one. I saw several dead people as soon as my eyes adjusted to the gloom, including three children. The bodies were bloated but appeared otherwise undisturbed. I was about to turn back and call in some of the others when I heard the sound again, a stirring that could have been anything. I might not have stopped if I hadn't then heard a single word. "Damn!"

My next thought was of looters, although a supermarket was not likely to be a prime target. Still clutching my makeshift weapon, I made my way through the maze of tilted and mangled display racks until I reached the frozen foods department. One bank of freezers had tilted forward and a glass fronted door had broken, sending a sharp spear of thick glass down to the floor. And through the body of a young woman.

The young woman was trying unsuccessfully to extricate herself.

It was just possible that someone – someone normal I mean – might have survived being stabbed through the chest. If it missed the heart and did little or no damage to the lungs, and was pressed tightly enough to cut off most of the bleeding, then it was just possible that this woman could have survived for a while. But not for three or four days. Particularly since this area had been completely underwater for most of that time.

I wasn't able to shift the canted freezers either, so I used my pipe to shatter the jagged glass shard. She drew it out of her body without assistance, panting slightly, and eyeing me warily.

"It's all right," I said. "I know what you are."

But that was a lie. I didn't even know what I was.

Sophie – her current name was Sophie Denberg – accepted my jacket. "Use it to hide the blood," I said. "And if anyone asks, you survived in an air pocket. You're just one lucky kid."

"I'm older than I look," she said humorlessly, but she did as I said. The other members of my work crew showed only mild interest. They'd carried so many corpses out of the wreckage already that they only recognized her as someone they didn't have to bag and tag.

It was no trouble getting her past the aid station. Wearing my jacket, she looked like just one more weary volunteer. "Where are we going?" she asked as we got into my jeep.

"My place."

She shrugged but didn't object.

Her massive chest wound was ugly looking but closed and not bleeding by the time we reached my cabin. I lived alone, for obvious reasons, at the end of a short dirt road. By unspoken agreement, we didn't say much while she carefully showered and dressed. She was a petite woman and looked lost in my jeans and shirt, but she appeared little the worse for her long ordeal.

You might think that I would have been delighted to find another like myself, to realize that I was not alone in the world. In truth, though, I'd become comfortable with my uniqueness, rather smug about it in fact, and my initial reaction was as much disappointment as elation. My balloon was already deflated when she finally admitted what we both already knew, that she shared my recuperative powers and my longevity. "I was born in 1751," she told me. "I'm the illegitimate child of Catherine the Great."

I was frankly skeptical, but she outlined her two and a half centuries of life so persuasively that I was ultimately convinced. "I told you I was older than I looked."

Sophie had been single and unattached, a reclusive young woman working as a bank teller in Duddleston. "I wanted to live in a nice dull place where nothing would ever happen." She laughed, but as always in her case, there was not the faintest trace of humor. It was a gesture of self deprecation rather than a sign of amusement

My cabin was roomy and she settled in even though we never really spoke of the arrangement. Her job was gone but, she assured me, she had ample funds stashed away. "The job was just camouflage." While I had started over fresh with each new identity, Sophie had worked out detailed plans for every transition. She was actually quite a wealthy woman, though it was hidden away under various assumed identities and blind trusts.

She had also given more thought than I to the nature of our unique abilities, and after quizzing me about my first resurrection in France, she felt more confident of her theories. "It must take a near death experience to trigger whatever it is that retards aging. I was sixteen when a horse threw me and I broke my neck." She twisted her head to show me that there were no lasting effects. "And that's when I stopped ageing. You weren't much older when you almost died."

"I think I did die," I rejoined. "At least clinically."

Sophie nodded. "Perhaps I did as well. We're remarkably well preserved corpses though."

The habits of a lifetime or longer are hard to drop. Sophie was often uncomfortable talking about her past, and I never did tell her the details of my experiences during the Hitler War or Vietnam. I know that she served as a nurse during the American Civil War and that she had left Europe before the colonies declared independence, but other than on that first day, she spoke very little about her past. We grew only slightly more comfortable with one another, knowing that we didn't need to keep our guards up, but doing so anyway out of force of habit.

We got married two years later. It was a practical decision not because we'd been intimate but because it provided a smoother mechanism for living together and for easing the transition when one of us needed to change identities. The widowed Mrs. Westcott could move to another state, re-marry my new persona, and no one would be unduly suspicious. Or I could be the bereaved partner.

We performed this leapfrog act roughly every fifteen years through the 21st Century. I'd like to be able to say that we shared the greatest and longest lasting love affair of all time, but in truth, we were never particularly attracted to one another, and after the first few months, we had separate bedrooms. We rarely quarreled and never over substantive issues, but our relationship was one of tolerance rather than liking. The shared secret was a bond of sorts, but we became increasingly like two prisoners on the same chain gang, mildly irritated by the inconvenience without actively blaming the other party for our situation.

Although we watched for others of our kind, we never found anyone. There must be more than just the two of us, we reasoned, but so few that the odds against mutual discovery were astronomical. That realization only made us chafe at our mutual bonds more actively.

One evening during a thunderstorm I became uncharacteristically expansive about my family and told Sophie a good deal about my past. She wasn't particularly responsive although she was clearly interested, and unbeknownst to me she took to the internet over the course of the next few days and did some genealogical research. A week after our initial conversation she dropped the bombshell.

"According to my research, you are in all probability my grandson, a few generations removed."

She had never mentioned having lived in England or having given birth. I thought at first it was some elaborate joke, but Sophie had never shown any sign of having a sense of humor. "I never intended to get pregnant, but I had too much to drink that night and I let my guard down. I paid another couple to raise the boy as their own and lost track of him when I came to America."

That boy was my great-great grandfather, according to her chart. If we hadn't already stopped sleeping together by mutual consent, this would have led to the same result. It also suggested that Sophie might have hosted the original mutation, a recessive which she had passed down to me. But she had never gotten pregnant again, I had neither siblings nor children of my own, nor any cousins that I knew of. Could it be that we were then the only two people so endowed in the world? If so, what possible quirk of fate could it have been that brought us together?

For a while it became more difficult to change identities, but then considerably easier. Sophie had mastered the intricacies of computerized record keeping and had constructed a dozen or so potentials for each of us, which she constantly updated. World conditions helped. The flooding of many coastal regions in the late 21st Century had resulted in worldwide chaos despite decades of warning. Governments more concerned with the current election cycle than long term consequences had grown increasingly short sighted. The Two Hour War in the Mideast had resulted in an acceleration of worldwide petroleum shortages. The Chinese invasion of Taiwan generated a protracted rift between America and China which had adversely affected the economies of both countries.

Happily, neither of us experienced any potentially revealing accidents during this period. Sophie was in a minor traffic accident that cost her the little finger on her left hand – to our surprise it did not grow back – but we avoided awkward questions by simply not appearing for the follow up visit at the medical clinic. The increases in air pollution and the decline in effectiveness of most antibiotics rendered the clinics permanently overwhelmed so no one cared.

Another century was about to turn when I noticed Sophie – although she was no longer Sophie and I was no longer Nathan – paying more attention to her appearance than usual. She didn't dress any differently but I often caught her peering at herself in a mirror and she seemed even more taciturn than usual. I finally asked her about it. At first she dissimulated, but finally she turned away, not meeting my eyes. "I found a grey hair."

I was tempted to dismiss this as female vanity, but it was very much unlike her and I fancied I did see something different about her appearance, a maturity that had been visible only in her eyes until now. A few weeks passed and I was sure of it, but I didn't know how to broach the subject. She relieved me of the responsibility one evening over supper.

"I'm starting to get older." There was no emotion in her voice but I sensed something I had never felt from her before now. Sophie was frightened.

"It's probably just a passing thing."

But it wasn't. Six months later she looked like a forty year old. Two months after that, we had to relocate. My "young" wife looked like my grandmother and she moved stiffly, although she insisted that she felt no pain.

We took up residence in Butte, Montana. I was looking after my grandmother, who suffered from arthritis. The first night we were there, Sophie came into my bedroom. "I don't want to die." Her voice was that of the young girl that I'd first seen in the drowned supermarket, but her body was frail and trembling. She spent the night beside me but neither of us slept very much.

Sophie died – really died – that winter. There was no dramatic ending. She simply passed away in her sleep. I found her body, cold and stiff, the following morning. I did wait all that day, on the chance that it would somehow rejuvenate itself, but I think I knew from the outset that this was the final death. For the two of us the ending had been deferred but not defeated. Assuming that our life spans were comparable, I had another century to go, but would probably end up in much the same fashion.

A century is such a short period of time. It doesn't seem fair.

Although we hadn't been a romantic couple for decades, I found myself missing her almost immediately. Possibly I delude myself and what I was missing was confidence in my own immortality, now banished forever. The question I kept asking myself over and over again was why had we been given this amazing gift, if all it was to accomplish was to extend our not very uplifting or rewarding lives?

I've developed a couple of explanations since then. One, of course, is that it wasn't a gift, but just a fluke, a chance mutation that didn't breed true despite its potential advantage. I've never been much of a churchgoer but I'm more agnostic than atheist. If there is a God of some sort out there, he must be a cruel one to dangle such a possibility and then snatch it away at the last moment.

But I like my other answer better. The purpose of life is to live. Whether it's a gift from God or simply the inevitable consequence of some mechanistic form of evolution, the result is the same. We aren't alive because we need to accomplish some spiritual or material goal. Living is itself the goal. Possibly Sophie and I squandered this gift by keeping it secret, and by becoming so obsessed with our uniqueness that we took no pleasure from it.

So tomorrow I will stop hiding what I am. It's likely no one will believe me, or if they do, that they'll tear me limb from limb so that I can't regenerate. But no matter what happens, I plan on enjoying it.

THE WORD MILL

Arthur Friar's first novel, *Thunder Ridge*, sold more copies than any other book published in 2004. In 2014, he had written every work of fiction that made it to the bestseller list, although most appeared under pseudonyms. Which is all very surprising since Arthur was a slow, meticulous writer who had spent nearly a decade creating *Thunder Ridge*.

It all started when Sarah Chambers showed up at a bookstore signing.

The chemistry between them was so palpable that even casual bystanders noticed that something unusual was going on. They talked briefly but warmly, and when the signing was over, they left together. A month later they were engaged, and a month after that they were married.

All of this would have been just a nice romantic story except for one thing. Sarah Chambers was a brilliant computer programmer who owned her own laboratory, and she'd quietly developed a method of replicating human personalities in code. A year after their wedding, Arthur was halfway through chapter one of his new novel and Sarah was nearly bankrupt because she had spent too much time and money on pure research and not enough on practical applications.

"I wish I could write faster," said Arthur one day.

"Maybe you can," was Sarah's rejoinder.

They spent two weeks uploading Arthur's personality into her network. "Time doesn't have quite the same meaning in the virtual world," she told Arthur. "Your replicated personality can experience several years in what is from our point of view a single day."

A week later, they printed out the first copy of *Banners of God*, Arthur's second novel. The six figure advance restored their solvency, though just barely, but a week later *Riders of the Dawn* gave them a comfortable cushion. When the publisher expressed reluctance to purchase a fourth novel so quickly, Arthur sold *True Visions* to a rival house, along with his first murder mystery, *Death Trip*.

In 2006, Arthur had eight titles on the bestseller list, all under his own name.

If it had been just a matter of money, that might have been the end of it. They were already rich enough to live comfortably for the rest of their lives, even if Sarah continued with her expensive programming projects. But unfortunately, the biggest fan of Arthur Friar's writing was Arthur Friar. He had an insatiable appetite for his own work, even if it was written by his proxy self, and was egotistical enough to believe that everyone else felt the same way.

They expanded the network and replicated the Arthur module several times. A new novel began appearing every day.

Arthur expanded into science fiction in 2007, men's adventure in 2008, romance novels in 2009, young adult and children's books in 2010, and started producing film and television scripts in 2011. He had over three hundred pseudonyms and could no longer read everything that he was writing. The various Arthur modules were interfaced regularly to avoid creating duplicate work after Sarah decided it would be unwise to assign them specialized duties.

By 2012, most of the writers' organizations had disbanded because there were so few active authors remaining, and the Friars controlled the fourth largest private fortune in the world. Sarah wrote linguistic programs for the Arthurs and in 2015 they began producing original works in Russian, French, and Spanish. By the end of 2020, writing as a profession had ceased to exist, and the few individuals who still produced fiction posted it on rarely visited websites.

Disaster struck in 2025. A technician noted that Arthur #223 had failed to produce the latest Lee Carson detective story on schedule and ran a diagnostic. She was waiting for the results when another red light appeared on her board. *Juggernauts of Saturn* was overdue from Arthur #151. Frowning, the technician started to request a second diagnostic, but a third light came on as her hands hovered over the keyboard.

Then another. And another.

The last complete Arthur Friar novel left the print queue an hour later. By then the entire board was red, and the Friars were flying back from their vacation in Baluchistan. It took less than a day to discover the source of the problem. The Arthurs all had writer's block; it had spread through the interface to infect each and every module.

Sarah tried restoring from backup, but the backup was so recent that the block returned after the Arthurs had turned out exactly the same text as on the previous day. They tried a new replication, but the organic Arthur hadn't written a word of fiction in over twenty years. His virtual copy went into block after two sentences.

Publishers began to panic. The steady influx of manuscripts had been of such high quality that they no longer employed editors. The supply had been so reliable that no one held any significant unpublished inventory. In less than a month, bookstore shelves began to empty. Reprints filled some of the gaps, but the reading public wanted new material, and there was no one left to write it. Hollywood was similarly devastated.

The world economy went into a tailspin. There were riots in most of the major capitals of the world. War broke out in the Mideast and spread throughout the world. Modern civilization collapsed into barbarism by 2030.

In the spring of 2146, Ted Graham of the Shoeless Clan set quill to parchment in a stone hut in what used to the Southwestern United States and wished that he could write more quickly.

PASSIVE RESISTANCE

Even as a child, Kristina was very meticulous about recording her murders. She had a red notebook for crawling insects – ants, caterpillars, grasshoppers, a blue one for those that flew – flies, mosquitoes, bumblebees, and a green one for warm blooded creatures – field mice, birds, and the occasional squirrel. Her entries were all printed, never in cursive, neatly and accurately. She looked up the spelling when she was in doubt, sometimes paging through her father's books about wildlife to make sure she had the proper species.

Her earliest entries were simple body counts. "Squashed two caterpillars on the back steps." "Burned seventeen ants with my magnifying glass on the patio." "Swatted six flies in the living room, nine in the kitchen, and one in the bathroom." By her tenth birthday, however, she had grown more expressive and more ambitious. "Knocked a squirrel out of the oak tree. It had a broken leg. Nailed its feet to a board and kept it in my playhouse. Used a paring knife to cut off its skin. Died after two hours." She filled the last page of her green notebook on her twelfth birthday. By then she was already working on the third volumes of the other two, but less assiduously. Insects no longer held much interest for her. They died silently and too quickly.

She was fifteen when she added a new color to her collection of journals. This one was jet black and the initial entry was titled "Bobby Fairlie."

The first seventeen years of George Foley's life were unremarkable, chiefly because he displayed no evidence of actually possessing a personality until he won the scholarship to Michigan State University on the strength of his astonishing mathematical talents. That allowed him to escape a home where he was constantly criticized by both parents, who loathed each other but invariably transferred their feelings to the son whose unexpected and unwelcome existence had more or less trapped them into marriage.

In a twisted sense, George blossomed in his new environment, but along with the blossom came a number of thorns. Although George had no friends, he wasn't aware of the fact. He showed up at the student union and interposed himself in conversations, usually regurgitating the pseudo-Marxist clichés that he'd adopted as his personal philosophical system. Lacking any experience of friendship, he had no qualms about characterizing the arguments of others as "stupid" and "uninformed", and insisted that any view contrary to his own was a product of "societal brainwashing". If he had no ready rebuttal to an argument, he literally failed to hear it.

Alan Sheffield didn't particularly like George, but he had also lived an isolated childhood, home schooled by his parents who spent most of their lives in one remote part of the world or another, excavating ancient ruins and studying relics that were more important to them than the modern world. They probably knew several members of the ancient royal dynasties of Egypt as well as or better than they did their own son, whom they generally treated in the same fashion as the local hired laborers. Alan had only been on campus two days when George found him sitting alone in the student union, drinking coffee. He had taken a seat opposite without waiting for an invitation, and pointed directly at the paperback copy of *Toward a Psychology of Being* by Abraham Maslow that Alan was reading.

"Most of that's bullshit, you know."

Alan was taken completely by surprise. "Come again?"

"He's got some of it right, that stuff about the best minds setting their own standards and ignoring those imposed by society, but he cops out at the end. People with superior minds like that have an obligation to help others see the truth. Maslow thinks they should just wander off and do their own thing."

"You're a fan of Ayn Rand then? *Atlas Shrugged*?"

George recoiled as though something had bitten him. "Ayn Rand's a fascist. Her characters are all trying to help themselves, not the world."

It had only taken a few minutes to determine that George's familiarity with both writers was superficial at best, but he was the first person Alan had met socially at MSU, and even after he had found other friends more in tune with his own nature, he had felt an obligation to maintain what passed for amity between them. And they did share one common bond. They both distrusted authority figures.

Alan met Dalton Maynard under very different circumstances. They were both majoring in computer science and during their second semester, they were randomly paired as a team for a series of programming exercises. There was no warmth between them, but neither was there animosity. Dalton seemed incapable of feeling any strong emotion except impatience. He was never angry or nervous, even when their work together was going badly, but neither did he ever express any pleasure when they solved a problem or completed an assignment. They almost never spoke of anything other than their class work, but on rare occasions Dalton would allude to his extracurricular activities. He was an active member of the ultra-conservative Young Americans for Freedom as well as the ultra-liberal Students for a Democratic Society.

When Alan questioned the apparent contradiction, Dalton simply shrugged. "They're not as dissimilar as you might think. They just use different words."

During the third trimester, Alan met a girl he liked, Paula Pfeiffer. She was from a small town and had never actually dated before, at least not without a chaperone, so she only agreed to go out with Alan if they doubled with someone. None of Alan's close friends were available, so in desperation he asked Dalton, with no real hope of success. They'd been working together for several weeks and his partner had never once mentioned a female acquaintance. Or a male one for that matter.

"Sure. When and where do you want to meet up?"

The answer had taken Alan so completely by surprise that he had stumbled over his words, but eventually arranged a rendezvous in front of the library. He and Paula had arrived early, and his nervousness was less anxiety about impressing her than it was concern about Dalton.

To his amazement, Dalton had appeared right on time accompanied by a stunningly attractive brunette whose manner and clothing shouted "Money!" as loudly as Paula's simple attire whispered the contrary. "Hi, guys! This is Kristina Kirk."

Kristina was possibly the most direct and unsettling person Alan had ever met. Her clothing was expensive but fit so badly that he couldn't decide whether or not she had a nice figure. Her manner was vaguely aggressive and her words frequently sarcastic; she met his occasional stare unblinkingly and he was the one who always looked away. Although she spoke the proper words of greeting and pleasure, it felt as though she was reading from a script. There was no hint of intimacy between her and Dalton, although they were obviously on good terms, and if anything she seemed more interested in Paula than anyone else. She had the eyes of a predator.

The date was not a success. Paula disapproved of the violence in the movie, the latest James Bond, ordered milk while the rest drank coffee because her minister had cautioned his flock about the dangers of over-stimulation posed by caffeine, and had been openly offended when Alan used the word "hell". His ambivalence about asking her out a second time was never resolved because Paula disappeared less than a week later. Her mutilated body was subsequently found in a woodlot in nearby Grand Ledge after a golden retriever brought home a well chewed human hand.

It was Alan who introduced George to Dalton, during his sophomore year. Although they no longer were officially partnered, he and Dalton had discovered that their talents complemented each other well and they often consulted each other. If asked, Alan would have described their association as friendship, but they never interacted socially after that single occasion. He wouldn't have minded Dalton's company, but Kristina had made him feel less than human somehow, even though she'd hardly spoken to him. They were still a couple, or at least as much as they ever had been. Alan saw them walking together on campus from time to time, but never exchanged more than a wave or a hasty greeting. He did notice that they never touched one another, not even to hold hands.

Dalton had come knocking on Alan's door one Saturday morning. Alan invited him in and started to ask how things were going, but his guest cut him off. "How much do you know about data matrices?"

Alan knew enough not to be offended by the abrupt tone. Dalton had tunnel vision when he was working on a problem and was frequently though unintentionally rude. For that matter, even when he was between projects, he generally rubbed people the wrong way – but it was a lack of awareness rather than a conscious decision. "Not a whole lot. Why?"

Dalton described his current project in very general terms. "There's a humungous amount of data, but that's okay. The problem is that the relationships aren't always linear, and some of them are conditional. I could write the code easy enough if I could just understand how the fields are supposed to be linked. And just to make it even hairier, the conditional statements have nested sets of overlapping criteria."

Alan shook his head. "I can take a look at what you've got, but I'm not so good at complex mathematical arrays." His brow furrowed. "But I think I might know someone who can help, if we can talk him into it."

And so it was that George Foley met Dalton Maynard, and in due course, Kristina Kirk.

Alan transferred to Cornell at the end of his sophomore year and lost track of the three of them. After graduating, he worked for Microsoft for a few years, then for a consulting firm in Chicago, and eventually founded his own company based in Providence. Years passed, and then quite a few more. Every once in a while he would see Dalton's name somewhere; he had founded his own consulting firm and specialized in political and sociological profiling, had landed a few government contracts, worked for think tanks on both the left and the right. Of Kristina and George, he heard nothing at all.

And one day he found someone sleeping on his doorstep.

Alan had married, unwisely, when he was in the early stages of building his own business. One day he had come home to an empty house and a brief note. He hadn't contested the divorce and Grace had declined to accept alimony. They had never seen one another again, although once a year or so he did some clandestine checking to make certain she was all right.

So he was living alone, in the same house he'd once shared with her, still sitting on the sofa she'd picked out, peering out at the world through her curtains, and sleeping exclusively on his side of the bed. He had a maid service visit twice a month and kept the house neat, but no one else had been inside since the plumber's last visit two years before.

Alan's first reaction to the sight of his unwelcome visitor was embarrassment. He assumed it was a homeless person. The figure wore mismatched, worn but not shabby clothing, with a scraggly beard to match uncombed hair and skin that seemed abnormally pale. Although he hadn't kept in shape, Alan was a big man and he felt no sense of personal danger, but he backed away, not wanting to risk a potentially awkward confrontation. He decided to go around to the back of the house and enter through the patio.

But the sleeper must have had some preternatural proximity alarm because his head came up and he rose smoothly to his feet. "Hey, Alan! Long time no see."

"Do I know you?" It seemed unlikely.

"Sure, it's me. George. George Foley, remember?"

Old memories stirred. "George, is that you?"

Foley stood up, tugging on his beard. "Yeah, the chin whiskers are new. My old man thought it made me look like a goat, so I grew them just to piss him off. By the time he croaked, I'd gotten used to them. How've you been?"

It had been a long Friday and Alan was tired. Even on a good day, he might not have welcomed George Foley back into his life. He had settled into a pattern and he liked it. But there was no way to avoid inviting George inside and offering him a drink, which he declined. "Pollutes the brain cells and makes them more receptive to government propaganda." It was as though he'd stepped into a time machine and jumped back to the early 1970s. Alan felt a growing sense of unreality and responded to each conversational gambit with short, banal replies.

"So you're probably wondering why I showed up again after all these years."

Alan admitted that this was in fact the case.

"Well, I kind of need your help."

Alan's immediate thought was money and he reached for his wallet. "I don't have a lot on me, George, but I'd be glad to lend you something." It was a lie, the kind of polite lie that George had always characterized as a moral flaw inherent in capitalist societies.

"No, put it away. I don't need your money, Alan. Money's just an illusion anyway. You can't reduce wealth to a piece of paper. The value of something is in the labor that goes into it."

Alan blinked. "So what do you want?"

"Me and some old friends are working on a big project and we're kind of stuck. Dalton wanted to hire some big name programmer named Colton but I heard you had your own business up here so I decided to look you up. You and Dalton always got along back in the day, and he's still a little hard to take sometimes."

"Dalton? Are you talking about Dalton Maynard?"

"Of course. How many Daltons do you know? So I thought maybe we could drive up to Boston tomorrow."

That was pretty close to the last thing that Alan wanted to do over the weekend, but George retained his ability to selectively tune out anything he didn't want to hear and Alan eventually found himself agreeing unenthusiastically.

"Great! I can sleep on your couch here and we can leave right after breakfast."

Dalton's company, MFK Associates, occupied a mid-sized, two story building in Brookline. It was technically closed, but George had a key and led the way inside.

"Welcome to Motherfuck Ass," he said cheerfully as they entered.

"What's the MFK stand for?"

"Maynard, Foley, and Kirk."

Alan stopped in his tracks. "You and Dalton are partners?"

"Sure are. Almost ten years now."

"So who's the 'K'?"

"Kirk. You remember Kristina, don't you?"

Alan winced. He did indeed,

Dalton was sitting at his desk. Kristina was sitting on his desk. George may have been almost unrecognizable, but Dalton looked very much the same even after more than twenty years. He had put on a few pounds but not enough to matter and still wore his hair in a crew cut above plain, solid colored clothing. His vaguely supercilious expression was as annoying as it had always been. Kristina looked both the same and different. She retained that hard, cool air with which she'd always surrounded herself and there were few signs of age in her face, but her glasses had given way to contacts, her hair was now stylishly cut, and her clothing was designed to draw attention to her well proportioned contours.

"It's like a class reunion," said Dalton, pumping Alan's hand.

"Except that none of us graduated together," Kristina objected mildly.

"Shit, I didn't graduate at all," added George amiably. "A diploma is just another chain tying you to the establishment."

"Nice place you've got here, Dalton. So what is it exactly that you do?"

He shrugged. "Public opinion polling and modeling. What-If scenarios for politicians. You know, do I gain or lose votes if I come out in favor of banning flag burning? But that's all old hat. There's a couple of hundred other guys doing the same thing and it's all just data pushing now. No challenge to it. Our current project's going to change all that."

"Oh? So what is it exactly? George wouldn't talk about it on the drive up."

"Proactive population response modeling," said Dalton.

"We're going to change the world," said Kristina.

"And screw all the motherfuckers in Washington!" said George.

It took a while before Alan understood even the basics of what they were working on. First of all, their terminology was often alien to his experience. Kristina was actually Dr. Kristina Kirk, now a recognized authority specializing in mass psychology and crowd behavior. Dalton handed him a copy of her book, *Panic Reactions in Heterogeneous Populations*, but Kristina took it out of his hands and tossed it casually aside. "Not bad for a dyslexic author. But that's old hat. We've moved way past that now."

Even more bewildering was the inability of any of the threesome to let the others finish more than a few sentences without jumping in. They talked over one another constantly and at times Alan felt as though he was dealing with a single, unfocused individual rather than three very disparate personalities. He finally threw up his hands. "Too much, guys. How about one of you giving me the rough outline and then the other two can fill in the details later?"

They all looked at each other and Dalton finally nodded to Kristina. "You go ahead. It all started with your idea."

She waved an acknowledgment and uncrossed her legs, leaning forward over the edge of the desk. "We were doing bellwether targeted public opinion sampling twelve years ago when we noticed an anomaly."

Alan held up a hand. "Stop right there. You've already lost me."

She smiled humorlessly. "Do you know what a bellwether is?"

He shrugged. "Some kind of standard of measurement? A control in an experiment?"

"No, not at all. The term originates with shepherds. They discovered that certain members of a flock which seemed otherwise ordinary had disproportionate influence on the other sheep. If you could lure a bellwether through a gate, the rest would follow."

"Trend setters."

She nodded. "Exactly, except that the analogy doesn't work well with humans. Most of us are just as easily influenced but the mechanism doesn't function as smoothly. We interact, either actively or passively, with a very large population – both in person and via the media – and since we're exposed to multiple bellwethers their individual influence is diluted. We're also affected by things we read and other stimuli. I'm sure you know from your own personal experience that some people are more convincing than others. Some of them are bellwether aggressives, the kind of person we tend to think of as natural born leaders. Aggressives have short term influence, partly because they can change what they advocate so easily. A politician can reverse his stance and carry people along with him, but only for a limited time. When they change an opinion, it is almost always for external rather than internal reasons. The other type are the bellwether passives. A person whose quiet example influences friends and co-workers. We're not as conscious of their influence, but it's just as real and sometimes far more effective. With aggressives, we're aware when they contradict what we're predisposed to believe. Passives are more insidious and it takes a great deal of effort to make them change a strongly held position. Most of their changes are generated internally."

"Kristina is a passive," interrupted George. "And I'm an aggressive."

She smiled at him with what almost seemed to be warmth. "You're an aggressive, George, but you're not a bellwether. If anything, you're an anti-bellwether." She turned back to Alan. "We developed a method of statistical analysis that allowed us to identify a high percentage of passive bellwethers in the general population. By confining our sampling to this group, we were able to improve the accuracy of our polling dramatically. Our margin of error is less than a percentage point."

"All right, I understand so far. What was the anomaly you mentioned?"

"We were conducting a follow up on a survey about global warming, sampling four separate populations of passives. All four groups had returned nearly identical results on the initial survey, but when we collated the returns from the follow-up, we discovered that we'd made an error. One of the populations had inadvertently been given a set of questions that had later been discarded. Since the questions differed, the results were incompatible and we had to repeat the follow up two days later. One of the four populations – the one which had received the incorrect survey – now varied by a small but mathematically significant amount from the other three."

"Something must have happened during the interval to change their opinion."

Kristina shook her head. "Not exactly. We concluded that the primary cause of the variance was the botched survey. The manner in which the questions were phrased actually influenced the opinions of the people who responded to them. We hadn't just recorded public opinion; we had changed it infinitesimally."

She let the words rest there a moment. Alan thought about it. "The act of observation changes the object observed."

"Exactly!" Kristina beamed at him, the first time she'd actually granted him a friendly or even approving look. "Our first thought was that we had stumbled onto a way to influence the public will on an unprecedented scale. Unfortunately, we were wrong. For one thing, it was too difficult to identify a large enough number of passives to have a significant impact. For another, not all passives have the same predispositions, so efforts to sway one subset for a particular proposition might well sway an equal subset in the opposite direction. Passives are not a homogeneous group."

"They've been brainwashed by the establishment just like everybody else," interposed George.

"But we thought of a way around the problem," added Dalton. "Virtual passives."

Kristina's lips had thinned. She was obviously displeased by the interruptions, but there was no hint of irritation in her voice when she resumed. "I never liked that term, but it'll do. More precisely, we've been constructing proto-passives. Bellwethers influence opinions but they don't create them in a vacuum. Like everyone else, they're exposed to innumerable stimuli, many of them contradictory, and the degree to which they are able to resolve these contradictions is reflected in the strength of their individual opinions. No two individuals experience the same stimuli, obviously, but if the preponderance in two cases is the same, the opinions of those two passives will be essentially identical. It would take enormous resources to directly influence a large enough body of passives to ensure complete control of a population. It is far easier to alter a portion of the stimuli they're exposed to."

"I think you just lost me. Are you saying that in order to influence the opinion of the bellwethers, and through them the public, all you have to do is acquire complete control of their environment? Sounds like you're trying to hammer the board down on the nail instead of vice versa."

"That's what I said when this all started," said Dalton excitedly. "But I was wrong."

Kristina ignored him, looking directly at Alan. "It's much easier than that. On the basic level, people have only two desires – sustenance and shelter." Alan flashed back to his reading of Maslow and nodded agreement. "So we needed to implant proto-passive elements within that context. We spent years experimenting with advertising media – on the screen and in print – before we started getting measurable results."

"Are you talking about subliminals?" Alan's eyes jumped from Kristina to Dalton and back. "Isn't that illegal?"

"Not subliminals. These are more subtle. The way a commercial for eggs is phrased and presented could affect a woman's maternal instincts. The presentation of a house in an advertisement for home improvements could either reinforce feelings of comfort and security or raise doubts about the competence of the man of the house. The cumulative effect, and more importantly the interactive effect, of these stimuli can have a tremendous amount of influence on passives.

We're still learning how many of these mechanisms work, but we've already had several remarkable successes."

"But how did you get the advertisers to agree?"

"They don't know. Only the advertising agency is aware that we're shaping the message, and even they don't know the whole truth."

"And how did you manage that?"

"Ever hear of Kirk and Weir?"

"Sure. They're the biggest ad agency in the world..." He made the connection. "You're related to the Kirks?"

"I am the Kirks since Mother died. And Weir is retired now. I have a management team that runs the agency for me."

He let that sink in. It had always been obvious that Kristina had money. But so much money? "Okay, why am I here?'

Kristina sighed. "You're here because Dalton is such an unbearable prick when he's working."

Dalton looked slightly abashed, but he was laughing. "I've run through three programming directors this year alone. You remember how impatient I used to get back at MSU?"

"Yeah, I just ignored you."

Dalton nodded. "Exactly. And you were always good with complex conditionals. I just never could get my head around them."

"If you're offering me a job, I'm sorry but I have my own business now and I'm doing pretty well."

"We wouldn't want you full time," said Kristina. "Probably one day a week. Dalton and the staff programmers can handle the scut code. But sometimes it takes him weeks to get through a particularly complex subroutine, and then we have to spend almost as long debugging it."

Dalton shrugged. "I get impatient. I hurry sometimes."

Alan turned to George. "And how do you fit in to all this?"

George fairly beamed at him. "I do the math. These two are clueless once you get past simple arithmetic."

Kristina actually smiled. "He's right. I have a problem with numbers. Even when I was a kid, I had to keep my locker combination on a card in my purse. I'd forget it almost every day."

They talked about it for another hour. Alan was reluctant, but some of the things they were doing sounded intriguing and he knew Maggie could run the shop back in Providence for one or two days a week. Maybe better than he could; she was more customer friendly. He finally agreed to return the following Monday to look things over in more detail, but wouldn't commit himself any further.

Alan ended up spending at least one day a week in Brookline for the next three months. Sometimes he worked so late that he stayed in a hotel room for the night and drove back in the morning. Dalton and Kristina had an apartment near the office and they offered use of their guest bedroom, but Alan always declined. There was something odd about the relationship between the two that he didn't care to explore further. They displayed very little affection for one another, and neither wore a wedding ring. He wondered if they shared a bed and, if so, what they did there.

Fall passed away and winter arrived. Alan felt as though they were making progress, although his own work was so abstract that he often forgot about the project's ultimate goal. His first hint that something might be wrong came in early January, and even that didn't seem significant at the time.

Peggy, the receptionist, tracked him down in the server room one morning and told him that he had a phone call. "It's Maggie from your office. She says it's important."

The noise level was so high that he didn't want to use the nearest phone. "Where can I take it that's private?"

"Use Kristina's office. She's not in today and I'm sure she won't mind. It's never locked."

So he sat at her desk and listened to Maggie's side of a dispute with Norman Conroy, and then Norman's side, plus rebuttals. It was an old argument and Alan knew from experience that if he just let them have their say it would blow over by itself. Half listening, half bored, he noticed a notebook sitting on the corner of the desk and began to flip through it.

Most of the clippings were from newspapers and magazines. The earliest was six years old, the most recent only a few weeks. Alan was familiar with the subject matter – the riots in Sydney, the wave of suicides in Toronto, the bloody coup in Singapore. There were multiple clippings for each event, and someone had highlighted portions of the text.

Once Maggie and Norman had calmed down enough that he felt confident they'd patch up their latest set of differences, Alan returned to work.. He was preoccupied for the rest of the afternoon, though. Why had Kristina collected these particular stories? Was she searching for patterns that could advance her work? If so, why choose such disastrous events? Maybe she's trying to find a way to prevent them, he told himself. But it felt wrong.

His next hint that something might be amiss came two weeks later. He'd been fighting off a head cold for the better part of a week, and had taken so many remedies that it felt as though he was encased in a soft layer of gauze that filtered and distorted all sensory input. He was walking down a corridor with Kristina when he stumbled and went to one knee, so dizzy that he couldn't stand up. She touched his forehead and almost visibly recoiled.

"You're running a fever, Alan. What were you thinking? You could have given it to all of us."

That led to the first argument he had ever witnessed between Dalton and Kristina. Alan refused to go to a hospital, but he was obviously too sick to drive home. Dalton wanted him to spend the night in their guest room, and Kristina objected. They went off together while Alan tried to rally himself, and when they returned, neither looked happy. But Alan was bundled into their Lexus and driven eight blocks to an apartment building he'd never seen before. Dalton held his arm while Kristina painstakingly punched numbers into a coded security lock, reading them from an index card she'd taken from her shoulder bag. Then they were inside and even though disoriented, Alan wondered if this was a good idea.

He did get to answer one lingering question, though. Kristina and Dalton had separate bedrooms.

Alan fell asleep as soon as he lay down on their couch, but his hope that a night's rest would make a difference disintegrated in the morning when he tripped and fell trying to get to the bathroom. Dalton helped him while Kristina made coffee. She didn't say anything but even through the haze of fever, Alan could tell she wasn't happy about his presence.

"Look, you spend the morning in bed. I'll tell Maggie what's up. If you feel better this afternoon, call and I'll send someone to get you. But don't rush it. We can't afford to lose you for weeks while you recover from pneumonia."

Too tired to argue, Alan went back to sleep.

It was noon when he woke up, feeling weak but otherwise much better. He showered and reluctantly put the previous day's clothing back on, then rummaged in the kitchen for orange juice, tea, and a couple slices of toast. His stomach felt queasy but the food stayed down.

Then he gave in to temptation.

The apartment was very large and sparsely furnished. The common areas were all black, white, and various shades of gray. Everything appeared to be expensive but functional. There were no pictures on the walls, no live plants, no magnets on the refrigerator, nothing expressing any personality except the den, which was filled with books – programming manuals and psychology texts, mostly the latter.

He hadn't intended to look into the bedrooms, but Dalton's door was wide open and he couldn't resist. The bed was unmade, there were dirty clothes strewn about, and the closet was disorganized and stuffed to capacity. A desk sat in one corner with a state of the art PC. The shelf under the work station was filled with pornographic magazines.

Invading the privacy of one of his hosts made it easier to continue. Kristina had closed her bedroom door but it didn't have a lock. Her bed was made up neatly, and her dresser looked like a prop for a fashion magazine. She had a private bathroom and deep closets lined two of the four walls, with mechanical racks that rotated to bring the clothing in the rear forward. She also had a PC but her workstation was otherwise unencumbered. There was a single picture on the wall directly above the bed, an innocuous landscape, and a corner shelf held a row of inexpensive notebooks in various colors, red, green, and blue.

The incongruous picture was a dead giveaway. He wasn't at all surprised to find a wall safe behind it. He almost passed up the notebooks, but on impulse he picked up a red one and flipped it open, read a few entries, then recoiled in disgust and put it back with the others. Apparently Kristina had been just as weird a kid as she was an adult. He called for a ride a few minutes later.

That night he dreamed that a giant sized Kristina was standing astride the Providence waterfront, using an oversized magnifying glass to burn scurrying pedestrians to ash.

Alan's uneasiness turned to outright suspicion shortly after the Islamic Republic of Iraq invaded Saudi Arabia. The animosity between the two Muslim states had been growing perceptibly for the previous several weeks, catching the world by surprise. The grievances seemed vague even by regional standards, charges of mismanagement of the holy city of Mecca, rumors of attempts to undermine Iraq's new oil pricing scheme, and unsubstantiated reports of atrocities along their long and largely unpopulated border.

Alan arrived that morning to find the threesome sitting in Dalton's office, watching CNN's live coverage of the conflict. He joined them for a few minutes, but there wasn't much new to report and he quickly lost interest. "I guess I'll get to work guys," he said genially, expecting them to follow. But they remained where they were.

It was only later that Alan remembered one remark Dalton had made, his eyes fastened to the screen, a remark that reverberated oddly. "The Saudis weren't up and running soon enough. I told you they fabricated their readiness reports."

Alan tried to set aside his suspicions, but little things continued to bother him. Dalton and the others had expressed no interest when fighting had broken out between Israel and Iran in December, but they were completely captivated by the short lived war on the Arabian Peninsula. When he finally started actually looking for something wrong, he told himself that it was only to set his misgivings at rest. What actually happened was that he grew increasingly alarmed.

He had always remained narrowly focused on the portions of the code which he was supposed to be correcting, or more commonly of late, writing from scratch. Now he started scanning the other modules, supposedly to make sure that the interfaces and go-to statements were valid, but actually analyzing their purpose. Everything seemed to be as described, and he was actually beginning to feel better the day he opened a data archive, hoping to save time by finding out how his predecessor had solved a particularly complex hierarchical ordering problem.

What he found instead was that the innocuous test data that had been there originally – an attempt to shape consumer desire for the color blue instead of the customary red – had been replaced by a much larger and more complex data matrix. Most of the content was too abstruse for him to decipher, but there were unmistakable references to Islam, Mecca, and the Saudi royal family.

Alan broke out in a cold sweat.

He knew what he had to do next, but it took a while to find an opportunity. He normally went to lunch with Dalton and Kristina when he was in Boston; George never came along, brought his lunch to work every day in a bag. "Those fancy restaurants are the worst kind of capitalism. The common man can't afford to eat there."

When they invited Alan to join them on the first Friday in February, he declined. "I want to finish up and go home early. I have plans for the weekend."

"Suit yourself," said Kristina, clearly not disappointed. She turned to Dalton. "Do I need to bring my bag?"

"No, I'll treat. You can get it next time."

They'd barely left the building before Alan realized the opportunity that had just announced itself. He got up from his workstation and walked back to the office area. Peggy was at the front desk, eating a sandwich she'd ordered from the deli down the street. Three of the staff programmers and one technician were playing cards in the lunch room. Dalton's office door was closed and probably locked. Kristina's was also closed, but probably not locked. Moving cautiously, feeling like a criminal, Alan tried the door.

It opened.

Kristina's bag was on the floor behind her desk and it only took a few seconds to find the index card tucked inside an inner pocket. There were eight numbers hand written on the top line, five more two lines down. Alan copied both sequences into his address book and hastily returned to work.

The second part of his plan required some maneuvering. Two weeks later, he worked for about an hour, then got up and went looking for Dalton.

"Hey, guy! What's up? Solve that indexing problem yet?"

"Pretty much. Still need to finish up the code. Look, is there anything doing today that can't wait?"

"Not that I know of. You got plans?"

Alan rubbed his belly. "I'm not feeling so hot. I stopped for bacon and eggs this morning and I think maybe I got a bad one. I probably should go home so I don't end up sleeping on your couch again."

"Hey, man. Do what you have to do. We're ahead of schedule anyway. I'll tell Kristina you were half dead."

"I'll call later and let you know I got home. Will you still be here?"

"Sure. We've got a full load today. Don't worry about it. Take care of yourself."

Alan drove out of the parking lot a few minutes later, but he didn't turn toward the interstate. He went to the apartment.

A stroke of good fortune helped at the last possible moment. He'd been about to punch in the first string of numbers from the card when he remembered that Kristina was dyslexic. When he entered them in reverse order, the blinking red light turned green and there was an electronic click as the lock released. He drew a deep breath and went inside.

The second string of numbers was the combination to the wall safe, similarly reversed. It opened smoothly and an interior light went on, but it revealed little of interest. There was some jewelry and a handful of legal papers, and a notebook very similar to the colored coded ones he'd already seen, except that this one was black.

He took it out and began reading.

Alan had to sit down on the bed before he'd finished the first page. The account of the death of Robert Fairlie, aged twelve, abducted, tortured, and killed, was described in sickening detail. In one margin, apparently a later addition, was mention of a vagrant named Howard Osterman, convicted and imprisoned for the crime. Alan assumed that he was responsible, but when he turned the page he found another vivid account of the death of a child, this one without annotation.

Each page that followed had a similar entry, sometimes brief, sometimes lengthy. Two more of the first twenty were embellished with accounts of arrests, one resulting in conviction, one not.

He began skimming through what he at first assumed was Kristina's early fascination with death until he saw another familiar name. Paula Pfeiffer. The girl he had dated once during his sophomore year. The girl whose mutilated body had turned up less than two weeks later. Kristina's account described the body in minute detail, far more detail than the newspapers had published. He told himself she was using her imagination, making things up, but he knew otherwise. Appalled but fascinated, Alan continued to turn the pages. Kristina's father had apparently died of natural causes, but her mother's "accident" was apparently not, and it was described with her daughter's usual precision.

Each victim had a number next to his or her name, up until page 220, near the very end of the notebook. Where 221 should have appeared was instead a very brief summary of the riots in Sydney. The last line read: "One hundred and eighteen dead. Should have been more. Need to tweak the emotive index." The next page similarly treated the coup in Singapore. "Nine hundred and twelve known dead. Probably many more." The last entry was even briefer and was titled "Toronto Suicides". The entry was chilling. "Six hundred and forty reported, probably others listed as accidental. Actual rate should have been in the low teens. Better than expected results. Need to sample surviving passives."

He closed the notebook and sat there for a long time, his face frozen into a mask. Then he returned the notebook to the safe, closed it, reset the electronic alarm, and drove back to Providence.

Alan considered approaching the authorities, but even if he hadn't instinctively distrusted them, he wasn't sure he could convince them of the truth and any abortive attempt would certainly tip off the others that he was onto them. Kristina's motivation he could almost understand, but why were Dalton and George going along with her? It was possible that George didn't grasp the implications of their work, but Dalton certainly must have known. Was it a sense of empowerment that made him cooperate with what was almost certainly a campaign of mass murder?

It didn't matter what their motives were. They had to be stopped. Alan began to increase the time he spent at MFK, very gradually at first. He didn't want to arouse suspicion. It took more than two months before he had a basic understanding of their delivery mechanism, and another four months to crack the proprietary coding they used to disguise the specific targeting elements. And when he finally felt confident that he had mastered their technique, it took most of his personal savings to pay for the advertising blitz required. Specially designed circulars were delivered to various neighborhoods in Brookline and an unusual television commercial appeared twice nightly during the local news program. Posters went up on telephone poles and were displayed in several storefronts. A telephone canvassing firm conducted an odd public opinion poll whose questions had been very specifically phrased and ordered. A billboard formerly advertising new cars now asked the question "Do you trust your neighbors?" and there were radio spots, newspaper ads, and two people with sandwich boards who paraded their messages within a block of MFK.

Someone threw rocks through the windows of MFK on a Saturday night, setting off the alarms. The residents of Kristina and Dalton's apartment building presented management with a petition demanding that they be evicted for unspecified "immoral and unneighborly activities". Dalton's tires were slashed twice, one at home, once at work. They began receiving hate mail. To Alan's satisfaction, neither of them seemed to suspect that they were the targets of an actual conspiracy.

"Most people are barely more than animals," explained Kristina. "That's why they're so easy to manipulate."

Their arrogance proved to be their undoing because neither of them took the mounting threats seriously until it was too late. Dalton was fatally stabbed one evening when he impulsively stopped at the bar and grille near their apartment. Although there was a good sized crowd at the time, nobody admitted to having seen the actual attack and no one was ever arrested. Kristina may have suspected something, because she stopped coming to the office and wouldn't let anyone visit her. Most of her acquaintances assumed she was mourning Dalton's death, and it is possible that she was grieving in her own bizarre fashion, but since she had no real friends other than George, if he counted, no one inquired too closely.

She was beaten to death by four women when she ventured out to buy groceries. They insisted that they'd seen her attempting to molest a ten year old boy and his eight year old sister. Neither of the children confirmed their story, but both identified the victim as "that bad lady everybody hates".

George just disappeared. He was such a non-entity that Alan hadn't been able to develop the right parameters to target him. It was just as well. His crime was probably no more than ignorance and without his partners, he posed no danger. MFK was liquidated by the administrator of Kristina's estate, since Dalton had predeceased her. Alan volunteered to help with the evaluation of the assets, which made it possible to destroy their more dangerous discoveries.

He felt no remorse for what he'd done, but he still found it difficult to sleep well. For no apparent reason, students at UCLA rioted and burned down several buildings on campus. The growing labor problems in Japan boiled over into open rebellion even though the government had met most of the protestors' demands. Prohibitionists had emerged as an independent political party in several southern states and had captured two state legislatures, vowing to outlaw all alcoholic beverages.

In each case, the change in public opinion had been sudden and extreme. One commentator noted that it was almost as if someone was moving behind the scenes, dictating what other people thought.

That was the last time Alan listened to the news. Or read a newspaper. He disconnected his television, refused to look at his mail, and had groceries and other supplies delivered to his house so that he didn't have to go outside where he might be exposed to any different viewpoint.

For as long as possible, he preferred to think his own thoughts.

FINDING ARIADNE

Ariadne might have died during her fourth performance at Scalawags, but it wouldn't have been her fault. Some drunken lout wandered backstage and fell against the lighting panel hard enough to cause a flicker. That's all two of the airsnakes needed to escape the hypnotic spell of her dance and break from the graceful pattern they'd been flying around her gently swaying form. One darted at her face, the other toward an upraised arm.

I'd been watching out of the corner of my eye, not really interested. Ariadne wasn't the type I ordinarily find attractive. Every woman I'd been involved with had been big, busty, and broad in the hips. Not that Ariadne was skinny exactly. She had a firm dancer's body with long, slender legs, but her torso was boyish and her face had the delicate features of a Tyrian festival doll. I figured she was human stock, although some of the other races are close enough that they could pass.

It was surprising that she eluded both of them. Most of the air dancers I'd seen, even those who draw the big crowds at the Royal Emporium, would have taken at least one hit. Of course, at the fancy places, there's always a technician standing by with the antitoxin just in case, but it's still bad for the image to get stung in front of an audience. Anyway, Ariadne just did this little dip and spin, and both airsnakes missed their strike, then hovered indecisively. Before they could make up their tiny minds to have another go, she swept toward them, improvising a few new movements that somehow managed to keep the other four hypnotized into following her while she beguiled the two rebels back into the fold.

If she'd moved away while they were befuddled, chances are that they would have lost sight of her. Their perceptual range is less than a meter. Her first move had captured my attention, and now she earned my admiration as well. Still keeping time with the background music, she closed the gap and swept both arms above her head, arched her back, and slid between the recalcitrant creatures. They fell back into the pattern of the dance, which she then completed without further incident.

I was impressed enough to applaud.

Scalawags is in the lower levels of Lucidia, not the kind of place tourists get to visit. The relaxed attitude the Androsian government has toward trade - no tariffs, no inspections, no questions, and minimal port fees – serves them well. All of the big intercorps have a major presence on the planet, and most of the smaller ones. The planetary authorities also ignore the less public commerce - flesh, drugs, weapons, biophages, implants, stuff like that - that takes place in the bowels of their major cities.

Under the mantle of the largely symbolic Androsian metro government, the city of Lucidia was currently being run by three organizations. Rudger Vik was human, more or less, from somewhere out in the Canopy Worlds. He controlled the upper levels of Lucidia, which had been built adjacent to and inside a mountain that overlooked the small but very busy spaceport. The spaceport itself was run by a Clicker triumvirate, whichever part of the gestalt happened to be dominant at any given time. The rest of the city had changed hands recently. A Valdosian named Koomberlos had ruled for more than a standard human lifespan until his recent assassination by a mysterious entity known only as the Spider, a particularly ruthless newcomer who'd executed virtually all of the Valdosian's lieutenants rather than recruit them, which was the normal practice. In slightly less than one local year, the Spider had become the most feared and hated of Andros' many petty warlords, even though no one claimed to have actually met him. Or perhaps because of that very fact.

Dinka showed up on time, and I spent the next two drinks arguing prices with him.

"You're a thief, Logus. You know that, don't you?"

I spread my hands and smiled. "You're free to shop elsewhere, Dinka. Some of my competitors have lower prices."

"For outdated technology," he growled.

We settled on a figure that had us both scowling, although it was actually more than I'd hoped for. I'd dealt with Dinka before, and I knew that if I gave any indication that I was pleased, he'd argue endlessly the next time we did business together. I offered to buy a final round and we were waiting for the serviton to bring our drinks when Ariadne came out from behind the stage.

She'd been wearing a skin tight glowsuit during the dance, but had changed to a halter that left her midriff bare above a scatterskirt that provided tantalizing glimpses of her bare legs as she walked. Without glancing to either side, she headed straight for the exit, passing almost within reach of my admittedly longer than average arms. I glanced up with casual interest and had already begun to turn away when an Androsian stood up from the next table and stepped into her path.

Androsians are human derived, but they're one of the less attractive variations. They were among the first genetically altered colonists and the bio-engineers were somewhat clumsy in their gene splicing. Androsians were quite broad at shoulder and hip, with heavier bones and more muscle mass. The gravity on Andros was slightly lighter than standard, however, so most of the muscle ended up as fat. This particular individual, who had the typical cratered complexion, had done nothing to reverse this process.

"My friends and I would like to buy you a drink." His speech wasn't slurred, but its odd precision told me he'd been taking nanoregulators to combat the effects of whatever he'd been drinking.

"No thanks," Ariadne answered politely but firmly, slipping gracefully away from the arm he was attempting to throw around her shoulders. He moved quickly to interpose himself and managed to block the entire aisle. Like I said, Androsians are broader in the beam than most of us.

"The boss wouldn't like it if you were impolite to some of his best customers." The man's tone was ponderously light, and it offended me. I'm not a champion of the downtrodden, mind you, and I've ignored worse, but there was something about Ariadne that appealed to me, and something about the Androsian that didn't. I felt my fingers curling into fists and wondered if I was going to intervene. I can't always predict my own reactions, so I'm constantly surprising myself.

"I do my entertaining on the stage. If you're looking for a joygirl, the serviton can summon one for you."

"Now don't be like that." And then he made his mistake. One huge paw reached for her shoulder and Ariadne acted as gracefully as she had on stage. She eluded his hand effortlessly and her arms moved so fast the Androsian never even had time to raise his guard. He fell back, clutching his throat, and crashed to the floor. Two of his companions jumped to their feet and started to move in her direction, but Ariadne just spun around with a dancer's grace and one long leg shot out with such force that the closest Androsian's armored genital sheath cracked audibly and he fell back. The remaining man pretended that he hadn't meant to do anything. Ariadne surveyed the damage and walked out of Scalawags.

She wasn't even breathing heavily. The Androsian who'd accosted her never moved again but no one much cared other than his friends, and they didn't care very much.

My business was brisk for the next few days. A delegation from the Tenebran Empire had arrived looking for technology that might help them suppress the latest wave of rebellions. I deal primarily in security and intelligence systems, so we met several times to negotiate their purchase of the latest model Autonomous Mechanical Guardian. It was my most profitable single deal since arriving on Andros, but I surpassed it four days later selling a nanoplague to their enemies which would incapacitate the AMG's.

There was also local unrest because of the Velvet murders. Serial killers who choose their targets from the richest and most powerful strata are very good for my business. Velvet had claimed twelve victims in the last local year, including two politicians and three highly placed intercorps executives. Each had been strangled, and the murders had attracted considerable attention because the killer covered the faces of his victims with a velvet mask. I was selling personal defensive systems as fast as I could import them.

I can't say that I was actually thinking of Ariadne the next time I visited Scalawags, but once I was seated and the serviton was downloading my second drink, I remembered her.

"Is Ariadne performing tonight?'

The serviton froze while its programming analyzed my non-standard question. The better places have more sophisticated equipment, but since it was not unusual for a patron of Scalawags to pour drinks into the staff's input jacks, the management here employed only the cheapest models.

"Yes, patron."

I sat through the performances of a singer with a piercingly shrill voice and a Clicker juggling act that was perfectly executed but boring. Then Ariadne came out on stage, wearing the same outfit I'd seen the first time. As she started her routine I counted six, seven, eight airsnakes, two more than she'd used during earlier.

Snake dancing requires absolute concentration. Airsnakes respond primarily to the physical movement of the dancer's body, but they're also mildly telepathic. A waver in concentration not visible to the audience could still shatter the equilibrium. Most performers used four or six airsnakes. The better ones could keep eight in thrall for short periods. Divadara, who defined the art form, had occasionally performed with ten, as did a few of her close competitors.

Ariadne performed flawlessly and there was appreciative applause. I felt a quickening of my interest and left with the intention of returning the following evening. As it happened, I spent the next several days in custody when the Androsians rounded up every offworlder who fit their profile for the Velvet killings, about six hundred of us. I'd arrived two months before the first murder and had been on planet ever since. We were threatened with deportation and kept incommunicado until the Clickers closed down the spaceport in protest, the Spider sabotaged the sanitation system, and Rudger Vik pulled strings attached to some high ranking locals.

Once released, I spent a hectic couple of days rescheduling all the appointments I had missed. Then I was forced to make a trip off planet to negotiate new deals with three of my suppliers. When I finally returned to Scalawags, they'd redone the interior. The stage was bigger now, and looked as though it had been rebuilt. Risers had been installed strategically so the stage was visible from almost every table. Even more significantly, there were no empty seats, and the audience itself had changed. In fact, many of them sported the azure chevrons of the Androsian petty nobility and they didn't look like they were slumming.

I asked the serviton about the changes, but it couldn't parse my question. Then Ariadne came out to perform and I figured out the answer on my own. She was accompanied by ten glittering airsnakes, and she and they performed flawlessly. Scalawags had a major attraction to offer and the audience was appropriately impressed.

I think that's when my obsession started. Like I said before, Ariadne was not the type to which I normally feel attracted. There was something about her that spoke to me, something I never was able to define.

I started visiting Scalawags every night, arriving just before her act, leaving as soon as it was over. I tried to schedule my appointments so that I was free whenever she was performing and only missed two shows. The second one was the night Velvet killed one of Vik's top lieutenants.

Ariadne rarely mixed with the crowd. Once in a while she would emerge afterward and have a drink at the bar, always by herself, politely declining the free drinks that were offered by her admirers. There was only one other physical confrontation that I saw, a spindly man from Grecha who had once purchased some surveillance equipment from me. Ariadne broke his arm. I made no effort to approach her, although on two occasions, she caught my eyes from the stage and held my gaze for just long enough to tell me it wasn't accidental.

Then, one night toward the end of second summer, a six armed juggler from Komus performed in her place.

"I do not possess the required information." The serviton's response to my question was less than satisfactory. I tried the more sophisticated model tending the actual bar.

"Ariadne will not be performing this evening, patron."

"Will she be performing tomorrow?"

The serviton's processing pause was almost a human hesitation. "I do not have access to that information."

The juggler was back the following evening, and the night after that a man I'd never seen before danced with four airsnakes. A significant portion of the audience walked out during his routine. I finished my drink thoughtfully, then strolled over to the armored door set unobtrusively in an alcove. A thin spray of nano-agents subverted the lock within a few breaths and I eased it open.

An AMG stood inside, but it was an old model and went into idle as soon as I touched the override in my pocket. That sent a signal to the monitor, of course, which I could have prevented had I wished to do so. Instead I waited patiently while two heavily armed flesh and blood guards showed up and escorted me to the manager's office.

"I thought you told me that new lock was state of the art, Logus." It was Scalawag herself, real name unknown, who rose from behind the massive autodesk.

"That was weeks ago, Scally," I answered easily. "We've had three upgrades since then. I did suggest a service contract, remember?"

"At an exorbitant price," she sniffed, but I could tell she wasn't really annoyed. "What can I do for you? I'm not in the market for more security right now."

"This isn't a sales call. I'm buying not selling this time." She raised an eyebrow and waited. "I'm looking for one of your employees. The dancer. Ariadne."

She sighed, and I thought it was genuine. "So who isn't? Business is up forty percent since she started. She misses a performance and I don't hear from her so I look her up. Address in the lower levels. Bad neighborhood, but not the worst. Inside's about what you'd expect. But no Ariadne. I'm having it watched but…"

"You try Surveynet?"

"Official and premium level. No data, recent or otherwise. She must've spent a good portion of her take on screening technology. She one of your clients?"

I shook my head.

"Well, she's got hot stuff protecting her privacy, including at least one false trail." This time it was my eyebrow that went up. "Records say she immigrated from Cawdor after the big flare there a year back. That mole program you sold me found a contradiction though. So we don't know where she came from. Or where she is."

I nodded, then turned to go.

"If you find her and she comes back to work, your tab's free here forever."

"I'll find her. Can't promise more than that though."

It wasn't as easy as I'd expected. I already had a probe into Surveynet, the secret government level, but learned nothing new. I salted her quarters with nano-monitors on top of those Scalawag had already planted and had a few discrete words with some of my more reliable contacts throughout Lucidia. Ariadne was a celebrity, so I expected to hear something within a day or two. Six days passed in utter silence. Even the wyrm program I'd uploaded into various city data grids reported steady nulls.

My organic contacts were more expressive but less reliable. First I heard she'd been seen leaving Andros on a freighter under an assumed name. Then there were rumors that she'd moved to Tempella on the southern continent and married an Androsian noble or that she'd contracted Ched's Disease and was dying in a private clinic. None of the stories stood up.

Dinka was the first to mention another possibility to me. "I hear you've been asking about the missing dancer." We had met on our usual business and, distracted, I'd let Dinka argue me down to considerably less than my usual margin. He knew it too, and the victory made him expansive. "I heard the other day that Velvet got her."

I considered my answer. "She doesn't fit the profile. Velvet only preys on the privileged class, the rich and famous and powerful."

"She was a level ten dancer. There's only two others on Andros can handle that many."

"Maybe Elithia or the Grande Dame would qualify, but I can't see Velvet stooping to murdering a dancer from Scalawags, no matter how good she was."

I heard the same rumor three more times over the next few days, but never bothered to check it out.

I resorted to more subtle methods. If Ariadne was dead, I was wasting my time. If she was still alive, there had to be pointers in the data system. Virtually everything that happens in Lucidia is recorded there, although not always in a recognizable form. I piggybacked a very expensive data coordinator onto my tap into Surveynet and monitored all live feeds from the city's data collection system, searching for approximations of her image, references to airsnakes and dancers. I placed over a hundred eavesdroppers in likely places throughout the city, all linked to a sophisticated program that watched for key words and phrases.

The rumor about Velvet ran its course in four days and fell below the threshold I'd established. In its place came another suggesting that Ariadne had been seen in the lower levels of the city. Although I expected that one to fade as well, it persisted, and I was already taking it more seriously when, to my surprise, one of my afterthoughts paid off.

A dead airsnake clogged a filter in the city's sanitary filtration system. It was mentioned in a routine maintenance report but the key word triggered the wyrm and sent me a summary. A few hours research allowed me to trace a path back through the sanitation system to a relatively small portion of the undercity. The most significant structure in that part of Lucidia was the virtual fortress that had been built by Koomberlos and which was now occupied by the enigmatic individual known as the Spider. Coupled with a low level rumor that the Spider had abducted her after visiting Scalawags incognito, I decided this was the hottest lead I was likely to get.

I was more circumspect than usual in the days the followed. Unobtrusive organic guardians, human and alien, were scattered around Spider's fortress along with a handful of relatively simple AMGs. I wasn't fooled, though. Koomberlos hadn't been a pushover, and his successor wouldn't have lasted long without a topnotch security system. There were too many ambitious sentients in the second tier of the Androsian underworld. If there were soft spots in his defenses, they'd have been penetrated long ago.

The fortress itself was a large, ugly, shapeless building built right on the periphery of the city, the edge gouged deeply into the mountainside. Two of its walls were, in fact, solid rock, although my detectors found a narrow tunnel that was probably an escape route to one or more boltholes elsewhere. There was a single visible entrance, no windows, and an array of nodules that housed surveillance equipment and automatic weapons. The Androsian military could have overwhelmed it in less than an hour, but not without taking serious casualties.

Although the equipment was top of the line, it was at least a year out of date. I tailored a nano counter agent that would not compromise the Spider's security except in my case and managed to introduce it into the water supply. Getting past the organics - three humans and a Clicker triumvirate - took a little effort, but I only had to seriously hurt one of the humans, and she would recover. The front door took a bit longer; it was even older than I had expected and my nanos had to run through several generations before they could neutralize the locks. Then I was inside.

It took longer than expected to circumvent the rest of the defenses, which remained formidable despite the inhibiting nanovirus. Using methods which must remain my little secret, I disabled several AMGs, passive and active alarms, a really ingenious electronic snare, and various other devices, some of which were practically antiques. There were no organic guards inside. Eventually I reached, and broached, the door to the inner sanctum, deep in the heart of the building, and rushed inside with my weapons ready.

I found myself in the Spider's personal living quarters and, confirming the information I'd gathered, Ariadne was there, sitting unrestrained on a large cerebroform capable of changing from bed to chair to lounge as required . There was no one else in the room and the only movement came from a row of electronic cages set against the far wall. Airsnakes hovered in several of them. I blinked and thought about it, then smiled and lowered my weapons. "I might have guessed."

"But you didn't." She seemed perfectly relaxed. "I've been expecting you for two days now."

Quite deliberately, I deactivated my electronic defenses, most of them anyway. "I'm a cautious man. The airsnake was deliberate then?"

She shrugged. "A tiny sacrifice. I reached twelve, you know."

I raised an eyebrow. "I must have missed that performance."

"There was no performance. I don't require the admiration of others to validate my achievements. No one has ever seen the Spider until now. Success is its own reward."

"Then why am I here?"

"To entertain me. That's why I didn't neutralize your inhibitor, although I did take my better equipment off line. You might have damaged some of it."

"So this time I provided the entertainment and you were the audience, is that it?"

She smiled and the cerebroform responded to her unspoken desire and transformed itself into a bed. "The show is just getting started."

And for a while, excitement made both of us feel more alive.

I'm usually restless after sex and this was no exception. Ariadne grumbled sleepily and rolled over as I slipped out of bed. Her quarters were furnished in spartan fashion, like my own. I strolled over to the habitats and watched the airsnakes for a moment. One of the cages held Tyrian fire lizards. A bright green one spat a tiny flame in my direction. I moved on, passed a Denebian spidercrab waiting patiently in its luxuriant web and a swarm of flugelflies from one of the Canopy worlds.

"I notice you like beautiful and expensive things." I turned and gestured broadly, as if I'd just noticed that the curtains and bedding were all made from Corinthian velvet. There was enough in that single chamber to balance a planetary budget.

"You don't think I'm Velvet, do you?" I turned, saw her sitting up on the cerebroform, watching me calmly.

I considered my response as I rejoined her. "No," I said honestly. "I don't."

She didn't say anything after that, and after a while I gathered my gear and left. Ariadne was the most extraordinary and in some ways the most beautiful person I'd ever met. If she'd been simply the dancer I'd first believed, the outcome might have been different. But when word got around that the Spider had been Velvet's latest victim, business would be brisk and profitable for a considerable time to come.

PRE-PIRATES

Prepubs.com made a splashy entrance to the internet, offering – for a nominal fee – the complete text of forthcoming novels by Stephen King, Nora Roberts, and J.K. Rowling. Individuals who stumbled over the site assumed that its owner had somehow come into possession of review copies, but no such copies yet existed. In fact, the King novel was undergoing a major revision, the Roberts was only half complete, and the Rowling consisted of little more than an outline.

DMCA notices were dutifully sent, but ignored. A polite email response from the site manager suggested that if the works in question were in fact not yet written, they could not have been stolen. This legal technicality caused understandable confusion. A few days later there were new offerings including the next installments in two popular mystery series and a tell-all book by an ex-White House advisor who had not yet resigned her position to write the book..

Spencer Hastings of the Hastings Detective Agency was hired by a consortium of publishers to get the goods on the as yet unidentified owner of the website. The person in question was one Teresa Grant, a mid-twenties free lance computer programmer. Hastings looked further and discovered that she had been a good but uneven student. "She always aced the written exams, but she was terrible at oral presentations or during class interactions." Grant had attended Michigan State, majoring in computer science with a minor in psychology. This pairing struck Hastings as unusual so he flew out to East Lansing and looked up some of her former professors. "It was parapsychology she was interested in." said one. "I always had the sense that she was looking for answers but didn't want to ask the questions."

It was only by chance that he ran into an instructor who had briefly been Grant's roommate. When Hastings asked her about Grant's interest in psychology, she smiled. "She was always trying to understand her foresight."

"Foresight?"

"Sure. Teresa could look into the future, sort of. All she could see were written documents though. When I was lazy, I'd asked her to read me my next letter home to my parents and she'd reel it off while I copied it down. Nice parlor trick, but no practical application."

When Hastings reported, it created consternation among the legal staff hired by the various publishers. Could you steal something that didn't exist yet? If Grant wrote it down before Stephen King, which of them owned the copyright? Could she sue the publishers for pirating original works published on her website?

Finally someone suggested a face to face meeting. To their surprise, Grant indicated her willingness. To their even greater surprise, she seized the initiative at the subsequent get together, overriding the array of high caliber legal talent. She already knew what they were going to propose – it had been written down beforehand – and she had a counter offer of her own. She asserted that she had no interest in claiming ownership of any of the work she was offering her customers. "How many people are going to download a Teresa Grant novel instead of one by J.K. Rowling?" She was even willing to pay a royalty on every download to the relevant publishers. "But in return I want a notice in every printed copy that the author's next book will be available first at prepubs.com."

There was a great deal of negotiating, but in the end, Grant got pretty much everything she wanted.

Several authors, whose royalties would now be problematic, objected to the terms of the deal. Many of them refused to turn in contracted novels, only to discover that they were soon available on prepubs.com anyway. Technothriller author Clive Clancy was chosen to approach Grant as the authorized representative of the authors. They had dinner together a few nights later. Grant did most of the talking, and at the end, Clancy was satisfied.

Most authors now make far less money per book than they did in the past. On the other hand, they are much more productive. The 700th Eve Dallas novel appeared last week and the adventures of Harry Potter's children have now reached twelve. Writers can be much more productive when all they need to do is access a website, download their next book, and mail it off to their publishers. Writing, after all, used to be hard work.

TRAPS

Ted had underestimated how much it would affect him to set foot on Mars once again. Planet sized memories assailed him with an almost physical force and he swayed slightly as he descended from the shuttle, prompting Janice, nominally his secretary, to lean toward him solicitously. "Are you all right?"

"I'm fine, Janice. I just need to adjust to the lower gravity." That was an obvious lie since their ship had been artificially generating the appropriate conditions for the past several weeks. She was certainly aware of that fact but she didn't contradict him. They had worked together for three years now, long enough for her to understand his personal quirks and defense mechanisms, perhaps better than he did himself.

He tried to taste the local air, which would be mixed with that provided by his rebreather now that they were outside the ship, but he couldn't tell if the hint of dryness was actual or part of his imagination. There was a measurably higher percentage of oxygen now than there had been when he'd last been on Mars, but it still wouldn't sustain human life for long without a secondary supply.

There was a delegation waiting for them on the paved walkway, of course, but it was small and tolerable. "Welcome to Mars, Mr. Loder." Harvey Wechsler shook his hand vigorously. Ted had never actually met any of the delegation before; he had left Mars in his teens and this was his first trip back. Nor had any of them ever visited Earth. That didn't make them strangers. They'd video-conferenced several times, a tedious process because of the extensive time lapse between comment and response and he'd frequently grown tired of watching their studiously neutral faces as they endured the intervals with feigned patience.

More hand shaking followed. Ted had the oddest feeling that he was meeting characters from a holodrama rather than real people. The formalities were completed and after a short walk and passage through a personnel lock they were inside the terminal where the atmospheric pressure was closer to Earth normal. There was a chorus of clicks as personal respirators shifted to standby. The unfamiliar weight on his shoulder made Ted feel unbalanced, but he acknowledged that at least the unit was half the weight of the one he'd worn as a teenager.

They took a tubeway into Burroughs, the largest city on Mars although Bradbury and Weinbaum were both potential rivals. Ted closed his eyes during the short, rapid trip through the tunnel. He had always found the tubeways mildly claustrophobic and a familiar hint of nausea stirred in his gut. Janice must have sensed his mood because she engaged Wechsler in conversation to divert his attention.

The terminal and the city beyond bore little resemblance to his childhood memories. The city's population had increased tenfold in four decades and the borders of the settlement had been extended by additional modules in every direction except upward. There had been only four domes when he'd left Mars; there were sixty now, all interconnected by portals which would automatically close if there was a breach in any one section. The underground levels had increased from three to twelve in some places.

Wechsler turned around in his seat to address the visitors. "We've made arrangements for you to stay at the Tars Tarkas. It's not as sumptuous as the John Carter Inn, but it's quieter. You said you wanted to keep a low profile."

"That's fine."

They exited the tube at a station Loder did not recognize. Someone had reserved an electrocart which stood parked in the service area and both his and Janice's luggage had already been loaded aboard. There wasn't much. His diplomatic status entitled him to a larger mass allowance than ordinary passengers, but he had not wanted to flaunt his privilege. Most of Ted's baggage weighed nothing and was visible only to him, but it pressed down on him despite its insubstantiality. We carry our heaviest baggage inside ourselves.

"Jankowski and Garcia will go along with you to make sure everything is acceptable. I imagine you'll want some time to adjust before our first formal session." Wechsler gestured toward a cadaverously tall man with a pale complexion and a shorter, slightly overweight but quite pretty woman. Ted had been introduced to both but he couldn't remember which was which. Jankowski must be the man, he thought; the woman looked vaguely Hispanic.

"We'll adjust to your schedule, Mr. Wechsler. But I would like a chance to settle in first."

"Naturally. Why don't we meet informally for dinner in, say, two hours. We can map out our schedules then and begin tomorrow morning."

Ted was still thinking in terms of ship time. He's eaten breakfast shortly before boarding the shuttle. After weeks in transit, Ted felt a sudden impatience, a need to begin negotiations immediately and dispense with the diplomatic niceties. As always, he mildly resented the feeling that he was being managed, but admitted to himself that Wechsler was only being a considerate host. Perhaps it was for the best, he thought. They were committed to remain on Mars for at least two months, even if they settled everything within a few days, which was unlikely given their carefully devised strategy. Now might be a good time to confront and banish a few ghosts. The negotiations would go better if he wasn't distracted.

The ride took longer than he'd expected. The passageways had not been designed for the current traffic level, and since most people traveled on foot or bicycle, there was a good deal of apparent anarchy although Ted was sure that conventions had evolved and that patterns existed which he could not yet perceive. The electrocart moved in fits and starts, skillfully managed by Garcia while Jankowski pointed out landmarks in a voice so devoid of interest that Ted felt no guilt about ignoring him.

They'd been given a suite. Ted suspected that their hosts were uncertain about the nature of his relationship with Janice and had deliberately left the sleeping arrangements flexible. The term "suite" would have been a misnomer on Earth since their combined space was about the same as they would have enjoyed in an average hotel back home, but the beds were separated by a door and they had expected no better. He was fond of Janice and thought sometimes that she reciprocated, but there was nothing physical in their relationship and, he was quite sure, never would be. Romance with a subordinate rarely ended well.

Although he usually unpacked hurriedly, never feeling at ease until his quarters were arranged to his satisfaction, he stood at the suite's single window, staring down onto a crowded promenade, and hadn't moved when Janice knocked and then entered before he could answer.

"It must have changed quite a bit since you were last here."

Ted nodded. "It's almost unrecognizable. And I'm looking at it from a very different pair of eyes in any case." He turned from the window. "First impressions?"

"Wechsler's on edge. As we surmised, he's more at ease negotiating from a distance. He's sharp but slow. He'll be used to having several minutes to respond to anything you say, so if you nudge him a bit, there's a chance he'll reveal more than he intends to. I don't know who among his entourage will be at the negotiations, but I'd keep an eye on Rajapaska. She doesn't miss a thing and she has self control and intelligence. It's possible she's the power behind the throne, so to speak."

Janice Voigt's ability to accurately assess people after only the most cursory encounter was her greatest asset as far as Ted was concerned. Her organizational skills and other talents were exceptional, but there was an endless supply of skilled bureaucrats back on Earth. "We always knew this wasn't going to be a walkover."

She shrugged. "I prefer things to be interesting."

"As long as they're not too interesting."

Dinner was elaborate by Martian standards, which meant that it included wine imported from Earth and meat from animals that hadn't spent their entire lives immersed in aqueous fluid. Ted complimented his hosts even though he preferred the consistency of the latter. The conversation brushed the periphery of the purpose of Ted's visit, but neither side was prepared to unsheath swords just yet. The trade and support pact was more important to Mars than to Earth, which theoretically gave Ted a big advantage, but there were ameliorating circumstances. If Wechsler and his people failed to wring any significant concessions, the nascent separatist movement would benefit enormously and there were strong anti-colonialist sentiments back home, directed primarily at China's political domination of the African subcontinent at present, but volatile enough to embrace the red planet's dissidents given the proper combination of circumstances.

Ted's job was to make sure they received no such socio-political reward but without granting excessive concessions to the colonial government.

The dinner party broke up early. Janice suggested that they review the previous three years' worth of production and trade data but Ted demurred. "We've gone over it more than enough times already, and we know it's not going to have that much impact on the final agreement. They'll insist on looking forward rather than back, and I don't blame them. I think I'm going to take a walk and clear my head."

She didn't ask if he wanted company, just nodded, understanding that his stress had nothing to do with the object of their mission. "Don't get lost."

"I won't."

But he did. Burroughs had changed so dramatically that he became disoriented as soon as the Tarkas was out of sight. In the early days, there had been rigid planning governing the layout of the city. There were still very exacting restrictions on what could be built and where so that the atmospheric reconditioning and circulating system would work properly, but inevitably exceptions were made and these multiplied upon each other. The passageways were no longer constructed on a regular grid, dwelling units were interspersed with multi-functional or commercial structures, and the city had been forced to adapt to these new conditions. Some of the environmental controls had been tinkered with and air quality was no longer consistent throughout the city, for example, a relatively small problem that could easily become a major issue.

Because of the flexible workday employed in most Martian institutions, the traffic level remained fairly constant on the main thoroughfares. When he'd been a child, clothing had been predominantly practical, undistinguished, and rather plain. Some of that tradition remained, particularly among older people, but much was also flamboyant, even more so than back on Earth. Dyed and sculpted hairstyles were apparently popular among the younger crowd here, in contrast to the shaved heads and painted domes of teenagers in North America and Europe. Ted's jumpsuit was unusual but not so much that it attracted attention.

At first he'd followed the crowd, listening to snatches of passing conversations, trying to get a feel for what preoccupied the thoughts of the colonials nowadays. He was rather disappointed to discover that their concerns were largely the same as those he might have detected in any busy metropolis back on Earth – family problems, complaints about working conditions, disillusionment with the government's economic policies, the trauma of unrequited love or lust or both. Disappointed but not surprised, he turned into a less frequented passageway and found himself walking alongside a bank of air spargers that huddled around one of the supports for the dome high overhead.

That's where he got lost. Not very lost actually. For all its complexity and growth, Burroughs was still a contained community. As a last resort one could walk to the outer perimeter and follow the curve of the dome back to familiar territory. Ted retained enough of his childhood pride to eschew that solution once he accepted that he was indeed disoriented. No, he would negotiate a more direct route back to the commercial district. He could no longer hear its heavier traffic sounds because of the thrumming of the machinery around him, but it was easy enough to glance up at the supporting struts and determine his relative position from their curvature.

It had been a different Mars back here near the shell when he was a child, and he was irrationally pleased to discover that some things were much as he remembered them. Most of the people who lived in Burroughs were acutely aware of the neutral but relentless hostility of the desert sands that lapped against their plastic and steel islands of life, but they preferred not to think about them. No one lived near the perimeter unless they had no other choice – and yes, Burroughs had its homeless minority although they were not an exact equivalent to their cousins on Earth.

Ted found a set of stairs that led up to a maintenance catwalk and climbed them. From that vantage point, he'd be better able to plot a course back toward the center. As he rose above the clutter, he found himself looking out through the transparent dome toward the Martian landscape. As a boy, he'd never recognized its beauty and had spent countless hours imagining he was surrounded by an ocean of water rather than sand, that he was a pirate searching for booty, or an explorer seeking new worlds to explore and exploit, or a shipwreck victim trapped on a deserted island. Well, he'd seen real oceans now and impressive though they might be, their beauty was only different, not superior.

Laura had tried to infect him with her love for this world, he remembered, but he'd refused to listen.

That was the first time he'd consciously thought of Laura since landing, although memories of their time together had hovered at the periphery of his consciousness ever since the departure from Earth. The intensity of his memory had grown steadily as they crossed the gap between worlds. He had long believed that part of his life had been set aside permanently but circumstances had changed. Ted had missed her fiercely at times after he'd first emigrated to Earth, but he had remained determined to sever every link that bound him to the past and when he'd refused to respond to her sporadic messages that first year, she'd stopped sending them. More than a decade later, he had impulsively inquired about her, discovered that she'd married someone he'd never met, and he had thought that knowledge had finally closed the book of their relationship forever. But it had not.

He turned away from the panoramic view and spied out a route that would take him back to the Tarkas.

There was no progress at all during the first day of the conference, but that was to be expected. Wechsler introduced the members of his negotiating team – nine of them, outnumbering Ted and Janice handily, even ignoring the small army of statisticians and miscellaneous staff people who sat at another table, waiting to be called upon. Ted considered that an advantage. He and Janice would speak with a single voice while the opposition was fragmented. The interests of the labor representatives would not be entirely congruent with those of the politicians or the societal engineers or the terraforming commission or the scientific community, all of whom were represented. Wechsler was the titular head of delegation, but that didn't mean he was necessarily the strongest personality sitting on that side of the table.

Wechsler made a long, halting, disjointed speech which purported to lay out the position of the colonials but it didn't require Janice's perspicacity for Ted to take note when hints of disagreement rippled the face of the Director of Research - a white haired Asian woman named Gaipo – or the impatience of the labor delegate, Morrow, whose fingers tapped the table rhythmically throughout. Each of the colonial delegates then added supplementary comments, some of which came perilously close to contradicting Wechsler. Ted responded with a noncommittal acknowledgment of the truth of many of the complaints and concerns that had been expressed but cautioned that economic and political considerations rendered it impossible to grant all the concessions that had been suggested. "I'm confident we can reach a compromise that will satisfy if not please everyone concerned." Janice then presented a compressed summarization of the existing trade and support agreements between Earth and Mars, and finished with an analysis of the balance of trade for the past three years – Earth years.

Several members of the Martian delegation started to respond simultaneously, and Wechsler looked flustered, but Ted raised both hands and spoke forcefully, re-establishing control. "I'm sure there's a lot of room for disagreement and no doubt many of your concerns are valid, but it's getting late and we already have a lot to process. I suggest we adjourn for the day and take this up in the morning."

Morrow looked as though he might argue the point but Wechsler hurriedly interposed himself. "I agree completely. These are all complex issues and they won't be resolved quickly or easily. But they will be resolved." He stood up and reached across the table to shake hands. Ted responded immediately and their eyes met. Wechsler was no fool, Ted realized; he knows that this could get out of hand quite easily. It would probably be to their advantage to ensure that Wechsler stayed in control, at least for the time being, particularly if he was aware that they were supporting his authority.

Ted and Janice compared notes back in their suite. She had picked up a few nuances that he'd missed, but in general the attitudes of the colonists were not obscure. Ted felt a good deal of sympathy for them, not just because he had been born here but because it was no secret that they were being deliberately hobbled in their efforts to become self sufficient. It was partly simple economics; the authorities on Earth wanted the most profitable arrangement possible even if that discommoded the colonists and at present the colonization effort was running at a significant loss. But it was more than just greed. Everyone knew that sooner or later Mars would become an independent political entity. Almost everyone even granted that it would probably be best for all concerned. They just didn't want it to happen during their watch.

Ted found his attention wandering during Janice's summary, and she cut off abruptly, aware of his distraction. "Do you want to do this later?"

"Yes, please. I'm sorry, but I can't seem to concentrate." He stirred uncomfortably. "Would you mind if I left you to your own devices for a while? I have something personal I want to take care of."

"Going to visit some old friends?" She knew that his family was dead, of course. The insurance had paid for his passage to Earth.

He shook his head. "I don't have any friends here. Not any longer. And I never had any really close ones even when I was young." That was a lie. There had been Laura. "I just need to walk off some old ghosts."

Ted had quietly kept tabs on Laura over the years. He knew that she'd married, but that her husband had died before they'd had any children. He found a public directory but could not find a listing for Laura Balfour, then remembered that she'd be listed under her married name, turned to Berkovic. She was there, along with an address on Willis Boulevard. He touched the icon for a city map and requested the shortest route to Dome 34.

He could have hired an electrocart but decided to walk, telling himself he needed the exercise even though he knew full well that he was stalling. He had often dreamed of meeting Laura again. Sometimes his imagining took the form of a surprise visit during which they would take up where they had left off. It was possible that she wouldn't recognize him even if they did meet, although he knew that she had not changed all that much. He on the other hand was heavier, hairier, and less caught up in dreams, more grounded in reality, and that maturity must show in his face.

It was not as long a walk as he'd thought, or perhaps it just didn't seem long because of the lighter gravity and his growing nervousness. Dome 34 had been erected long after Ted left Mars so there were not even the ghosts of ghosts here to bother him. On the other hand, the architecture had not changed all that much in three decades. The components were arranged in different configurations, but the pieces themselves were all very much the same.

Score one for the Martians, he told himself. Their argument that Earth denies them proven technology that could make life easier was justified. He passed a bank of heat exchangers which were obviously newly installed, but they were technologically two generations behind those available in most cities on Earth, and the electrocarts still used old fashioned power receptors with limited range and wasteful bleed over. He was authorized to make certain concessions in that area and their strategic planning included several upgrades, though not all that the colonists would covet. It might even make good tactical sense to pre-emptively offer a bouquet of technical assistance. But it would be costly, both in financial and political credits, and he would have to wrest something from the colonials in return that they would be reluctant to concede easily.

He paused in front of her address, playing a scenario in his head in which they met, exchanged polite pleasantries, realized they still loved one another, and tore off each other's clothing in the rush to satisfy their passion. The absurdity of this fantasy made him flush and he was suddenly filled with a panic so intense that he felt physically ill. Shaken, he turned and walked on hastily, pausing only when he had rounded the corner into another common area. He felt as though he had just escaped from some devilishly clever trap.

Ted had been preoccupied with traps for most of his life. As a child, he and his peers had been subject to adult supervision around the clock, watched over in the community crèche while his parents worked, never allowed to leave home except in their company until he was old enough to act responsibly. Although his limits had expanded during early adolescence, it wasn't long before Burroughs itself – dramatically smaller at the time – had seemed just as much a prison as had the crèche. And when he'd finally been allowed to leave the dome for limited, solitary excursions among the dunes and plains of Mars, he'd decided that the planet itself was a prison, and unlike his parents and most of his companions, he was unable to reconcile himself to confinement.

And so, when his parents died in a tragic accident, he had emigrated to Earth, only to discover that he had carried his prison walls with him, that he felt just as constrained as ever and no longer had the consolation of his friends – of Laura at least – to compensate.

And now I'm back on Mars, he told himself, and my job is to make sure that the bars of the cage are loosened enough to satisfy the inmates, but without letting them actually escape.

He returned to the Tars Tarkas and went to bed, but it was a long time before he could sleep.

In one sense, the Martians were already self sufficient. They could break ties with Earth unilaterally at any time. There would be inconveniences but they could make do. The catch was that in order to survive on their own they would need to take the draconian step of reducing their population by almost a third. The colonial authority on Earth was more than generous with the staples of life because it was to their advantage to keep the population on Mars high enough that it became a self imposed dependence. None of this was secret, though it was rarely addressed openly. No Martian politician was going to risk his position by suggesting that his constituents should have fewer children, or perhaps live shorter lives.

Ted went through the motions of negotiating the initial elements of the trade compact, but in the end there was no significant variance from the rough agreement they'd worked out at long distance. This was all theater; the colonial negotiators could announce an early "victory" that would bolster their position and allow them to make later concessions to "balance" matters. Wechsler and his team were all aware of this posturing but since the illusion worked to their advantage, at least in the short term, no one tried to dilute the effect by appending substantive issues.

Ted was restless throughout the session and allowed Janice to do most of the talking. In part it was impatience with the whole process. He also felt a whisper of guilt, as though he was engaged in some unethical scam, as indeed he was. But most of all he wanted to escape the cramped conference room, even if only to the crowded streets outside. He and Laura were destined to meet again and he was impatient to get it over with. He had trouble concentrating on what was going on around him and twice had to ask someone to repeat a question before he could answer it. When Wechsler suggested that they defer starting on the technological exchanges until the following day, he agreed quickly.

"Is anything wrong?" Ted was aware that Janice had been glancing at him speculatively.

"Sorry, I'm off my game today, aren't I?"

Janice was always the consummate diplomat. "It must be strange. Coming back here after so long, I mean."

"Yes. More than I expected. I'll get over it. I know why I'm here and what I have to do." He smiled. "You won't mind if I leave you to your own devices again?"

"Of course not. I have a lot of work to do anyway. You have to do what you have to do." But this time there was a deeper emotion in her voice, if not her face. Ted understood and felt a flash of irrational resentment which she probably noticed.

"Don't wait up."

It didn't take as long this time. He felt more confident making his way through the crowds and this time he knew the way. It was only when he was in sight of her quarters that his steps faltered and he came to a stop half concealed behind a secondary pylon from which point he could watch surreptitiously. Laura worked an early shift. She might well be home now. Ted told himself that he was being foolish, that he should walk right to her door and tap the visitors' plate, but he stayed where he was. Janice would be both amused and impatient, he realized, if she saw him dithering this way. Hesitation and caution had rarely been a part of their relationship.

He never noticed that he was no longer alone until a hand touched his shoulder. Turning and retreating a half step, he found himself facing a handsome looking woman his own age, dressed conservatively and looking at him with considerable amusement. There wasn't the slightest hesitation when she spoke.

"Hello, Ted. I was wondering how long it would be before you showed up."

"To be honest, I wasn't sure if I should come at all." To his surprise, his nervousness had evaporated in an instant. He felt as comfortable in Laura's presence now as he had decades earlier, and the interval between his departure and their reunion shrank to insignificance. "You look the same as you always did. It's like I stepped through time."

She laughed. "Not quite. I've added a little padding and there are wear spots if you know where to look for them. You're looking a little soft, frankly. I thought the heavier gravity would have helped trim down some of that baby fat."

"It all turned to muscle," he lied transparently. "How have you been?"

"Married. Widowed. Lonely. And you?"

"Bachelor. Busy. Lonely."

"You never married?"

"The only woman I ever loved was millions of miles away. Long distance relationships never work well."

"You could have come back."

"Not really. I don't belong here, Laura. I never did."

She sighed. "No, you had to fly off and escape."

"I don't feel as though I escaped."

"I told you so, a long time ago."

"Yes, you did."

She invited him in and he accepted. Her quarters were neat and orderly, but even smaller than he had imagined, not much larger than the suite at the Tarkas. The furniture was sparse and plain but serviceable. There was a net terminal that obviously saw a lot of use and a vidscreen that obviously saw little. Even as a teenager, she had been the practical one, with little interest in holos or music or fiction or much of any light entertainment. He was slightly older but she had been much more mature, introducing him to sex which he had enjoyed immensely, and history and politics, which he had not.

"You're working for the city government now, I understand." He accepted the drink which she'd prepared from her limited assortment.

"Yes," she said drily. "One of the under equipped trying to satisfy the needs of the unappreciative."

"There were shortages before. Are they getting worse?"

She shook her head. "But they're not getting any better. My husband would probably have lived if he' d been on Earth. You knew about his accident?"

He did, but he preferred that she not realize how closely he'd followed her life. "I'm sorry to hear that. It's an endless game of catch up. First priority goes to the homeworld constituency, Laura. Self interest reigns supreme. That's not going to change."

"No, I suppose not." She looked away but not before Ted caught a glimpse of something in her face. Frustration, perhaps, or regret. "Are you going to help us, Ted?"

He knew what she meant. "My job is to negotiate the best possible deal for my superiors," he said quietly. "That doesn't mean it will be unfair."

"No," she laughed humorlessly. "It's never unfair. That would drive the population into the arms of the separatists, wouldn't it? You'll grant some small concessions that will mostly be window dressing, but the balance of the power will remain as it has been."

Ted allowed a hint of irritation to color his voice. "I'm just the messenger, Laura. I don't make policy."

"You could change sides."

He laughed. "Revert to Martian citizenship? No, I'm sorry. I might still be in a cage, but it's a bigger one and has more conveniences. And it wouldn't help. They'd just tell Janice, my secretary, to take over. She'd play by the same rule and I suspect she's a lot sharper than I am."

"No, I didn't mean that. But you could tell us about the Ares Simulation."

Ted raised his eyebrows. He considered playing dumb, but Laura would see right through him, as she always had. "Where did you hear about that?"

"Word gets around. You have an implant, don't you?"

He hesitated. "Lots of people have implants."

"You know what I mean, Ted. You have the demographics and projections all loaded up so that you can access them."

"I really can't talk about this." He shifted uneasily, as though he wanted to leave. He did want to leave, but he also wanted, needed to stay.

"Do you know what you're really carrying there inside your head?" She stood up and moved so that she stood between him and the door. It wasn't menacing, and might even be unconscious, but Ted couldn't help feeling that she knew exactly what she was doing. Laura had always been decisive; she had been the one who gave form to their games and fantasies, and sometimes their realities as well. "With those projections to work with, we could fashion a domestic strategy that would lead to real self sufficiency. We could identify which initiatives would work in our favor, enable us to shape development policies that would weaken the paternalistic domination of the colonial authorities."

"Earth won't tolerate an autonomous Mars. Not yet. They're not ready. You'll have to be patient."

"They won't ever be ready as long as they have a choice, Ted. And at the rate we're going, it will be generations before they let us go our own way. You can help change that. If you won't join us, you could just let us download a copy. No one would ever have to know."

He shook his head and started to stand up. "I'm sorry, Laura. I can't do that. I've changed my stripes once already. I can't do it again. I'd better go."

She suddenly looked contrite. "All right, I'm sorry. I had to ask. Please don't leave yet. No more politics. I promise. Let me get you another drink."

Ted let himself be persuaded. He really didn't want to leave, not yet, and he accepted the second drink. He was a bit disappointed, but not at all surprised, when his vision suddenly blurred and he felt the world closing in with a rush. "Trapped again" was his last thought.

He woke up all at once, as though a switch had been turned on. His head ached and his stomach was slightly queasy, but otherwise he seemed uninjured. He sat up slowly and looked around. This wasn't Laura's place any more. It was a good sized room filled with electronic equipment and he was lying on a bare table set against one wall. At first he thought he was alone, but then he saw Laura sitting in one corner.

"How is your head?" Her voice was low, faltering.

"I've felt worse." He turned and slid down onto the floor, rubbed the back of his neck. "I assume you got what you wanted."

"Yes, we did. I'm sorry we had to do it this way, Ted, but there really wasn't any alternative."

"There's always an alternative. So now what? Do I die in some freak accident?"

"Of course not!" There was genuine shock in her voice. "We're not violent people."

"No, just thieves and kidnappers."

"I'm not proud of that, but it was necessary."

He looked around. "So I can just go? What's to stop me from notifying the prefecture?"

"Nothing. But what good would it do? You never even saw my accomplices and you know I'd never betray them. You would also have to admit that you put yourself in this position, and your superiors would not be happy to know that their enormously expensive and effective resource had been leaked to the opposition. It would also mean acknowledging the existence of the Ares simulation."

"You have the projections, but not the simulation itself. They're of limited usefulness."

"But they're better than nothing. And they'll enable us to put together a strategy that could shorten the liberation process by decades. You know that as well as I do."

He started toward the door and she didn't speak again until he reached it. "If you say nothing, we'll never reveal the truth. Your career will be safe."

There was bitterness in his answer. "Do you think so little of me that you believe I'd betray the people I work for?"

"No, you wouldn't do that. But you'll find a way to rationalize this because you know we're right. You're not an Earthman any more than you're a Martian. You've lied to yourself for a long time but you have to know the truth of it."

"What particular lie are you talking about? I have to be one or the other."

"No you don't. You know that even your superiors don't consider you a real Earthman. You still believe that you're at least part Martian and you're not. You never were. You grew up wanting to escape this trap, remember? You were always the exiled prince or the captive of pirates in our games."

"So I just jumped from one trap into another."

She shook her head. "No, Ted. You carry your trap around with you. That's why you will never really be free." He was shaken by the fact that her words so closely mirrored his own thoughts, but he kept his face still.

"We all fool ourselves sometimes, Laura. Even you." And he left.

He had little trouble orienting himself and set out on the long walk back to the Tars Tarkas. He did not call the prefecture. Back at the hotel, he walked up to his room, entering quietly to avoid disturbing Janice, but she was there waiting for him.

"You look terrible." She stayed seated, watching calmly as he sat down on his bed. "I gather they acted even more quickly than we expected. How did it go?"

"Just the way we thought it would. They believe they have the leverage they need now and they know we won't go public because to do that we'd have to reveal just how much we've been concealing." He rubbed the back of his head. "I always get a headache after a probing." He carried painkillers in his medikit, but on some level he was enjoying the ache in his head. Betrayal merited some punishment, after all.

"How long do you think it'll be before they show their hand?"

Ted shrugged. "Not long. They'll have at least one person on the negotiating team. We might catch a change of attitude as early as tomorrow."

"They'll know we know that."

"But they won't know that we planned all of this in advance, that we knew Laura was part of the independence party, that the information they extracted was pre-selected to mislead them, and that this was an elaborate trap to nudge them into a path that will hobble them even more tightly than before."

"A job well done then." She stood up and started back toward her own room. "If the rest of our visit goes as well, I'll be recommending you for that promotion once we get home."

"Thanks, boss."

He lay back on the bed as soon as she was gone. Laura had been right, of course. He was caught thoroughly in a snare that he could not escape because it was inside him. What she didn't realize was that her case was even worse because she actually thought she was free. Ted had long since come to terms with his situation. If he had no choice but to live in a cage, then at least he was going to have as many toys as he could squeeze in there with him.

He slept well that night.

DRIFTER

This is not the world I was born into. Sounds like a truism, doesn't it? The world is always changing so obviously none of us are living in the same world as that into which we first arrived, or even the one we inhabited yesterday. Almost goes without saying. But I mean it more literally than that. This is NOT the world I was born into. It's an alien place that simply bears a good deal of resemblance to where I spent my childhood, or at least part of it.

I'm not really sure when I started to drift.

I was a pretty ordinary boy up through my early teens. My grades were all right and I wasn't a disciplinary problem by any means, although I did have to stay after school a few times, mostly for fooling around when I should have been paying attention. I knew politics and history existed the way kids my age know that Brazil exists; it was a foreign country about which I knew little and cared less. When campaign signs appeared on lawns in my neighborhood, they were a new target for petty vandalism but had no inherent meaning.

But when I entered seventh grade - that would have been 1958 - I was quite sure that Eisenhower had defeated Adlai Stevenson for the Presidency. When told otherwise, I was puzzled for a while, but the issue had no discernible impact on my life and I was much more interested in Muriel Bates, who had moved into the neighborhood and who was very cute.

I have never been able to perceive the actual moments when the world changes around me. For all I know, it happens constantly in small ways that I cannot detect. If a spider catches a fly in Panama that it would have missed in my original world line, I could hardly be expected to know, or care. Lives could be changing all around me without my ever realizing that anything was different. Unless, of course, the life in question is that of someone famous.

The first time I realized that something strange was going on was the day I heard Elvis Presley sing "Are You Lonesome Tonight?" I was double dating with Dave Driscoll, whose date was actually Muriel Bates. I was with Susan Grayson, who dumped me a few days later. Dave had the car radio on and when I heard the deejay announce the next song I wondered aloud if it was the last he'd recorded before his death. Muriel was a big Elvis fan and was devastated by my announcement so the subject came up off and on all night. It wasn't until the next day in school that I got soundly told off for getting my story wrong. Elvis, it appeared, was alive and well.

Now I know with absolute certainty that I saw the news story about the crash on television. No survivors. Him and the Big Bopper and Buddy Holly and Richie Valens. I also remember that everyone at school was talking about it the next day. But now I was told that while those other singers had died as I remembered from a year earlier, Elvis had not been on the plane.

My divergent memories – I refuse to call them false memories – bothered me for several weeks but with decreasing force. Like I said, Susan dumped me and then my father nearly died in an auto wreck and my grades slumped for a while and I had to study like crazy to bring them back up and other stuff like that happened and Elvis Presley was no longer that big a factor in my life.

Graduation came and went and I was off to college at Cornell where I lasted as a biology major for about fifteen minutes before switching to history, without telling my parents, who would have thought it a very impractical career choice. Or maybe they wouldn't have by then, because when I came home after my freshman year, they were different. Yeah, I know. That's a complaint made by a lot of college freshman. It's not that the family changes but that we're looking at them with fresh eyes, right? Wrong! My father had been a chain smoker all his life, but not only was our house suddenly smoke free but he and Mom both insisted that it had always been that way.

This time I figured it was them who were crazy, not me. I got a full time job stocking shelves at the Patience and Prudence thrift store for the summer, dated Gale Davis off and on, and was greatly relieved when the summer ended and I was back at Cornell.

And then I started failing my courses.

Does the name Germany mean anything to you? How about the Panama Canal? Did you ever hear of the Boer War? Probably not, since no one in the history department at Cornell ever heard of such things. They spoke instead of the Lithuanian Empire, the Nicaraguan Canal, and the Australian Civil War. Two of my professors suggested that I seek counseling and a third told me I should change my major to creative writing. The weirdest thing is that I looked back at my old tests and found that I'd correctly stated on a midterm that Greater Bavaria was the head of the Axis powers during World War II even though I'm sure it was Nazi Germany. Oh, the Nazis were a fascist political party of the time, or at least in my world. You've probably never heard of them either. At least that was a plus.

So I dropped out of college. I mean, what's the point? If history can change at any moment, then no amount of studying would ever keep me current. I thought about switching to English, but I'm pretty sure that Ernest Hemingway and John Dos Passos were not famous for their collaborative novels, at least when I was in high school. Or I could have gone back to biology, except the phyla aren't defined or named exactly the way I remember, and I thought the Dodo was extinct, not just endangered.

I lived with my parents for a few weeks, but only until I got a job as a day laborer at one of the local factories. Dad still wasn't smoking but Mom had lung cancer because she'd been doing two packs a day since high school. They gave me odd looks when I asked about my brother. Apparently I was now an only child.

My first job worked out pretty well until the day I showed up for work and no one knew who I was. I couldn't collect unemployment – they had no record of me – and after one of the clerks made veiled allusions to illegal immigrants I never went back. I drifted out west and became a migrant farm worker, which worked out pretty well. The one time I tried calling home, some complete stranger picked up and told me that he'd had the same phone number for ten years.

I gave up trying to rent rooms near wherever I was currently working. The pace of change was obviously getting faster and I'd come back from work to find strangers ensconced in what I thought was my temporary home. I switched to a mix of flophouses, motels, and YMCAs, and sometimes they even recognized me a second night. It was obviously impossible to develop a relationship with a woman – or a man for that matter – so when I felt the need to do something about it I paid my money for professional if not compassionate relations.

Ten years passed and I had almost gotten used to having the world re-order itself at random intervals when suddenly things got worse.

I spend a lot of time in libraries, reading current newspapers or websites to keep at least somewhat abreast of the situation in the world variant I'm currently inhabiting. I almost got arrested once because I didn't know it was illegal to wear hats in public buildings, and when automobiles started using the left hand lanes rather than the right it took me weeks to get used to the new traffic patterns. I gave up driving a long time ago but I still have to cross the road to get to the other side.

But one day I bought a hotdog from a street vendor and told him he'd given me the wrong change. He looked at the money in my hand and insisted that it was right, but I'd given him a ten dollar bill for a two dollar dog and he'd returned only a five and two singles. He was bigger than me and a lifetime of not being certain of much of anything had conditioned me to accept whatever I was told, so I slunk away with my tail between my legs, feeling victimized.

And you're wondering why, right? Because ten minus two is seven. At least it is now. I've tried it myself and there's no question. I put ten pennies on a table and then pick up two. There are seven left behind. But I swear that there used to be eight. It was bad enough when history kept changing, but now even the laws of nature are no longer immutable.

A few months after that, I started having trouble breathing. I thought it might be allergies or asthma, but it got much worse and I blacked out a few times and was tired almost constantly. I went to a free clinic once but they couldn't find anything wrong with me and just told me to take things easy for a while. Two days later I collapsed and that's how I ended up here.

It's not clear to me exactly where "here" is. When I first woke up, it looked like a hospital, but every morning I notice little differences now. Different faces, different uniforms. And it's getting harder than ever to understand what people are talking about. The language you people use sounds like English most of the time, but a lot of the words are completely different and there's this odd kind of inflection you use that makes everything sound like a question. I hate questions, because I don't have any answers.

But I did understand a lot of what the doctors were saying about me this morning when they installed the oxygen tent. It's been getting harder and harder to breathe and at first the tent didn't help but they made some adjustments and for the past few hours I've recovered enough strength to write down this account. I don't know why I bother, since it won't be here when I wake up tomorrow, or at least it's not likely to say the same thing.

But just once I have to protest. Despite the physical evidence from this morning's examination, it is absolutely not true that I am a visitor from another planet and that's why I can't breathe the air without assistance. And when I was younger, everyone had an appendix, at least unless they had a surgeon remove it.

I'm still the only constant in a universe that is in constant flux. My lungs are just the way they have always been. It's the air that has changed. I am not an alien from another world.

Or then again, maybe I am.

ORWELL'S OTHER NIGHTMARE

It was a bright cold day in April, and the clocks were striking thirteen. Marlboro Smith surveyed his desk with satisfaction. The monthly reports were done and he'd responded to all recent requests under the Public Accountability Act. His workload was current once more.

Smith enjoyed being a public employee, even though he knew he should be ashamed of that fact.

He carefully assumed a pained expression and turned toward the omnipresent Public Oversight camera. It was mounted to look over his shoulder so that it could record exactly what Marlboro wrote, read, or filed away. The placard beneath the lens warned:

LITTLE SISTER IS WATCHING YOU.

Smith sensed someone standing just outside his office. There was no door; no government official had worked behind a closed door since the Governmental Scrutiny Amendment's ratification.

"May I help you?"

Discovered, the other man entered, his expression one of undisguised distaste. "I'm here in an official capacity, Bureaucrat Smith."

"But I've already been audited this month!" He protested without hope. Under the Federal Reorganization Act, all government functions were divided among Central Services, Implementation, and Administrative Operations. Each agency was obligated by law to monitor the others.

"We've had a complaint."

Smith felt his stomach clench. "What kind of complaint?"

"Bureaucrat Myrtle Dagosian reported that you said to her, and I quote, 'We ought to do something about the inefficiency around here.' Is that an accurate version of your remark?"

He hesitated. Obviously his visitor was an agent of the Ought Police, devoted to suppressing any secret wish to transfer power from the people to elected or appointed officials.

"Yes, I did. But the pronoun 'we' referred to the American public and not my official position, Mr....?"

"O'Brien." The interloper appear dissatisfied. "Is your desk always this clean?"

"Well, I can't stand disorder."

"Have you caught up to your workload?"

Smith saw the trap. "Of course not, I've just placed it in a drawer. Catching up would imply excessive intrusion into the public realm."

"Are you aware that you have the highest efficiency rating in Washington?"

"My predecessor cleared things up during the transition. When I arrived, there was no backlog. I've been much less productive."

O'Brien nodded skeptically. "Your attendance is also extraordinary. An excess of zeal is cause for disciplinary action."

"I'm an early riser and I catch the early train to avoid the crowds. If you check my lunchbreaks, you'll find that I'm rarely punctual about returning, and I frequently leave early."

"You could wait outside, smoke a cigarette."

"But smoking is illegal!"

"The rule of law is a rule of crime," O'Brien quoted. "A healthy disrespect for intrusive regulation is the mark of a true patriot."

"I guess I never looked at it that way. The price of freedom is eternal vigilance."

O'Brien left shortly thereafter, leaving Smith distinctly unsettled.

EFFICIENCY IS WASTE.

The banner was draped across the elevator lobby. Smith waited impatiently. He considered himself a patriot, knew that the government that governed the least governed the best. But it was hard to let things slide. It was an unspeakable crime but in the secret recesses of his mind, Marlboro Smith knew he was guilty.

He loved being a government employee.

There was a new lobby placard the following morning. GOVERNMENT SERVICE IS A CONTRADICTION IN TERMS.

O'Brien was waiting in Smith's office.

"Good morning, Citizen O'Brien. May I be of limited assistance?"

"I'm here to issue you a writ of mandatory refresher training."

"Refresher training?" Smith was bewildered. "But I thought everything was in order."

"I reviewed your present and prior performance. You were demoted after several warnings about a high intrusiveness rating, and one violation of the Limited Implementation law."

"I was just trying to help!" Smith responded emotionally. "There were conflicting rules and the state agencies kept contradicting each other. The disaster victims needed assistance and invoking federal jurisdiction was the only solution."

"So you concluded that a government official had the right to determine the future of American citizens,"

"Not exactly. I was trying to fulfill their requirements of the government."

"Your superior didn't see it that way."

"Molinski didn't understand that the federal statute took precedence."

"And you did?"

"I consulted legal experts first."

"You feel justified then?"

"Yes." Smith froze, realizing he'd just indicted himself.

O'Brien smiled. "Bureaucrat Smith, you have just admitted believing that official action can have positive results rather than being a necessary evil. I will therefore recommend your immediate suspension pending mandatory attitude adjustment therapy."

Fury swept away the last vestiges of Smith's reserve. "All right, I admit it. I love my job. Why should that be a crime? I'm trying to help. That's what government should do."

"That's the kind of thinking that made America lose sight of the fact that central authority necessarily strips away freedom."

"But nothing ever gets done now! Government service is the career of choice of the inept, the incompetent, and the indolent. We need to reshape government to reshape our future."

O'Brien scowled. "You want to know what the future holds for government employees, Smith. I'll tell you. Picture a giant glove, ripping your balls off forever. That's the future, Smith."

Six weeks later, Smith was released from retraining, wearing a graduation pin that said "Order is Chaos". He returned to his job the following day, showing up fifteen minutes late, sorted all of the paper on his desk into four priority piles but failed to deal with any of them lest he interfere with some citizen's freedom to sicken and die, or starve, or infringe on a neighbor's rights. After his two hour lunch, he carefully polished the lens of the Public Oversight camera, and noticed with satisfaction that he no longer had to fake his smile when he looked in that direction.

He had won the victory over himself. He loved Little Sister.

GOTHIC

I know how this is going to sound but I sensed that my visit to Sibiu was going to go badly almost from the moment we landed. It was a difficult, unusually turbulent descent and even though I had been briefed about local conditions, I hadn't expected such a dramatic demonstration right at the outset of my visit. Even the shuttle attendant looked concerned as he moved about the cabin, making sure we were all properly secured in our seats. But we did land safely, to everyone's obvious relief, and within moments we were standing in line, waiting for the outer door to open.

The umbilicus was water tight, but it shook violently as we made our way into the spaceport terminal. There was a rumbling sound that I thought briefly might be the shuttle's engines. That was nonsense, of course; we wouldn't have been allowed to debark before they were completely shut down. The malevolent rumbling was thunder. "Looks like we've landed in the middle of a storm," one of my fellow passengers shouted.

The attendant glanced at him. "Actually, the weather is unusually mild today."

That sobering observation dissuaded the rest of us from speaking until we were inside the building proper.

The terminal was small by my standards, clean and orderly and decorated in bright colors, apparently as a contrast to the view outside the regularly placed windows. There wasn't much to see since we were looking out toward the artificial plain that had been created to handle off world traffic, but even if there had been a scenic landscape, it would not have been possible to enjoy it. Rain swept past the windows in successive waves, falling at a sharp angle because of the high winds. There were landing lights in the distance, barely perceptible blurs of paleness in the all encompassing dark. Most of what illumination there was came from jagged flashes of lightning that fractured the sky in the distance. Sometimes not so distant. At least the thunder was no longer audible; the terminal was well insulated.

The bright, cheery décor emphasized the chaotic unpleasantness rather than offsetting it. I felt illogically depressed and a bit anxious, even though everything so far had gone as I'd planned.

The official formalities were superficial. The immigration officer told me that I'd been cleared for entry while still aboard the *Demeter*. There were few visitors to Sibiu thanks to its unpleasant climate, and if it hadn't been mineral rich and wrapped in a surprisingly human compatible atmosphere, there would probably be no resident population. I was cautioned to apply for an extension if I chose to remain more than ninety local days, and I nodded, having no intention of remaining beyond five. The *Demeter* would depart for Varna after that and I fully intended to be on it. My business at the Zakili estate should not take more than a day to complete, two at most.

A human rather than robotic attendant showed me where my luggage was waiting and as soon as it recognized me, it trundled obediently in my wake.

Although it was early evening, the clerk at the Services desk told me that there would be no public transportation until morning. I asked about renting a private lifter but she shook her head vigorously. "No one will rent to offworlders, Ser Hokker. You must understand, the roads here are treacherous. They are always being undercut or washed away or buried in landslides, and the winds make air travel hazardous. Even our most experienced drivers are always at risk. Where is it specifically that you wish to go?"

I told her and the eagerly helpful look on her face lost some of its vivacity. "That area is very lightly settled, I'm afraid. Let me see what I can find for you."

Her fingers played across an interface and she frowned. "There's a cargo lifter traveling that way tomorrow, but it won't be able to take you into the heights. The wind is quite violent in the mountains. I can get you as far as Fagaras, but you'll have to make arrangements locally if you want to go farther."

I tried to be insistent but she was obviously unable to help, so I stalked off to the spaceport hostelry to get a room for the night, my luggage trundling obediently behind me. Doctor Zakili wasn't expecting me until the following day in any case, so I decided to put as good a face on the situation as was possible.

I spent a restless night despite the perfectly acceptable accommodations. Perhaps somehow I sensed the wind pressing against the building or the rain which ran off the top of the structure in glassy sheets. Breakfast was adequate but uninspired and the half dozen or so of us who ate in the communal hall kept to ourselves. My spirits improved slightly when I found the cargo lifter bay without difficulty, and a very large, hirsute man in a stained uniform came perilously close to being pleasant as he processed my credit implant and stowed my luggage.

The cargo lifter wasn't really meant to carry passengers, but this one had been modified to hold seven in addition to the driver. Since I'm chronically early, I was the first to arrive and therefore took the seat with the best view. An older woman boarded just before departure time and took the seat adjacent to me. She nodded pleasantly but didn't immediately initiate a conversation, and I responded in kind.

It was still raining when the outer door rolled open, not quite as violently as the night before but I would not have enjoyed being exposed to the wicked crosswinds that sprayed our windows for the next two hours. We made painfully slow but steady progress, traveling across the most unwelcoming landscape I've ever seen. At times I felt as though we'd shrunk to insect size and were crawling across a field of gravel. There were trees of a sort, thick limbed, lumpish, and with enormous spatulate leaves that curled into funnels to channel the rainwater into internal sacs where the peculiar bacteria of Sibiu performed their equivalent of photosynthesis. We saw none of the native fauna during the morning, not surprising since most of the animal life lived in caves or artificial burrows, emerging – if ever – only to hunt down and kill one another.

I exchanged a few words with my fellow passenger, Lucinda, who seemed perfectly happy to respond to my questions but asked nothing in return. She told me that she was returning from a business trip to the capital, that she operated a small hostelry in Fagaras, which was the final stop for the day, and also my destination. I gracefully declined her invitation, insisting that I already had a place to stay.

"I'm visiting a client who lives just beyond the Borgeaux Pass," I explained. "I don't suppose you could recommend a local carrier who'd take me there."

Something odd had come over the woman when I spoke those last few words and her voice was strangely altered when she

answered. "There's no one who'll risk a lifter in the passes. Old
Armin might rent you a landcar, though I wouldn't count on it.
That's dangerous country, even for those that live in it."

"Then possibly he could be persuaded to take me there, and
retrieve me in a day or two."

"Possibly," she answered, but her tone and expression said
she doubted it.

We arrived safely, although not entirely without incident.
One natural bridge had partially collapsed and we had to back track
to find an alternate route. Apparently there had been several serious
earth tremors recently. I also saw my first native Sibian wildlife, a
pack of vargulves kept pace with us for a while and I could tell they
made Lucinda uneasy even though they posed no threat to us so long
as we remained inside the cargo lifter. They moved silently and
almost effortlessly over the ground. Their longish, grey bodies were
covered with dense fur, but their six-limbed gait seemed almost
insectlike.

"I can feel them touching my mind," she told me nervously.
"They have vile, filthy thoughts full of blood and violence. Even
when they mate, it's all blood and pain." She shuddered as she
spoke. I think it was the first time I ever saw someone actually do
that.

Lucinda was exaggerating, of course. The vargulves do have
a limited shared consciousness. Their disquieting howling is
designed to frighten their prey and has nothing to do with
communication, according to the brief discussion of them in the
orientation chip I'd processed prior to the trip. There was no proof
that they could sense human thoughts, or vice versa, but many of the
locals were convinced that it happened.

Fagaras was, as near as I could tell, a small, well maintained
community hunkered down in the shelter of an overhanging cliff. It
had almost stopped raining by the time we arrived at dusk, although
the wind was still brisk and unpredictable. Lucinda tried once more
to convince me not to venture into the Borgeaux Pass, at least not
until the morning, but I had no intention of being late for my
appointment. I would walk if I had to, and that was almost my fate.
Armin Vambery did indeed have a landcar available, but he
wouldn't rent it to me and he wouldn't take me any further than the
head of the pass. Reluctantly, I used his communicator to call Doctor

Zakili's home and explain my situation. The call went through, audio only, and a heavily accented voice told me that transportation would be provided if I waited at Dragon Rock. I conferred with Vambery, who agreed to take me there, and that seemed to settle matters, but when I suggested that we fortify ourselves with a hot meal first, he demurred, insisting that we must leave right away.

"The pass is too dangerous once it is full dark. If you want to go tonight, we go now." And so we did.

To be fair to Vambery, he continued forward even as the night closed in around us, fulfilling his promise to deliver me to Dragon Rock, but I had barely stepped out of the vehicle before he backed away, negotiated a tight turn, and roared off back the way we'd come without so much as a word of farewell.

It was raining – still rather than again – but I'd purchased a weather cloak in Fagaras and it kept me dry and warm. There was no sign of my promised ride, so I settled down to wait. I had barely managed to find a comparatively comfortable spot when the eerie cry of the vargulves came from the distance, not distant enough to please me, and I realized that I had nothing with which to defend myself if they really could scent my thoughts and decided I qualified as prey. I searched my surroundings, found nothing more formidable than a fist sized rock, and contented myself with that as best I could. At one point the ground shook beneath my feet and I had to leave my shelter to escape a shower of mud and gravel. The small quake had set off landslides on every side, though none were serious.

Fortunately, Zakili's promised ride arrived before the vargulves found me; it was an all-terrain rover of unknown vintage, dented and caked in filth, but I was in no position to be critical. The driver's bubble was dark and I glimpsed only a shadowy figure there as it waved for me to enter the passenger compartment. I did so promptly; the cries of the vargulves had been growing steadily louder and more frequent. The intercom was inoperable, so I settled back to relish the safety if not the comfort of my new surroundings.

The last leg of my journey was uneventful, although I did catch occasional glimpses of the vargulves, who loped along on either side, keeping pace easily, a silent and unsettling escort. The last leg of my journey took longer than I expected and I was beginning to get restless when the road finally leveled out and, moments later, we entered a sheltered courtyard. By the time I had helped my luggage out of the passenger compartment, the driver was gone and I found myself alone. I was in fact growing increasingly irritated when a door opened facing me, light spilled out, and a dimly perceived figure waved for me to approach.

"Welcome to my castle, Ser Hokker. It is inside a mountain rather than on top of one, but it is my castle nonetheless." I had never seen a holo of Dr. Zakili, but I assumed this must be the man himself. He was tall, surprisingly tall, but somehow fragile, a lace spider in human form. His hair was shoulder length and so white I wondered if he was an albino. We shook hands as he closed the door behind us, shutting out the awful din of the rain and wind, and I almost flinched away. His flesh was cold and dry.

"I hope that your journey was uneventful. Given conditions on Sibiu, I can hardly hope that they were pleasant."

"I have no reason to complain, Doctor Zakili. I am only sorry that I was unable to reach you sooner."

"No matter. This way please." He led me through a succession of dimly lit passageways into a larger chamber and it was only then that I began to realize that this was not a completely artificial structure, that Zakili made his home in a series of caves and tunnels, some natural, some manufactured. "I've had a meal prepared for you."

The next chamber was so exquisitely furnished that I had to remind myself that we were not in some elegant pleasure palace back on Whitby. An elaborately decorated table stood in the center of the room, surrounded by at least a dozen chairs, although only one place had been set. A stasis server sat near at hand, transparent so that I could see the food waiting within. "Aren't you joining me, Doctor?"

"I will keep you company, but I'm afraid I could not wait. My physical condition makes it necessary for me to be very regular about my meals."

I hadn't realized how hungry I was until the stasis was raised and I smelled the food. There was some kind of cutlet – I knew better than to ask its source – and a variety of vegetables. There was very little conversation for the next few minutes, but I soon felt boorish and glanced around the room. "Is that a relative, Doctor?" I nodded toward a holo portrait mounted on one wall. The subject closely resembled my host, but was of a much older man, his flesh sagging, cancerous nodules speckling his face, the hair thin and lifeless. There was something vaguely unpleasant about his expression, I thought, as though he was smirking at me.

"Only in a manner of speaking. He only exists as an abstract, a potential averted. You know my background, of course?"

It was a somewhat difficult question to address, since I was well aware of his clouded past, but I answered truthfully if sparingly. "We respect the privacy of our clients, Doctor Zakili. I know that you spent most of your life on Novotny, that you are a noted biophysiologist, and that you retired here on Sibiu approximately thirty standard years ago. That is the extent of my knowledge."

Zakili smiled, not entirely pleasantly. "I specialized in anti-agathics, Ser Hokker. I was on Novotny for nearly sixty standard yeas, but that was not most of my life." He glanced up at the portrait. "I have managed to slow the aging process dramatically using both orthodox and unorthodox techniques. What you see there is a simulation of how I would appear if I had let nature take its course."

Lacking an appropriate response, I resumed eating, trying not to let my eyes drift back to the portrait. I wondered if my host had entertained such morbid fantasies before arriving on Sibiu or if he just succumbed to the aura of his environment.

We moved to a small office after I'd eaten and took up the business that had brought me to Sibiu. Doctor Zakili had engaged my employers to purchase property for him on Whitby. He wished to have a large, well appointed house in Quincy and a smaller retreat somewhere in the Morris Archipelago. The task had been passed to me and I had brought virtual tours of several properties which I thought might satisfy his requirements.

I had barely begun my presentation, however, before we were interrupted. A younger woman, by appearance approximately my own age, came into the room so silently that I was only alerted to her presence by a flicker of motion at the corner of my vision. She was clearly related to Zakili; their features were quite similar although hers were softer. Her skin was so pale she might have been a ghost, an effect heightened by a white sarong; her hair had the faintest hint of color, an almost bluish tint.

I stood up immediately. Zakili remained seated, his face betraying no reaction. "Ser Hokker, allow me to introduce you to my grand-daughter, Madlin."

I shook her hand and found it as cool and dry as that of my host, apparently a family characteristic, and expressed my pleasure at making her acquaintance. I even went so far as to invite her to join us in watching the next virtual but Zakili intervened.

"It is past Madlin's bedtime, I'm afraid. Her health has not been good recently and she needs her rest."

Something passed between them. I wouldn't care to characterize it, but I could feel the sudden tension as though it had reached out and touched me. They looked at one another, and then Madlin turned to me, thanked me for my cordiality, and left without another word. She moved so silently that I didn't even hear her footsteps.

"I hope her illness isn't serious," I hazarded once she was gone.

"It's incurable," he answered bluntly and for a second I saw tragedy and loss in his face. "She would have been taken from me long ago if I hadn't imposed a very strict regimen." He obviously wished to discuss her condition no further, so we returned to business.

Whatever further response I might have made was forestalled by a sudden shifting under my feet, a sickening sensation that ended almost as soon as it began. "Don't be afraid, Ser Hokker. The entire base of my mountain is ringed with stress compensators. They measure the magnitude of the tremor and exert a balancing force before it can cause any damage."

It was very late by the time we had finished. I tried to cover a particularly expansive yawn and Zakili noticed and apologized for keeping me up so late. "We so rarely see the sun here that I confess I'm oblivious to the hour. We will resume this after you have rested. With luck, there will be a lull in the weather and I will be able to show you the sights, such as they are. The view from the parapet above us can be breathtaking."

Zakili conducted me to my room personally, a surprisingly long and torturous walk through a series of narrow tunnels and small chambers, and it was only then that I realized that I hadn't seen any indication of servants, human or mechanical, since arriving, other than the enigmatic driver, whom I had not properly seen either. "Someone will come for you in the morning," he told me. "I'm afraid the passageways are rather bewildering to those not accustomed to them. It would be safest if you didn't wander off by yourself."

I was exhausted. Not only had I been up all day and most of the night, but the days themselves are considerably longer on Sibiu than on Whitby. I ascertained that my luggage had been delivered – by what means I never did discover – and ordered it to open itself and prepare my night clothing, but I had barely managed to change before I lay back and fell instantly asleep.

The chamber was inky black when I opened my eyes some time later. To this day I cannot say just what it was that disturbed my sleep, but as I lay there in the darkness, I became quite irrationally convinced that I was not alone, that someone else was in the chamber. I called for light, but Zakili either did not use voice activation or it was keyed to only the permanent residents. Tentatively I rose and crossed to the manual controls near the door.

Except for my luggage, which squatted in a corner waiting for instructions, there was nothing else capable of movement in the room, but I would have wagered my credit balance that something had done so within the last few moments. Cautiously I opened the door to the corridor, which slid aside so quietly that I judged it entirely possible for it to have opened and closed without waking me, and took a step out into the corridor. Movement or heat sensors registered my presence and a very faint illumination stretched a few meters in either direction, but not as far as the curve at one end or the junction at the other.

Despite my conviction, I was about to dismiss it all as a bad dream when I heard a brief, inarticulate sound from my right. It had sounded like a woman's voice. Madlin? One of the servants? I couldn't imagine such a sound coming from the stately Dr. Zakili.

Against my better judgment, I decided to investigate.

At the first chamber I saw a slim, feminine shape disappear into another passageway. Having come this far, I was determined to satisfy my curiosity, so I followed. It wasn't far. The corridor turned sharply to the right and ended at an elaborate doorway. Something shimmered in the air and I approached cautiously. It looked very much like the stasis field that had preserved my dinner, but more intense, the colors deeper, the field at the opaque end of translucence. It was theoretically possible to create a stasis field this large, but I had never actually heard of anyone having done so.

I stood there for some time, eventually felt like a fool, and returned to my chamber.

I pretended that nothing out of the ordinary had happened when Doctor Zakili showed up to conduct me to breakfast. He joined me this time, although he restricted himself to some kind of thick red liquid. Although I had completed my presentation the night before, he had a great many questions this morning and we worked through them, eliminating almost two thirds of his choices very quickly. We took a break then and Zakili gave me a guided tour of his castle, starting with the control room in the lower levels. The equipment was quite evidently state of the art.

"A big enough earthquake would overwhelm my resources," he admitted, "but we've had no serious damage since I had the compensators installed."

The parapet was at the summit, accessible by means of an old style elevator, partially exposed to the elements but worth the visit. During the intervals when the rain was less overwhelming, we could see for miles across jagged rocks, deep cup canyons, and lines of serrated hills.

He suggested I enjoy an early lunch while he took care of some private business, promising that we'd wind things up during the afternoon. I was picking at the last of my food when I had a visitor. Madlin Zakili. She was dressed exactly as she had been the previous day, but she seemed much more animated.

I started to greet her but she raised a finger to her lips, cautioning me to silence. "Don't talk. Just listen. I need your help. You have to get me out of here."

"I don't understand." I started speaking normally but she gestured frantically and I softened my voice.

"He's a tyrant. He's been holding me prisoner ever since we came to Sibiu. You have to take me away with you!"

I thought about it, but only for a moment. "That's impossible, I'm afraid. But once I get back to Fagaras, I promise you that I'll alert the authorities. They'll protect you."

She laughed, a sharp, unsetting sound. "The magistrate is paid to leave us alone. He won't do anything to stop him."

I felt doubly confused. "Then I'll notify the Governor's office before I leave. That's the best I can do for you. They'll deal with your grandfather."

"Grandfather? He's not my grandfather!" I must have looked very confused because she laughed again, with a hint of genuine humor this time. "He's my brother."

Madlin could not possibly have been more than thirty standard. I immediately concluded that she was mad, but I was wrong. At the opposite end of the chamber, Doctor Zakili had entered quietly. "She's telling the truth, Hokker. I'll explain in a moment." He turned toward Madlin, who stared at him defiantly. "You're violating our agreement, Madlin. Return to your room immediately." His voice was soft, regretful rather than commanding.

For a second, I thought she was going to refuse, but then she turned and flung herself into a passage and was gone.

Zakili's shoulders slumped and he suddenly looked much older. He seated himself at the table and waved for me to do the same. Even from a distance I could see that his hands were shaking and when he spoke, strain was evident in his voice. "It seems I must explain things to you, Ser Hokker. Please don't think harshly of me until you've heard what I have to say."

"Madlin spoke the truth. She is my sister. No, don't interrupt. This is hard enough to explain. Ser Hokker, my sister contracted Murray's Syndrome when she was thirty, a genetic defect. It was then and is now incurable and terminal. With treatment, she might have lasted as long as two standard years, certainly no longer."

"But she's alive!" I protested.

"In a manner of speaking. The disease causes premature, greatly accelerated aging. It was Madlin's illness that shaped the course of my career. I was determined to effect a cure, although to date I've found only palliatives. I have added to her projected lifespan but not significantly."

"But she's alive today," I repeated.

"Is she? In a sense, perhaps. I didn't show you Madlin's suite during our tour. You probably wouldn't have guessed its purpose even if you'd seen it, but you'd have known something was wrong. Madlin lives in a stasis chamber, all biological functions frozen to prevent deterioration from the disease, or from the normal aging process. "

I knew very little about the mechanics of stasis, but enough to argue the point. "You can't keep someone in suspension for that long. You'd never be able to revive them."

Zakili nodded. "Perfectly correct, which is why Madlin becomes animate once every thirty days. She spends a few hours, her body decays ever so slightly, and then she returns to her dreamless sleep. At least, that was our agreement until recently." He sighed audibly. "I think she has grown tired of fighting and wants the struggle to end, so she resists the process and revives prematurely. I could suppress her will by strengthening the stasis field, but that would require more frequent periods of wakefulness to avoid deterioration. What time was given to her by one hand would be stolen away by the other. I cannot let her waste what is left of her life, Ser Hokker. I believe I am close to the solution, close to the knowledge that will set her free from this terrible dependence." His face crumpled and he looked suddenly profoundly sad. "But I have believed so before, and I have always been wrong."

I'm not sure how I would have responded, but I was spared the necessity. There was a distant, muted burst of sound and the floor shook beneath us. We both stood immediately. Zakili's wrist unit beeped and I heard Madlin's thin but recognizable voice.

"It's time for me to go, Herman. It's time for both of us to go." And then silence.

The floor shook again, and this time a holograph fell from the wall.

"It's an earthquake!" I shouted.

Zakili's eyes widened. "No! It's Madlin! She has tampered with the compensators. You must leave now, Ser Hokker. Uncontrolled they could tear this entire mountain apart!" Without another word, he turned and raced off.

I stood there only until the next concussion threw me to my knees, then scrambled to my feet determined to escape.

How I made it back down that treacherous trail to Fagaras I will never know. I think the vargulves were with me some of the time, but they didn't attack; if they really could touch my mind, perhaps they were repulsed by the chaos of horror and confusion that possessed me. I didn't really come to myself until I saw the lights and then the hunched shapes of the settlement. And even now, safe and en route to the spaceport to leave Sibiu forever, I cannot drive one final searing image from my mind.

Somehow I had found my way to the courtyard and from there the narrow road that led back down toward Borgeaux Pass. My precipitous flight from Zakili's castle had been accompanied by powerful shock waves and distant explosions and I hadn't looked back until a misstep sent me sprawling painfully across the muddy ground. The oppressive rain had paused for breath and I had a relatively clear view, clear enough to see the two figures, one clad in white, the other in black, as they struggled on the parapet far above me. Even as I watched, the entire mountainside seemed to shiver, hidden flaws in the rock finally surrendering to the relentless forces of gravity and erosion.

Whatever the cause, the looming shape that was both mountain crag and Doctor Zakili's castle disintegrated in a shower of rock and dust, carrying everything in it, and those two tiny struggling figures, down into the abyss, into the only peace that will ever be granted those two tormented souls.

www.ingramcontent.com/pod-product-compliance
Lightning Source LLC
Chambersburg PA
CBHW072140170626
46813CB00004BA/1628